Meg tied Don Juan to the same post as Whiskey. The horses didn't bother each other now, dripping with the sweat of the climb and hanging their heads low as they sniffed at the dry oat weeds. I met Meg's gaze and felt her waiting. She took a step closer to me. Our boots were only inches apart. We hadn't stood this close, not without a horse or a fence between us, since the night we kissed. I opened my mouth to speak but nothing came out. Meg pressed one finger to my lips then let it fall slow as honey down my chin and throat. She paused just at the spot where my collarbones left a space, where they didn't quite meet.

My breath came quick and hungry. I stepped back and Meg's finger slipped off me. She closed her eyes and turned away from me. I felt as if I'd slapped her and wanted to apologize but didn't say anything. Meg went over to the married oaks then, her hand tracing the splitting trunk, her thoughts closed to me.

Visit

Bella Books

at

BellaBooks.com

or call our toll-free number

1-800-729-4992

Whiskey and Oak leaves

Bella
BOOKS
2007

First Edition

Editor: Anna Chinappi
Cover designer: Kiaro Creative Ltd

ISBN-10: 1-59493-093-7
ISBN-13: 978-1-59493-093-5

ACKNOWLEDGMENTS

Thank you, Corina, again, for putting up with my crazy busy schedule and for being the best first-, second- and third-pass reader! Thank you, Lauryn and the Circle of Writer's Rio Caliente writing group, for sharing the experience. Keep writing, guys! Thank you, Anna, for the editing help. Thank you, Mom, for giving me my first leg up on a horse. And thank you, to my horse friend, for reminding me how much fun it is to run like the wind.

About the Author

Jaime Clevenger lives in Santa Cruz, California, with her partner and an ever growing number of furry friends. She works as an emergency veterinarian at night and spends her days riding horses, writing and playing in the ocean. Jaime has also written *The Unknown Mile, Call Shotgun, All Bets Off,* and *Sign on the Line.* She would like to thank you for reading this book and hopes that you enjoy it. If you would like to contact Jaime, please visit www.jaimeclevengerbooks.com.

Chapter 1
Meg
One year ago . . .

"Mrs. McCormick, can you hear me?" I rubbed my fist on the woman's sternum and watched impatiently for any response. The sun beat down relentlessly on the arena and my uniform clung to my legs. Summer hadn't officially started and it was already too hot to be caught outside after noon. Only her chest moved. Her breaths formed a labored pattern of three quick heaves then two slow sighs. She was sprawled out on her back with her left leg twisted sideways unnaturally. I slipped my stethoscope under her shirt and listened for a moment. Her lungs were clear and I decided the irregular breathing might just be a response to pain. I felt the pulse on her wrist, her skin strangely cool to my sweaty hands, and then checked her blood pressure. She was stable at one thirty over sixty.

1

I sat back on my heels and eyed the path I'd taken to the arena, hoping to spot my partner, Eddy. Unfortunately, he was a new EMT and painfully slow. To the right of the arena was a large gray barn. A gravel path led from the barn to a white-fenced pasture, scattered with a few oak trees and three grazing horses, oblivious to the commotion of the accident. I half expected some cowboy to come swaggering down the path but no one was in sight. Just beyond the pasture, a sprawling one-story house with a gray stone front and a big redwood porch loomed like a perfect ranch estate. I couldn't help but wonder what Mr. McCormick did to afford a place like this.

"Mrs. McCormick?" I rolled my knuckles over her sternum again. I'd been at this job long enough to not mind unconscious patients. They didn't complain. Still, we had protocol to follow. I yelled her name a third time. The woman's eyes flickered open and she squinted at me. "Good. Now we're getting somewhere." Her eyes closed again and no amount of yelling seemed to get her attention. I forged ahead anyway. "Mrs. McCormick, I need your help here. Nod your head if you can hear me. Mrs. McCormick? Please try and open your eyes again."

"I hate being called missus." Her voice reminded me of an ex who smoked too much. She leveled her gaze on me. "Who the hell are you, anyway?" Grimacing, she tried to shift up to her side, then cussed and sagged back again.

"It'll hurt less if you don't move."

"Thanks, I figured that one out on my own. Where's Gabe?"

"He'll be here soon, Mrs. McCormick." Gabe was the ranch hand who had called for our ambulance. He'd led me over to the arena and introduced the unconscious woman as Mrs. June McCormick, one of the owners of the ranch. According to Gabe, Mrs. McCormick had been thrown from Jericho, the dark bay horse pacing in a small corral at the other end of the arena. He'd given his account of the accident and then gone back to the ambulance to help Eddy carry our equipment. Knowing Eddy, Gabe was probably getting a tour of the ambulance.

"If you insist on saying my name over and over, call me June. Hearing missus makes me feel old and married."

I bit my lip and held back my smile. "Of course." I liked it when my patients kept their sense of humor.

"Where'd you say Gabe went?" June pressed her hand to her forehead. "Damn, everything's so bright. I've never had a headache this bad. Feels like I fell down a flight of stairs, on my head."

"I hate it when that happens."

"Damn horse." June shook her head slowly. "By the way, who'd you say you were?"

"I'm Meg, your paramedic."

"My paramedic?" June eyed me for a moment. "Well, you got a nice uniform, medic. Carry any pain medication?"

"It's coming soon. My partner's bringing our supplies." I guessed June had a concussion. It would explain the headache and her confusion.

June sighed and her eyes closed again. I quickly began an exam, trying to keep June talking with a series of questions. "Do you live here?"

"For better or worse."

"And you ride horses?" I quickly summarized the external wounds that I could see. June's left leg, turned out at an awkward angle, was likely broken at the tibia. There was an abrasion on her forehead, just above her right eyebrow with an egg-sized swelling under it. A deep laceration marked the length of her right palm and the wound was covered with sand and dirt.

"Mm-hmm."

"Does it hurt when you take a breath?"

June inhaled deeply. "No. It only hurts when I try to think."

"Yeah, I have the same problem." I got a smile from her with that.

"How long have you lived at the ranch?"

"Forever."

"Forever is a long time."

"Mm-hmm."

I shined a light in June's eyes and the left pupil constricted while the right one remained dilated. The leg would likely heal well with a cast but the head trauma could be serious. "How old are you?"

"Thirty-three. Can you turn off that light?"

"Sorry, I just had to check your eyes. Are you having any problems with your vision?" I replaced the penlight in my pocket when June nodded. "So, what does your husband do?"

"He lies."

"He lies? That's his job?"

"Mm-hmm. Full-time liar. With benefits. 401K plan. Stock options."

"Oh. I've met people in that same line of work." Semiconscious people were some of the most interesting people I meet. "And he lives here at the ranch?"

"No." June seemed to be upset by this question, the muscles at her jaws working as if she was clenching her teeth in pain.

I decided to change the subject. "Okay, I'm going to feel around a bit here. Let me know if anything hurts. Other than your head, that is." June's body was probably too full of adrenaline for her to sense the pain of the broken leg. I didn't try tempting fate by touching the leg, however. I felt her other limbs and checked for broken ribs. She cringed when I lightly touched the swelling on her head but didn't say anything. "Another minute or so and we'll get some pain meds for you." I put a hand on June's shoulder, rubbing gently, and felt her relax against me. June was attractive, distractingly so, and I thought of the details I'd like to add to the record for this call: nicely-defined muscles with soft curves in the right places; smooth, tanned skin, shoulder-length auburn hair; warm, amber eyes . . .

Finally, I heard Eddy's voice. He was following Gabe, trudging slowly down the path toward the arena, weighed down with nearly half of the equipment from the truck. "Why the hell did you bring all of that?"

"Hey, Boy Scouts are always prepared," Eddy answered, grinning.

"Boy Scout? I thought they hired you as an EMT." I shot back. I didn't try to hide my irritation.

He looked defensive and mumbled an excuse about why he'd brought the extra equipment. I was pissed about how long he'd taken but now was not the time to push him. The guy was still learning.

Gabe pointed to the fence post above where June lay. "She hit right there, when Jericho, that crazy stallion over there"—he pointed to the other end of the arena where the bay was standing—"bucked her off like a sack of grain."

"Wow. A sack of grain, huh?" Eddy whistled faintly as his boot knocked against the fence post with a dull thud. He handed the long board and the other stabilizing equipment over the rail to me. "You think she's got a spinal cord injury?"

Gabe answered quickly, "Probably. I had a friend that got bucked off a bronco the same way and never walked again."

After ten years as a paramedic, I'd seen enough trauma cases to have a good intuition about spines. June could move her arms, turn her head and shift her weight. The only thing she couldn't do was stand up and walk out of the arena on two feet. "Her spine is fine. She won't be walking out of here though." I pointed at the leg. "My guess is a tibial fracture."

Gabe looked doubtful but Eddy made his usual grunting sound of agreement. He grunted when he didn't know what the hell was going on but wanted to seem like he'd already guessed whatever I'd just figured out. The stallion in the far corral whinnied and June's eyes opened again. As she moved, I slipped a hand behind her back and helped her sit upright.

"Just sit tight, ma'am," Eddy said in an exaggerated western drawl. He was an ex-surfer from southern California and his attempt at an Old West accent was pathetic. He continued, "Ma'am, we're gonna take real good care of you. I'm gonna drive the ambulance and Meg, here"—he paused and grinned at me—"well she gets to hold your hand. Then before you know it, we'll be at the hospital."

I was ready to kill Eddy for that comment and gave him a good hard glare, which he completely ignored.

"I hate hospitals," June mumbled.

"Well, by the look of things, you're going to need a good doctor. That bump on your head . . ." Eddy switched from the western drawl to the sugary voice he used to talk to sick kids, "You know, our hospital has real good food and you get to keep the TV remote all to yourself." Eddy smiled dumbly down at June. "The doctors will fix you all up."

"Who the hell is this guy?" June asked, obviously irritated.

"I'm Eddy. I'm your EMT."

"My what? Well, can I get a new one of you?" Turning to me, she continued, "Hey, medic, does this guy have to be here?"

"June, they're both from the ambulance. Let them do their job." Gabe's voice was just as patronizing as Eddy's. I briefly considered sending them both back to the truck to wait there. Carrying the patient myself would save a lot of time but getting chewed out by my boss later made the idea less desirable.

"Gabe, how about you do your job, shut up and help me up." June reached up to brace herself against the fence and drew her left leg under her. The right leg was still stretched out. Gabe reached through the fence rail to stabilize her. With one arm hugging the lowest fence railing and her left leg tucked under her, she grimaced and tried to stand. I struggled against the urge to grab her. Unfortunately, if an alert patient refused care, we weren't supposed to intervene. A moment later June collapsed back on the ground, cussing. Her right foot pointed outward toward the barn while the rest of the leg faced the sky. The adrenaline was probably starting to wear off. June finally relaxed and looked up at me. "You look like you're saying 'I told you so.'"

"I think it'd be easier if you let us help."

"Fine. Go ahead and help. And can I get that pain med you

promised? Aspirin or something. Maybe a shot of morphine. I'd ask for a shot of whiskey but I have a feeling you probably don't carry that."

I struggled to ignore the notion that I'd like to ask June out, under other circumstances. "Don't worry, we'll get you something strong. Then we'll stabilize your leg and move to the hospital." To Eddy, I continued, "I'll radio ahead to the ER at Sutter Hospital and talk to the doc on duty about giving meds. Get her leg set on the board."

I radioed the dispatch center and got patched through to the hospital. A moment later, I had the morphine drawn up in the syringe. I pushed up June's shirt sleeve and rubbed her muscle with an alcohol swab. "This is gonna sting for a second here." She watched the needle sink in and then closed her eyes.

Chapter 2
June
Present Day

"She's got some spunk." Rhonda began, climbing up to the top fence rail of the arena just as the bay mare galloped to the other side.

I nodded, trying to keep my focus on the horse. Cassidy was in the far corner of the arena now, breathing heavily with nostrils flared. The sun had dropped to eye level on the horizon just behind where the mare stood and I couldn't look at her very long without being blinded by the bright rays. Her brown coat was darkened with sweat but her body was outlined in sunlight. In the distance, the hills were trimmed with the same gold hues. "Today's her first time on a lunge line with a saddle on her back."

"How's she doing?" Rhonda lit a cigarette and took a drag.

"She's acting like a yearling but she's almost three." The horse bucked, trying to throw the weight off her back. The saddle stayed in place despite her attempt to dislodge it, so she had craned her head to her side and tried biting it off. "She's too smart for her own good. But I like a smart mare." I cracked the whip to get her moving again. Rhonda took another drag and let the smoke curl out of her lips slowly. She had a way of smoking that made it seem like nicotine ought to be savored like something close to good wine. "I thought you quit last week."

"Rough day at work. We had two patients go into cardiac arrest and, well, you know . . . one more cigarette won't kill me. I'll quit tomorrow." Rhonda was dressed in her green hospital scrub top and blue jeans, as usual. "Tell me about the mare. Why haven't I seen her before?"

"Cassidy's been out in the east pasture with three other mares and two of my dad's retired geldings." She'd been the trouble-maker of the bunch since I put her out there and I had some mis-givings about training her. "When I get her in the arena, the only thing she'll do is charge in straight lines, rear or buck. Just like her dad."

"Who's she out of?"

"Jericho and Sassy."

"Why the hell did you breed those two? Didn't your father make you promise not to breed that mare? I can clearly remember him calling Sassy the Wicked Witch of the West. And Jericho? Only your crazy bronco riding pals would buy that stallion." Rhonda shook her head. "Your father is saying 'I told you so' from his grave."

"Probably." I'd given my dad a lot of reasons to say 'I told you so' and didn't regret not hearing the words now. I tightened my grip on the lunge line as Cassidy charged toward Rhonda's perch. The mare bucked again, sending a flurry of sand up in the air, then spun on her heels and bolted in the other direction. "Isn't she pretty to watch? She outruns all the other two-year-olds she's pas-tured with. I'd bet she'll be as fast as her dad."

"Great. We'll nickname her Butch Cassidy."

"Butch? Why is it that lesbians have to make everyone secretly gay?" I gritted my teeth to hold back my smile. Rhonda always got touchy when I teased her about lesbian idiosyncrasies. She pointed out my homebody tendencies just as often, which she'd somehow linked to divorcees, so I figured I had a right to tease.

"You could just agree with me. Maybe say it was funny." Rhonda sighed. "I think you woke up on the wrong side of the bed again."

"You've been telling me that for the past two years."

"Well, maybe you need to rearrange some furniture."

I looked over at her and grinned. "Now that was funny."

"I knew I could get a smile out of you if I kept trying." The mare suddenly spooked as a gust of wind rustled a tarp on the far side of the corral. She reared, ripping the lunge line out of my hands and tore down the arena, digging in her heels at the last moment in a sliding stop in front of the gate. Rhonda leaned back, trying to escape the brunt of the dust cloud. "Shit, June, you're in for it if you plan on breaking that horse yourself. Why don't you get one of the ranch hands to ride her first?"

"And miss all the fun? Hell no." I squeezed my hand into a fist, trying to numb the sting from the rope burn and then caught up with the tail end of Cassidy's lunge line. As soon as the mare glanced back at me, I cracked the whip to get her moving off the gate. She made a few erratic sweeps past me before succumbing to the whip's guidance and found the circular path I'd been trying to get her into all afternoon. She circled for several minutes, her pace gradually easing to a jog. She finally stopped on my command. I approached her, trying to push down the fear that inched up my chest. Yesterday we'd gone through a similar training session, minus the saddle, and as soon as I'd approached her then, she'd reared up and kicked her front legs a bit too close to my face. But this time I'd worked her longer. She was soaking in sweat and her head hung low, her breath still heaving in her chest. Speaking softly, I unclipped the lunge line from the halter and rubbed her neck. I placed one hand on the horn and the other at the back of the saddle, leaning my weight on the seat as if I might vault onto her back. Cassidy's muscles trembled at the touch but she didn't shy away. I loosened the girth and pulled off the saddle, smiling as Cassidy shook like a wet dog. "She's making progress."

"I think you're crazy." Rhonda hopped off the fence. She stamped out her cigarette and opened the gate, leaving plenty of room for the horse to pass out of the arena without coming too close to her.

"I've been called that before. They used to say that about you too, remember?"

"Yeah, but we're both in our thirties now. We can give up some of our daredevil ways when we're this old."

"Maybe you can." I set the saddle on the fence, keeping an eye on Cassidy as her lead line slacked. Earlier, the horse seemed to be looking for any excuse to act up. Now she seemed too tired to do anything but follow me.

"You know, if you break your leg again doing something stupid, don't count on me coming over all the time with dinner. I already fulfilled my best-friend obligations for you last year."

"Don't worry, I won't ask again." In fact, I hadn't before. Rhonda had no talent in the kitchen and I'd struggled through too many of her noodle casseroles.

"You could just stick to riding the horses that have already bucked off someone else. You don't have anything to prove, you know."

"I'm not trying to prove anything. As I remember, both of us used to ride the yearlings bareback. We weren't trying to prove anything. I think we just wanted a little excitement and a good ride."

"I don't need to tell you that there are better ways of getting a good ride." She arched her eyebrows and murmured smugly about a past weekend's affair with another nurse.

"Don't go there, Rhonda."

"What do you mean?"

"You're going to start in on a tirade about me needing to get laid."

She feigned a look of disbelief, then added, "Well, someone needs to tell you. Wouldn't you rather hear it from me than some stranger?"

"Is he a handsome stranger?"

Rhonda rolled her eyes. She'd told me more than once before that a good roll in the sack solved all problems. And of course, being the divorced homebody, how was I supposed to argue? I quickly interrupted her when she started in on the topic of my sex life. "Remember when you got thrown halfway across the pasture by that mean old Appaloosa? You got up, brushed the burrs off your overalls and smiled as wide as I can ever remember you smiling. Forget about sex. What happened to your lust for excitement?"

"I gave it to Goodwill along with my favorite pair of overalls. I miss the overalls." Rhonda winked. "Don't miss the bruises on my ass."

Rhonda had grown up on a ranch that neighbored ours and had been my closest friend since grade school. Her family eventually sold their land and moved to Sacramento, an hour southwest of here. Rhonda kept in touch until she moved east for college. I only got occasional letters then. After she graduated, she'd moved back to Sacramento and had apparently tried to look me up. By then, I was already a year into my traveling phase.

I'd dropped out of college to take up wandering. I went as far east as Maine for a job on a fishing boat and as far south as Florida for a job as a waitress at a friend's restaurant. The restaurant job didn't pan out so I decided to keep moving. I crossed all the way to Texas, hoping to reach San Diego in a pickup that broke down twice before I changed my mind and ended up in Aspen, Colorado, for a stint at a ski lodge. I'd sent postcards back to the ranch from all the pit stops. My father kept tabs on me and passed the post-cards on to my old high school boyfriend, Greg. Greg and I had gone to the same community college. He'd dropped out to take up bronco riding and then worked for my father training yearlings. My father and Greg both decided I'd eventually end up back home in El Dorado. After the ski lodge, I'd gone to Kentucky to work at a thoroughbred ranch where all the horses were racers or just plain crazy. A week after my twenty-fifth birthday, I called my dad to tell him I was catching a Greyhound to Sacramento. He didn't ask if that meant I was coming home for good. He just said, "Good, I bought you a new pair of boots and I've got a colt I want to show you. You'll want to start his training soon."

When I got home, Greg was waiting for me. He was still train-ing horses for my dad and convinced me to move in with him in the apartment he'd built above the barn. My dad wouldn't allow it unless we had a marriage license. So we talked about it and a few weeks later got married, quietly, by a justice of the peace. If my mother had still been around, things would have been different. My mother would have wanted the works—a wedding with guests, flowers and a reception. I was happy with the simple version. Greg and I were good for three years. Then we just started fighting about little things. The little things got bigger and neither of us could quite figure out what went wrong. When I finally told him to go, he left without an argument.

The day after I'd kicked Greg out, Rhonda showed up at the ranch, saying she was looking for a horse to ride. I handed her the reins of a black horse with a white blaze. His name was Don Juan because every one of the mares in his pasture followed him around like he was God's gift to the female horse. I'd just finished school-ing the gelding and was looking for a buyer. But I liked the horse and wasn't trying very hard to get rid of him. "Don Juan, the heart-breaker. He's yours, free of charge." She happily agreed and then said, "By the way, I'm a lesbian. Can you believe that?" I told her I didn't believe it but we were both tomboys and things like that happened, I guessed. Then I told Rhonda that I'd kicked Greg out that weekend. We had already signed the divorce papers and I was sleeping alone in bed for the first time in three years. She'd said, "Things like that happen, I guess. Will you be upset if I say I'm happy for you?"

I tied Cassidy up at the posts by the tomato bed and fished the hose out of the plants. Aiming the spray at the horse's back and inching it slowly up her neck, I tried every language I knew which was mainly English, some German and broken Spanish to tell her to calm down. Rhonda held her belly laughing at me and I ended up, as she predicted, more wet than the mare. After a rewarding brown cascade of water flowed from Cassidy's sides, I felt cocky and turned the spray near her head. She instantly reared up and kicked out at the hose, pointing out my mistake very plainly.

"Damn, girl." Rhonda whistled as she stepped back from Cassidy. She wasn't laughing anymore and her face was paler than I remembered. Seeing Cassidy's hooves from that angle would unnerve most people.

"Sorry about that."

"If you survive this bath, come find me over in the arena. I'll be grooming Don Juan. A friend from work is on her way here and I'd like you to meet her."

"Another nurse at the hospital? I thought you already dated all the available ones." I moved to the horse's other side and tried again with the hose turned on low. I'd met several of Rhonda's coworkers and found all of them boring.

"No, she's not another nurse. You'll be happy to know that after last weekend I'm giving up on nurses. Meg's a paramedic. And you can't tell me a paramedic is boring."

"So, your new girlfriend drives ambulances." The water inched up the horse's neck and her ears started twitching. I angled the spray the other direction before she had a chance to rear.

"She's not my girlfriend. We're not even really dating. June, I swear, sometimes I don't know why I tell you anything."

"Who else would you tell?" I kept my hand on Cassidy's halter and let the water trickle down its chest. Cassidy almost seemed to enjoy the cool rinse as long as I kept my distance from her head. "Anyway I don't really have time for small talk with your new romantic interest. The west pasture has a downed fence and I've got to make sure Gabe cleared out the storage shed. We're expecting a load of alfalfa."

"Well, when you change your mind, come find me over at the barn."

"Enjoying a roll in the hay with your new girl?"

"No, I'll just be giving Don Juan a rubdown." Rhonda turned and headed toward the barn. She kept talking as she walked away. "I think you'll like Meg. Come introduce yourself at least. Be sociable."

After finishing with Cassidy's bath, I cross-tied her to let her dry in the sun and then went to check in at the storage shed. As expected, the shed had been completely swept and the yard tools removed. Gabe was snoozing on a horse blanket, also as expected. Waking him was easy. My blue work shirt was still wet enough to get a few drips of dirty water off when I wrung it over his face and he shot upright like a jack rabbit.

"What the hell?"

"Morning Gabe. You still work for me?"

He nodded sheepishly. "It's siesta time. I'm allowed a break after lunch. Check the labor laws."

"There's a fence leaning in the west pasture and some of the barbed wire is bent. If you follow the Wrangler Path down to the gully, you'll find the spot under a couple of valley oaks. I think the deer have been working at it." The deer were dead set against fences, something close to how Gabe was to working in the afternoon. His stubbornness about siestas drove me crazy. "Go on, the siesta's over."

Gabe sighed and glanced at his watch. "You're right. Okay, I'll take a look at the fence." He shuffled off without another argument.

Having run out of excuses, I decided to make my way up to the barn to meet Rhonda's new love interest. The gray paint on the south facing side of the barn could use a fresh coat before the summer sun hit it and I added that to my list of things to do for the new ranch hand. The henhouse that bordered the barn also needed to be repaired but that could wait. I'd thrown a few planks of plywood over the hole that my neighbor's bull terrier had made trying to steal a chicken dinner last week. Fortunately, my collie Ajax had heard the terrier's scuffle with the rooster. Ajax was convinced the hens were his monarchs and protected the pen like a British guard. He'd chased the terrier out of the yard before the hens lost anything more than feathers. Unfortunately, the rooster had met his end in the terrier's jaws. Ajax had taken to sleeping at the gate of the henhouse and the neighbor's dog hadn't come near our property since.

Rhonda was brushing Don Juan and keeping one eye on the front driveway. I flipped a grain bucket upside down and took a seat, leaning my back against the barn door. "Don Juan's looking good. I think he likes that extra ration of grain we've been giving him." His black coat glistened in the sunlight. "You're taking him out on the trails tonight?"

Rhonda nodded, obviously distracted.

"So you really like this girl?"

"I've had a crush on her for about a year now. Finally got up the guts to ask her to come out for a ride. I couldn't believe it when she said yes."

It had been a long time since I'd seen Rhonda so interested in someone. I glanced at the sun, still high but inching toward the horizon, "If she doesn't show—"

"She'll show." Rhonda checked the road again, hearing a car coming over the hill. The car continued past the gates of the ranch and Rhonda turned back to Don Juan. She combed his mane half-heartedly. "I thought you had work to do."

"Someone told me I should be sociable. Anyway, I'm expecting a load of hay and they always deliver it here around six."

"It's not six yet, is it?" Rhonda nervously glanced at her watch. "Five thirty. She was supposed to get off work at four. I guess she could have gone home first to change. Do you think she got lost?"

"Relax, I'm sure she'll be here soon. Has a girl ever stood you up, Rhonda?" Rhonda had recently informed me that she'd had more dates in the past year than she had shoes. And she wasn't short on shoes.

She shrugged. "This isn't even a date, really. Meg thinks we're just friends."

"Uh-oh. That sounds like trouble." I knew that Rhonda had a tendency to fall for unavailable women. We had discussed the issue more times than I could count. "Does she drive a red Jeep?" A topless Jeep crested the hill and turned down the road heading for the ranch. The driver pulled up at the house and then looked around as if searching for some marker. The only way to know if you were at McCormick Ranch was by the sign on the side of the main road that said MC. Otherwise, no address was posted. Most people drove right on by and then had to turn back once they reached the main highway and realized they were twenty miles off course.

Rhonda dropped the brush in her tack bucket. "Yep, that's Meg. Okay, I'll admit it. I was a little nervous she might stand me up." She turned and headed up the path toward the house, waving to get her friend's attention.

I watched Rhonda greet the woman. They didn't hug, didn't even stand too close. Meg held up a pair of boots and Rhonda nodded, waiting for her to change out of her sandals. Then the two made their way down to the barn. I couldn't make out any of their words by lip reading but I did notice Rhonda pointing out the trails between the pastures and where the Sierra Mountain Range began, toward the east.

"Meg, this is June." She made the introduction with a nod of her head.

Meg smiled and shook my hand. She had a grip as strong as a man's and I squeezed back just as hard.

"We've met before," she said, letting go of my hand.

17

Rhonda looked at me. "Really? You two know each other?"

"I'm sorry, I don't remember . . ." I racked my brain, thinking there was no way I'd forget meeting a woman like her. Meg was tall, nearly Gabe's height, and he was six feet. She had disarming blue eyes with dark black eyelashes and was one of those women that anyone would catch themselves staring at.

Meg smiled. "I'm not surprised. You were out like a light. Did Rhonda tell you I'm a paramedic?"

I stared at her for a moment. "Yeah, Rhonda told me." It occurred to me that I had met a paramedic a year ago. Of course I wouldn't have been able to tell one thing about the woman who'd helped me then. "Don't tell me you were one of the ambulance medics?" As soon as I said it, the whole accident came back in unsettling flashes. I remembered riding Jericho. He had an easy lope and I'd just started to relax. A plane had buzzed low over the ranch and Jericho took this as an excuse to go into a bucking spree. One of my stirrups snapped and the next thing I felt was a fence post clocking the side of my head. I'd heard a loud crack and then was on my back wondering if the fence post had split. Then the nauseating pain in my leg started and I guessed the sound had come from my bone snapping. The rest of the details were blurry. I had almost lost vision in my right eye—the doctors were all ranting about brain swelling and nerve damage. Fortunately, I'd only lost peripheral vision. As long as I looked straight ahead, everything stayed clear. "To tell you the truth, I've tried to forget that whole incident."

"I won't take it personally." Meg smiled at me and continued talking to Rhonda, "It's funny that I'd heard you talk about this place and never realized I'd been here. But I didn't really have much time to appreciate it." She glanced at the green pastures where the young mares were grazing and then her head turned toward the golden hills dotted with oaks just past the edge of the barn. I followed her gaze. In May, the hills were just turning gold. By July, they were dry and brown. Spring never lasted long enough.

"So I'm just going to finish up with Don Juan and then we'll find you a horse to ride." Rhonda went over to her tack bucket and fished out a hoof pick. Meg was still gazing out at the lay of the land and I couldn't help but wonder what she remembered from the last time she'd been here. As Rhonda passed me, she whispered. "I know you don't go for women, but can you tell me truthfully that she isn't a thing of beauty?"

"Too clean for me. I bet she freaks when she chips a nail."

"Oh, no, sugar. She's way too butch for that."

"Who's too butch?" Meg asked, looking over at us.

Rhonda blushed, so I had to jump in. "Cassidy. One of the mares I'm training. Rhonda has nicknamed her Butch Cassidy."

"Butch Cassidy. I like it. Is she the horse I get to ride?"

"No." Rhonda replied. "Not if you want to walk tomorrow."

"She isn't broke yet," I added.

"You mean, she's not trained?"

I nodded. "You might never forgive Rhonda for bringing you out here if we put you on that horse." I might not forgive myself either. Then again, it would help Rhonda decide just how tough her new love interest really was.

"Do you train all the horses here? And run the ranch? Rhonda told me there are over a dozen horses boarding here and it looks like you have a dozen or so more out in the pasture. Do you have anyone helping you out with all the work?"

The question was pointed. She seemed to be asking, "Is a single woman running this place alone?" Ordinarily I would have been offended but it occurred to me that she was ready to be impressed, not thinking I was doomed to fail as most people did. "Actually forty horses total. We have some people that just retire the horses out to pasture, others board here to ride the trails. We've got a breeding stallion and some brood mares. I train all the young ones and sell the others."

"The ones she doesn't get too attached to," Rhonda added.

"I used to dream about working on a ranch when I was a kid." Meg paused. "Guess that sounds pretty stupid to you guys." I knew she meant to include Rhonda and me but she was only looking my way when she continued, "I was a city kid and the only wildlife I saw on a regular basis were pigeons in a city park. So I played with plastic horses until my parents sent me to horse camp one summer. I think they were hoping I'd get my fill of horses."

"You didn't?"

"No. I got thrown off the first horse I tried riding and broke my arm." She smiled. "My mom got scared and wouldn't let me go back, no matter how much I begged. I gave away the plastic horses after that. Once you see the real thing, plastic won't cut it."

Rhonda stifled a laugh and added under her breath, "I've never had a problem with my plastic toys."

Meg either didn't hear Rhonda's comment or was tactfully ignoring it. Her gaze was set on the two yearlings roughhousing in the nearest field. I decided to use my usual approach to late bloomers who came here with their dusty dreams of horse riding. "You know, it's never too late to learn to ride. We can set you up on a horse that won't throw you off unless you do something real stupid."

"June is always trying to recruit more women riders here." After a moment, Rhonda added, "Not that it's a bad thing, to have more women around . . ." A blush tinged her cheeks and she fell silent.

Rhonda had always been a big flirt. She was also prone to going too far and making others embarrassed for her. I glanced over at Meg and realized she was staring at me and at my hands in particular. I had picked up a bucket of grain, intended as a treat for Cassidy, though she didn't really deserve one. With Meg's eyes on me, I couldn't help but feel self-conscious. I never gave my appearance a second thought, so long as I was wearing a clean shirt and had brushed my hair that morning. This shirt had only been worn twice before and my hair was probably fairly tidy. I'd pulled it back in a ponytail after lunch. But I knew my hands were filthy. My sister used to ride me for not taking better care of my hands, the fingernails in particular. The idea of a manicure struck me as a good way to waste ten bucks. With scars crisscrossing the backsides of my hands from skirmishes with barbed wire fences, a blackish-blue spot on my thumb from a misplaced hammer and several split nails, I figured trying nail polish was a lost cause. And lotion didn't do a thing for the calluses that roughened my palms and every fingertip.

"I bet it's a harder job running a ranch then most people realize," Meg said finally. "I don't think I'd be cut out for it, even if I could ride."

"June's got help," Rhonda said. "There are two ranch hands you'll see roaming around the place. They do most of the work. Don't give June all the credit." She winked at me. "We'll run into one sooner or later and I'll introduce you."

"Yeah, I remember meeting a guy here last time who said he was a ranch hand. He had a thick black mustache and wouldn't shut up. Not really that helpful, either."

"Gabe." I smiled at her description, which was perfect. "He's been at the ranch for ten years now, though he'd rather be mixing drinks at a bar on some Caribbean island. And then Shank—his real name's Sherman but he goes by Shank. He runs the tractor and cleans the pastures. We just took on a new ranch hand last week." Rhonda perked up at this. She liked to stay in the know for everything that happened at the ranch and mostly I told her. This new addition I'd been trying to keep on the down-low until I decided if she was going to work out or not. "You haven't met Chris yet."

"No."

"She'll be here on Saturday. Maybe you could come by and introduce yourself."

"She? You hired a girl?" Rhonda furrowed her brow. Her eyebrows came together in a line whenever something didn't sit right with her.

"What's wrong with that?"

"Nothing. I'm just surprised."

Why would Rhonda care if I hired a woman? "Well, you won't

21

be surprised when you see her." I held up my arm and flexed my biceps, then pushed my fingers on it to make it look bigger. "Tough girl. She'll put Gabe to shame."

Meg grinned. "Now that sounds interesting. Can I come back on Saturday too?"

I shrugged. "Sure." Meg's smile made you feel that she wore every emotion honestly. I had to admit that Rhonda was right. Meg was certainly attractive, in a kind of androgynous way. If she'd had long hair, all the men would be after her. But her black hair was cut as short as a boy's, curling softly behind her ears. She seemed to have a carefree attitude and if she had any problems in the world I would bet she was good at hiding them. Her blue eyes settled on me and I realized too late that I'd been staring at her. I glanced over at Rhonda quickly.

"June, I was thinking of getting Meg up on Don Juan and taking Gypsy myself. Do you mind loaning her?"

Gypsy was one of my dad's brood mares that I had finally decided to train a few years ago. She was a little feisty but good on the trails. I'd considered selling the horse to one of my neighbor's kids but hadn't gotten around to it yet. My dad would have wanted to keep the old mare. He hated to sell any of the breeding stock. "Not at all. Gypsy needs the exercise."

"Good. Then we'll catch those two and give you some time to decide which horse you're taking out on the ride with us." Rhonda finished cleaning Don Juan and grabbed an extra halter and lead line, motioning Meg to follow her.

Meg glanced at me. "You're coming on the ride too?"

I didn't miss the hopeful tone in her voice. She acted like she didn't want to be alone with Rhonda. "Actually, I can't. I have to hang around here to wait for a load of hay."

"Why the hell do you pay Gabe, anyway?" Rhonda interjected. "He can wait for the truck."

"I think you should come with us," Meg said.

I felt my cheeks warm as Meg stared at me. I wasn't sure why I was blushing. A moment later I'd convinced myself that she hadn't noticed. I was glad Rhonda had already turned her back. She would have called me on it. I thought of joining them for a ride and liked the idea but couldn't decide if Rhonda really would want me tagging along. "Maybe."

Rhonda was halfway down the path toward the south pasture. "Come on, Meg," Rhonda called over her shoulder. "I'll probably need an extra hand with Gypsy. We'll give June some time to consider the trail offer."

Meg started to follow Rhonda then paused. "It's good to see you again, you know, under better circumstances."

"I agree." I followed Meg and Rhonda with my eyes until they had crossed behind the barn and disappeared from view. Remembering Cassidy, I went to untie the mare and return her to the pasture. Tanner trotted over to the gate, hoping for a handout, and then scuffled with Cassidy who was fit to be tied after the bath. I started to close the gate but changed my mind, thinking that Tanner needed some exercise. Tanner was a chestnut gelding with a white blaze on his head and four white socks. He was one of my father's retired racing quarter horses and always ready for a trail ride. Tanner also enjoyed a game of chase when it came to being haltered, which was no game to me. I tried to throw a line around his neck three or four times and he skillfully sidestepped just out of reach. Finally I resorted to lassoing him. After I caught him, he jogged over to me and rubbed his head on my side as if he'd been hoping I'd win all along.

By the time Rhonda had lectured Meg on the basics of leading, grooming and saddling a horse, it was half past six. The alfalfa had already been delivered and the load was in the storage shed. I'd left Tanner tied up next to Don Juan and the two geldings were nuzzling each other, patiently waiting to stretch their legs on the trail while Gypsy served time as Rhonda's demonstration horse. Gypsy was a dark bay mare with no interesting markings and worth a good amount mainly because her sire was a well-known rodeo champion. Gypsy wasn't much of a rodeo queen herself but I'd sold a few colts out of her for a nice price and now she'd earned the right to a relaxed life on the pasture. Gypsy clearly was frustrated with lifting her hooves for Rhonda's inspection, tossing her head and snorting as Rhonda explained the finer points of hoof-picking. Meg kept nodding in agreement whenever Rhonda asked her if she understood one thing or another, but I doubted she was paying close attention. She gazed at the north pasture and the valley beyond it, at the two colts romping in the arena and then over at Tanner and me, clearly distracted from Rhonda's lecture.

I interrupted Rhonda just as she brought up hoof fungus. "So, I think we better get a move on if we don't want to get caught on a moonlit ride home."

"Right," Rhonda said. "I guess hoof diseases can probably wait. Do you have any other questions Meg?"

She had already put her foot in the stirrup and slipped into the saddle like she'd done it a hundred times before. Turning to me, she asked under her breath, "So, is it really all that complicated? Seems like all I have to do is sit here in the saddle and hold on."

"It's not complicated. Don Juan will take care of you. With another horse, I'd be worried. But I'd put a baby in that saddle and slap Don Juan's ass."

Meg grinned. "I don't think we're quite ready for ass slapping."

"Just relax and stick behind Rhonda's mare. Don Juan won't shy from anything. If you point his nose right on Gypsy's tail, he'll follow like an elephant."

Rhonda untied the lead lines and slid into her saddle. "Everyone ready?"

We set off for the north facing canyon, Rhonda and Gypsy in the lead with Tanner and me picking up the tail. Meg was quiet for most of the ride, pointing out every bug that passed with her index finger. She was as happy with the horseflies and beetles as she was with the dragonflies and butterflies. I asked her about this and the only answer I got was, "Yeah, I'm into bugs."

"Why?" I couldn't see anything fascinating about a horsefly except the fact that it was big and annoying as hell.

She shrugged. "I majored in biology in college and I always planned on continuing on, getting a masters or maybe even a doctorate in entomology. The study of bugs, you know."

I nodded and almost said, "Although I live on a ranch, I'm not totally ignorant." Instead, I wondered how liking bugs would have led to a paramedic job. "So what do bugs and ambulances have to do with each other?"

"Nothing, really."

A bumblebee buzzed near a rosemary bush and that was the end of our conversation. I'd ridden the summit trail more times than I could count, always hoping to catch the perfect sunset but simple things seemed suddenly beautiful with a new pair of eyes noticing them. Bugs, however, I doubted if I could ever come to appreciate. I was surprised at how well she took to riding, given her brief experience. Most green riders sit in the saddle as stiff as a stick but Meg had relaxed almost as soon as her jeans settled on the leather. It helped that Don Juan was dead broke and could probably follow the trail with a blindfolded rider.

By the time we reached the summit, the sun had slipped from view and the low-lying clouds streaked the sky in shades of pink, purple and orange. We gave the horses a moment to snack on some clover grass and then turned the whole company around and headed home. Meg started talking then. She joked about the horse camp where she'd broke her arm and how she'd had this plan then to steal racehorses off the track and start up a retirement ranch. Rhonda claimed our ranch wasn't far from that, minus the stealing. She'd never liked the racing industry and wasn't happy when I'd agreed to take on the thoroughbreds.

I tried to give Meg and Rhonda some distance so they could talk and reined Tanner back from the group. He had a bad habit of riding too close to Don Juan's heels and was pushing for a race now. But leaving them alone didn't seem to inspire any intimate conversation. Rhonda was going on about the problems with horse racing while Meg was paying closer attention to the views of the valley. I found myself watching Meg and leaving Tanner to crowd up on Don Juan again. I wondered what she was thinking about and what little things she noticed that I'd overlooked growing up here. We got back to the ranch sooner than I wanted to and I didn't get a chance to ask.

"So, what do you think of her?" Rhonda slunk down in the sofa, pushing the magazines to the corner of the coffee table to make room for her bare feet.

I thought about my words, choosing carefully. "She's nice. And she can ride all right. Of course, she was on Don Juan and he can keep a baby in the saddle."

"I also gave her a good lesson beforehand." Rhonda smiled. She took a sip of her beer then set the bottle on top of the magazines. "Thanks for stopping me before I told her about hoof thrush. What the hell was I thinking?"

"Beats me."

"I'm too nervous around her," she admitted. "Half the time, I don't even know if she's the least bit interested in me. She's hard to read."

The light in the kitchen sent a feeble glow into the family room and Rhonda was mostly in the dark. I sat down on the rocker next to the sofa and switched on the lamp between us. We'd finished the ride just after dusk and Meg had only stayed long enough to see the horses unsaddled and brushed. Rhonda invited herself to spend the night at the house. I didn't mind the company for dinner. It wasn't unusual for Rhonda to stay over after a late ride. In fact, the hospital where she worked was closer to the ranch than it was to Rhonda's downtown apartment. Besides, it was easier for me to eat vegetables when I had someone else noticing what was on my plate. Otherwise a burger with ketchup and pickles qualified as a well-rounded meal.

Rhonda swiped her finger on the edge of the lampshade. "You ever think about dusting in here?"

"Not often. What are you suggesting?"

Rhonda shrugged. "Nothing . . . I clean compulsively. Vacuum twice a week and dust just as often, sometimes more. I think I like Meg."

"I don't see the connection."

"There isn't any connection." Rhonda took another sip of her beer. "What do you think—should I ask her out on another date?"

I got up and went to the kitchen to get a clean dishrag. I tossed it to Rhonda. "Well, asking her on another date can't hurt. You like her just as well as the others you've dated, right?"

"Why'd you give me this?" She paused, turning the blue check-ered cloth in her hands. "Trouble is, I like her better than the others."

Rhonda liked the women that were hard to get. I didn't want to tell her that she wasn't going to get Meg. What did I know, anyway? I motioned to the rag. "Figured you could dust for a while if it helps you think. My dad used to say cleaning dirty windows gives you a clearer perspective. Maybe that's what you need. Though I think he said that mostly to keep my sister and me from being lazy. Anyway, God knows I've got enough dirt here to give anyone a chance at cleaner thoughts."

"How is Karen? Haven't heard from her in a while."

Karen was my older sister. She worked as a loan broker for a big bank in the city and was co-owner of the ranch. "Okay I guess. When I hear from her it's always bad news but it's been six days now so I'd bet she's fine." The less I saw of Karen, the better I felt. I turned then and headed down the hallway toward my room.

"Where are you going? I thought we were gonna watch the news. You're not leaving me alone to dust, are you?"

We hadn't agreed to watching the news and right now it was the last thing I wanted to do. Meeting Meg and thinking about the accident had got my mind spinning. I couldn't believe a year had passed since I'd broken my leg. That was when Karen had decided we ought to sell the ranch. She'd picked the moment I'd gotten back from the hospital to show up with a horde of developers who wanted to talk about splitting the ranch into cookie-cutter lots. The developers were friends of Ned, Karen's husband. He was a real estate agent and as pushy as they come.

I never understood why my dad thought Karen and I should run the ranch together. We'd spent our whole lives finding ways to disagree. In the end, dad had left the ranch in both of our names thinking this would be a way we could resolve our differences. Karen went on and on about the easy millions that selling the land would bring. I'd made her a deal then. If the ranch was making money in a year, we'd hold onto it. If we were losing money, the developers could come have a second look. Karen agreed, so long as she was in charge of the books. She gave me weekly reports of how bad we were doing that first year. Barely breaking even. She was chomping at the bit to sell, repeating Ned's line about the hot market and how we had the perfect location for a gated community and private golf course. The idea nauseated me—but it also made me determined. I sold a few horses and advertised hard to get new boarders. A year later I was keeping Karen happy with our monthly totals. She even admitted we were making more money than when our father had managed the place and took all the credit for it on account of her managing skills.

I wanted some time alone to think. "I'm gonna take a shower. You can watch TV or dust, whatever your pleasure. Better yet, dream about your new girlfriend."

Rhonda sighed. "Fine. I'll dust. Take your shower, then come back and watch the late night show with me. I'm feeling lonely tonight."

I didn't remind her that I'd been lonely for much longer than a night. Instead, I agreed to the late night show. Rhonda had broken off her last fling a week ago. I couldn't even remember the last time someone had wanted to watch me undress. After Greg, I'd given plenty of thought to dating. But then I got used to sleeping diagonally in the double bed. I hadn't spoken with Greg since the divorce papers had been filed and for the past few years I'd only shared breakfast with the ranch hands and the occasional dinner with Rhonda. Rhonda spent more time at the ranch when she was between girlfriends. For the most part, I didn't feel lonely. But I noticed it sometimes. And then there was nothing to be done about it, like you notice the smell of a clear night sky after months without a drop of rain.

Mac, the fattest cat on the ranch, was curled up in an orange ball at the foot of my bed. I passed my hand over his head and got his purring started. He slunk off the bed after a minute or so, thinking of dinner probably, and padded down the hallway toward the kitchen. I stripped off my jeans and tossed them in the laundry bin, then unbuttoned my blue shirt and unclasped my bra. The mirror nailed to the bedroom door caught my reflection. I criticized the naked image, poking at my breasts that always seemed too small for the rest of me. Something made me think of Meg then and I wondered what her blue eyes had seen when she stared at me for so long that afternoon. I brushed back my hair, the same shade of brown as the dry oat grasses in summer, and tried smiling. The image changed imperceptibly. I thought of the sunset that evening and all its colors. I'd always wanted to be more colorful. My wardrobe was full of reds, blues and greens. As soon as I was naked though, the colors all disappeared. I'd had a physical last month and the nurse smiled as she'd pronounced me average. "Average height, average weight, average blood pressure. How nice!" Apparently that made her life easier. The mirror only accentuated the plainness, quietly proclaiming that I was a thirty-four-year-old woman, divorced and an average muted brown.

The first time I'd noticed the color of my body I was four or five years old and it was late summer. I'd been following my dad on his morning ride and had gotten distracted by a place off the trail where the grass was bent down in a semicircle. Later, I came to recognize these patches as a place where deer bedded, their weight causing the grass to flatten, but at the time I'd thought it was a little bed the wind had made for me. I'd laid on my back in the center of the patch and gazed up at a cloudless sky. A hawk had circled, his shadow crossing my belly several times, then he'd fly on as if he'd never noticed me. It was easy to imagine that the hawk had confused me with the weeds. Even my eyes were somewhere between weed brown and gold.

I took my time in the shower then found a clean shirt and boxer shorts before going back to the family room. Rhonda was sound asleep on the sofa, the late night show just beginning. I switched off the TV and instead of waking Rhonda, found a quilt to spread over her. I replaced her empty beer bottle with a glass of water, she always wanted water when she woke up, then swept my finger along the base of the lamp shade. My clean fingertip wasn't any surprise. Just like Rhonda. Not only had the shade been dusted, the coffee table, the fireplace mantle, the bookcase and my father's mounted rifle case were all clean testaments to Rhonda's busy mind.

Saturday came quicker than expected. That was the way of things lately. I was forever trying to catch up. Karen was due for a visit that evening. She'd called the day before to say we had a list of inventory items to discuss. I never cared for her discussion techniques. "For instance," she'd said, "why do we have to buy two types of hay? The alfalfa hay is two dollars more per bale than the oat." Sometimes I wished I'd never agreed to let Karen be the financial manager. I was thinking of this when Chris, the new hand, showed up. Right on time.

"Morning," she mumbled. She wore a cowboy hat kicked back on her head and carried a little bundle wrapped up in a bit of plaid cloth.

I guessed the bundle was her lunch but didn't ask. Instead, I asked her how she liked mornings. She grumbled a bit about the sun not being up yet. Chris was twenty-three and low on motivation. She'd told me this much about herself. The first time I saw her, the only thing I thought was, "Looks like she's wandering without a compass." It was something my dad used to say about me when I'd hitchhiked across the country twice before I found my way back to El Dorado County. It took me a while before my legs lost that itch for a new trail and I agreed to settle down. Sometimes I thought I should have wandered for a few years more. Chris had heard from a neighbor that I was looking for an extra hand. I wasn't, but I'd hired her for a trial run anyway.

My rules were few, one being the ranch hands showed up at the house for breakfast at six a.m. and we all started work at half past. Two being everyone cleaned stalls at least once a day. Three being payday wasn't arbitrary and I didn't give loans. Gabe was always late but he brought his wife's homemade biscuits, still warm, so I gave him leeway of fifteen minutes. Shank was already in the kitchen, watching the fry pan and waiting like a hungry puppy for his breakfast. I pointed Chris inside and the two of them got to know each other over mugs of coffee and plates of eggs and bacon. Then Gabe arrived and the house smelled more like morning with the warm biscuits he brought. Spread with a slice of butter and warm honey, the cornmeal biscuits were second to no other. We feasted quietly for a few minutes and then I started detailing our plans for the day. "Chris, do you like painting?"

"No, ma'am."

"Well, you do now," Gabe said, grinning.

"We're painting the barn. It's kind of yellow-mud colored right now. Used to be white. We almost decided to paint it red but gray was on sale. We power washed yesterday and we'll keep the horses out of the arena to keep down the dust. Gonna be a pain in the ass if the wind picks up before the paint's dry."

"We're all painting?" Shank asked.

I knew better than to let Shank paint anything. He wasn't good with inanimate objects and got distracted too easily. With my luck Shank would probably paint the dog and half the horses gray after an hour of sheer boredom staring at a barn. "Gabe and Chris will start on the painting. Shank and I will do the morning feedings. Then I'm gonna take a ride out to check the Hudson's north fence.

I figured you could make a run through the pasture and have a look at the foals."

Shank was happy with this plan. "I like foals better than fences anyway."

I had begun to detest fences as well. Mr. Hudson had dropped a note in my mailbox yesterday saying that our fence "might be down in one or two spots." We shared a fence on the north side of the property with the Hudsons and it was their terrier that had busted into the chicken coop. Not only was his terrier a burr in my sock, Mr. Hudson had an obstinate mama goat that was dead set against staying on her side of the fence. Instead of jumping the fence, she was determined to take it down. I'd had to replace nearly a hundred yards of the line because of that damn goat. Whether I liked it or not, I had to stay on good terms with the Hudsons, though. We shared a well.

"Shank, can you check on Trixie too?" She was one of our mares that foaled last April. "I noticed she was favoring one of her hind legs. Probably one of the others kicked her."

"I'll clean her up and let you know what I find. Her colt's looking good. Saw him running around the pasture happy as a murderer day before yesterday."

I didn't add anything to his comment and noticed Chris looking a little uncomfortable. Maybe she'd heard that I hired ex-cons. It was a rumor that the Hudsons had started and not unfounded. Funny thing was, Gabe, who had been caught smashing a bottle of liquor on someone's backside in a bar fight, was my ex-con, not Shank. Shank wouldn't harm a flea. Anyway, Chris would get used to all of our strange ways soon enough. "Then I'll need your help this afternoon with Cassidy. I want to get her ready for a buyer who's coming to have a look at the end of the month. She needs to be solid broke by then."

"No problem." Shank, an old bronco rider, had the best seat of any man I'd met. But his hands were a little rough. Gabe was better where this was concerned but I wasn't willing to put either of them up on Cassidy and have her mouth turned sour by a hard rein. Instead, I had every plan on riding the mare myself but I wanted his advice and good luck charm to keep me in the saddle.

"So, we're painting all day?" Chris asked tentatively.

"We take a break for lunch and another for siesta," Gabe answered. "It's too hot to paint when the sun's overhead so that's when we rest."

The last thing I needed was Gabe influencing the new hand on his mission to get two afternoon breaks. "We take a lunch break and then I'll need you to clean out the stalls in the barn this afternoon. No siesta, Gabe."

"No siesta, of course not. What was I thinking?" He smiled bravely. "I'm Italian, not Spanish. Italians don't take siestas. Then again, Italians don't start working at six a.m. either." He whispered "siesta at three" under his breath.

"Chris, don't listen to a thing this man tells you."

"Right. After lunch we'll find a nice shady stall and shovel shit. Welcome to the romantic world of ranch life." Gabe patted his mustache and stretched his arms. He yawned, showing off his silver-filled cavities.

Chris nodded, looking a little bewildered. Gabe slapped her on the back and added, "Don't listen to a thing any of us say at the McCormick ranch. We're all a little crazy from the horse manure fumes. That's why we need the siesta. Not that we take one."

"All right, breakfast is over. Let's get to work. Gabe, thank Janet for the biscuits. Perfect as always." I finished my last bite of honeyed cornmeal biscuit and started collecting the dirty dishes. The others filed out of the kitchen, Gabe still going on about labor rights and the necessity of four breaks a day and Shank noticing the colors of the sunrise. Chris was quiet, probably trying to decide if the meager hourly wage I'd offered would be enough to keep her here through the summer.

Mr. Hudson, among others, hadn't been happy with me taking over the ranch. They were hoping Karen would give up the bank job when our father died and take over. Karen was the successful one. She'd aced her way through college and married well. Ned's family had cattle ranches in El Dorado County and their name was well-known. I stood in Ned's way of taking the ranch and neither he nor Karen knew one iota about horse breeding. Karen had given up riding too long ago to remember why she'd once liked horses. These days, she heard the words horsepower and thought of BMWs. Ned hadn't ridden a horse, ever. He didn't even like dirt.

Still, the neighbors held out hope. They couldn't see a woman running a place alone. Mr. Hudson said he regretted my dad wasn't still alive, because he "didn't like to see the ranch go to hell." I decided I wasn't going to win any points with him by arguing. Mr. Hudson was just an ornery old man who didn't like change.

The fence was down, just as Mr. Hudson had claimed. I rode Tanner along the fence line for about a half mile before I found the bad spot. The wire was bent down but the posts were still in place. It was nearly the same spot I'd repaired last week and just a hundred yards or so from the well. This time I caught the mama goat on my side. I had to drag her kicking and butting back to the Hudson's property while I tried to rewire the fence. Obstinate isn't a strong enough word for a goat on a mission. I couldn't see what she found so appealing on my side of the fence. The yellowing oats and thistle brush looked the same on both sides. Then I noticed Don Juan tromping his way over to where I'd tied Tanner. He nudged Tanner with his muzzle by way of greeting and then continued in a more or less direct path to the fence. The goat's ears perked up as soon as she saw him getting closer. Don Juan paused and sniffed my tool belt, then hung his head over the fence. The goat started bleating like a maniac, her ears flapping back and forth. I bursted out laughing. Don Juan had charmed the goat.

Just as I'd finished with the repair, Mr. Hudson rode up on his nearly blind Appaloosa. The horse was as surefooted as he was sighted and a catastrophe waiting to happen but Mr. Hudson didn't seem to care. I waved but Mr. Hudson didn't return the greeting. He wasn't one for formalities.

"See you found the spot."

I nodded.

"And that wasn't the only damage your horses did to my property." Mr. Hudson punctuated his sentences with spits of dark tobacco juice. He still insisted that the fence was his property, not shared between the two ranches. Several years ago he'd had his land marked out by someone from the county and it was discovered that my dad had built the common fence two feet off the mark. The whole length of the fence was on Hudson's property. He was livid to find out that for the past thirty years, my dad had been using his land. The well that we thought we owned in common also ended up being solely on his property. My dad and Mr. Hudson had worked out some agreement to share the water regardless.

"There's hoofprints all through the garden bed. The greens are ruined as are the tomatoes. Do you know how much those damages are gonna cost?"

I didn't point out that either of his two horses could have trampled through the garden. Nor did I point out that it was the goat who had taken out the fence. I knew it was safer to blame it on the wildlife. "We've had some destructive deer this year, Mr. Hudson. The Clarks told me they were having the same problems and they've caught the deer red-handed in their garden. The deer are going for the fruit in the orchards too."

Mr. Hudson considered this for a moment, chewing on his tobacco. The Clarks were our neighbors to the south. They hadn't told me anything about destructive deer and I couldn't even remember if they kept a garden. I banged my hammer on a nail that I'd already driven into the wood, focusing on the wire that encircled the post and pointedly ignoring Mr. Hudson. After a moment, I noticed that the Appaloosa had turned around and was heading toward the well, away from me. Mr. Hudson was gone without any further conversation. I'd won the argument at the expense of the deer and hoped Mr. Hudson wasn't thinking of oiling his rifle now.

An hour or so after lunch, Gabe decided it was everyone's unofficial siesta time. It was heating up to be a warm afternoon and I wasn't in the mood for arguing. I'd been craving lemonade and went up to the house to mix up some.

Rhonda showed up with a bag of groceries. "Hi. You making that for me?" She nodded at the pitcher. "I invited Meg to come for a ride. Would it be okay if we had her stay for a barbecue afterward? We can invite the ranch hands too."

"Barbecue sounds fine." I wasn't in the mood to have a dinner party here but Rhonda liked to play hostess and she usually did most of the entertaining work.

"Where is everyone?"

I knew she meant "where's the new hand?" Ever since I mentioned that Chris had big muscles and had been working as a hired hand on local ranches, Rhonda had decided she must be gay and therefore couldn't wait to meet her. I didn't tell her that Chris was more than ten years younger than us and had mentioned an out-of-town boyfriend when I first hired her. "Shank's lunging Cassidy in the round pen. Chris and Gabe are taking a break from painting the barn."

Rhonda dropped her bag on the counter and got a glass, waiting somewhat impatiently for me to fill it. She took a sip, pinching her lips at the tartness, and started in. "So, what's the word? Is she gay?"

"All I know is that she paints slower than Gabe. I'm hoping she knows how to handle a horse better than a paintbrush."

"What does it matter if she paints slow? Sometimes slow strokes are good." Rhonda winked.

"Don't go there. She's too young and I don't think she's your type. Besides, I thought you had a girlfriend coming over." I poured a glass of lemonade for myself and filled three more for the hands.

"We're not even dating. I think she's only coming tonight because she wants to ride. A horse, that is . . ." Rhonda grabbed two of the glasses. "Come on, I wanna meet the new gal. How young is she?"

We met up with Shank at the round pen. Cassidy had worked up a good sweat and according to Shank, she was ready for a rider. I could see he was eager to jump on the mare but I handed him a glass of lemonade and thanked him for warming her up for me. Rhonda left us, saying she wanted to find the others. Shank and Rhonda didn't get along for reasons I never could understand, so they parted without so much as a hello. I grabbed a saddle and a bridle with a gentle snaffle bit and had Shank keep a good hold on Cassidy as I put on the tack.

Rhonda brought Don Juan out sooner than I expected. Apparently siesta had ended and Gabe and Chris were already painting again. She'd had to leave their lemonades without any excuse to stand around and chat. In that brief interaction, however, Rhonda decided that I had not underestimated Chris's muscles, she wasn't too young to be called a hottie and she definitely wasn't straight.

I didn't try to correct Rhonda. My thoughts were focused on Cassidy now. I waited impatiently for Rhonda to saddle Don Juan and we led the horses over to the larger arena. Don Juan was supposed to be Cassidy's moral support but she didn't seem to give him any notice. Rhonda hopped on Don Juan and she circled the arena a few times before I decided I better get in the saddle. Shank had already tried teasing me about being scared of the little mare.

"She's too tired to give you any trouble, June," Shank said. "And I already let her know you're the boss-woman around here."

"I don't think that will make a difference to her, but thanks. Cassidy still believes she is her own boss." I scratched Cassidy's sweaty neck and rested my hand on the saddle. Don Juan made a few circles around the arena before I finally placed a foot in the stirrup and slipped onto Cassidy's back. The moment she felt my weight in the seat, Cassidy reared and took off at a full gallop. I felt my heart rise up into my throat and had to struggle to swallow. Rhonda pulled Don Juan out of the way as Cassidy and I raced around the arena. Cassidy was bucking every other stride and I kept telling myself to let her run this out while Shank called advice from the sidelines like an irate coach of a losing basketball team. I wanted her to trust me. I knew I could stop her with a hard yank on the bit but I didn't want to risk injuring her mouth or beating her spirit into submission as Shank was ready to do.

Finally, she slowed down to a jog. When she wasn't bucking, she had the smoothest gait that I could hope for on a young horse. I tried steering her toward the rail but as soon as the bit moved against her tongue, she reared again and we were off at a mind-numbing speed.

"Slow her down, June," Shank hollered. "She needs to know she's got a bit in that mouth for a reason."

I want her to make the decision to stop and get rewarded for it. Shank gave me a look like he'd thought I'd gone mad—again. Don Juan and Rhonda had parked themselves in the center of the arena, more or less just as spectators. On one of our circles around the arena, I noticed Meg had joined Shank on the fence. Meg's face had a strange look—something between concern and disbelief. After too long, Cassidy started to wear herself out. I yelled whoa and got no response from her. If anything, the sound made her pick up speed. Shoving my boots into the stirrups and sitting back, I tightened the reins and tried "whoa" again, adding "and I mean it." She slid to a halt. Finally. We circled the arena at a walk for a few minutes. Once I had her under control, we worked on turning directions and leg commands. She picked up the signals with an amazing quickness. I ended the lesson before anything else set her off. When I dismounted, Shank was waiting to take the reins. He didn't hide his disappointment when I shook my head. I knew he wanted to try a spin on her. "She's done with the riding lesson.

Walk her out until she relaxes. Or falls down. At this point, I don't really care which happens first."

Meg and Rhonda took Gypsy and Don Juan out on the trails later. I knew Rhonda could use some time alone with Meg so I opted out of the ride when she invited me to come along. As soon as Rhonda's back was turned, Meg asked if I'd reconsider and join them. I gave the excuse of needing to pay the ranch hands and tried not to notice Meg's disappointed expression. I wanted to go on their ride—Meg was hard to say no to. Fortunately, I did have work to do.

Saturdays were payday and Gabe and Shank both started murmuring about quittin' time by five o'clock. I let them go, giving them my dad's old warning, "Don't spend it all in one place and don't bet on horses."

Gabe nodded. "The races are all a set-up."

I knew Gabe placed a bet every week. His wife told me as much, hoping I could convince him against it. One morning Gabe didn't show up for work and I learned the secret. He'd finally won on a no-name rider and a no-name horse. Gabe was back to work the next week. He'd gone through all of his winnings and his wife was pissed. We didn't get biscuits for a while after that.

Since Chris hadn't worked a full week, she wasn't supposed to be paid yet. Guessing she was living on nickels and dimes by now, I gave her a day's pay anyway. I asked if she'd mind hanging around to chat for a bit. She agreed to wait up on the porch swing by the house while I went to place a much less spirited Cassidy back in the pasture. By the time I trudged back up to the house, Chris was sound asleep on the swing.

I gave her shoulder a nudge with my hand and she turned to the side, eyes still closed. "Chris?"

She woke and rubbed her face against her shirt sleeve. "Oh. Sorry. Didn't mean to fall asleep." She stifled a yawn.

"Don't worry about it. You want something to drink?"

"I wouldn't mind another glass of lemonade."

I brought out the pitcher and some glasses, taking a seat on one of the wicker chairs by the porch swing. Chris poured her own glass and then stretched again, rubbing her arms. "Sore?"

"Mm-hmm. And I don't think I'll get the image of that gray barn out of my head any time soon. I feel like I could close my eyes and still be painting."

"No painting for you tomorrow."

"Really?" Her face lit up at this. "You know, we're only halfway done."

"I know but you're a really slow painter. I don't think it's your *thing*." She didn't have any comment to this and I was sorry I'd said it. Still, it needed to be said. Gabe had done most of the painting and Chris had labored over detail work for hours on end. Barns don't need detail work. By the look on her face I knew I should have delivered the news with more tact.

"Am I out of a job?" She wasn't looking at me anymore. Instead, she stared downward and nudged the toes of her cowboy boots against the porch rail to get the swing moving again.

"No. I think you might as well have a second chance. You ride horses?" She'd told me earlier that she had. Then again, she'd also told me she could do almost any handyman work and painting was a basic task.

"I do. That's one thing I do know how to do. In fact, I could train that bay mare for you real easy. She was giving you some trouble this afternoon. I think I'd try some tie-downs with her."

Tie-downs were supposed to keep the horse under more control. I'd never liked them. "Tie-downs, huh?"

"Yeah, and get a little more assertive with her. When you want her to stop, you have to show her who's boss, you know? And I'd try wearing a pair of spurs. A horse like that needs to respect you. She thinks she can get the upper hand with you."

Spurs would only make my problem worse, that much was certain. "You're selling yourself as a horse psychic now?"

"No, ma'am. I can just see that mare wasn't really listening to you. She's got her nose in the wind and thinking more about running than listening to you. She wasn't paying any attention."

"Mm-hmm."

"I mean, I'm not trying to tell you what to do. It's just I think tie-downs and spurs would work. Course, she's your horse."

"Yep."

Chris looked over at me and grinned. "Guess I overstepped, didn't I?"

"Mm-hmm."

She shifted her place in the porch swing. "So, what can I do for you tomorrow, boss?"

"That's better." I didn't like being called boss. Gabe called me that only to get on my nerves. But I didn't want a new hand thinking she could come in and do as she liked. "Morning feedings start at seven a.m. Then I've got to lunge a few of the boarding horses and groom the retired racers. You think you can give me a hand with that?"

She nodded.

"Good. Gabe has the day off. He likes to go to church. I don't know if it'll help his soul but he seems to think it might. Shank shows up around noon on Sundays to help with the afternoon cleaning and the evening feed."

"Who does the evening feeding the rest of the week?"

"I do, six days a week. Shank only stays late on Sundays."

Chris seemed to turn this information over in her head for a minute. "I could stay late and help with the feedings."

"Fine. We're having a barbecue tonight and I'm guessing you won't turn down a free meal."

"No, ma'am."

"We start feeding the horses in the barn at dusk. That'll give us time to get our own food on the coals." I noticed Rhonda and Meg coming up from the barn and glanced at my watch. It was almost seven. Then I remembered Karen was due to come by any minute and felt a rush of regret for agreeing to the meeting tonight. I had no interest in talking to my sister about money matters and hoped that the other guests would distract her. "You'll find the barbecue on the deck behind the house. Mind lighting the coals?"

"Not at all." Chris stood up then and stuck out her hand. "By the way, thanks for not firing my ass. I'll make putting up with me worth your while."

"We'll see if you last through tomorrow." I said, clasping her hand. "You're welcome."

"I'm thinking after tomorrow you'll be ready to keep me here for the next ten years or so. I'll be indispensable before you know it."

"Mm-hmm." It wasn't the first time I'd had to deal with the bravado attitude. My sister acted the same way when we were younger. Now she'd replaced the bravado with an annoying paternalism. I'd take bravado over her attitude any day. Chris had started to talk again about breaking horses but I interrupted. "Go figure out the grill. I want to eat before the cows come home."

Karen showed up just as we were setting out the plates. I handed her a bun and told her to go get a burger off the grill. She seemed irritated that we had guests but quickly forgot about it when she saw Rhonda was there. Rhonda and Karen had been close friends growing up but since Ned had been in the picture, they'd grown apart. I knew Rhonda didn't like Ned. No one did, except maybe Karen. Anyway, I was glad he hadn't come with her tonight. Ned got along with the rest of us about as well as a hunting dog and bunch of angry barn cats. Karen mentioned Ned was on another business trip that weekend. He traveled several times a year and I think it saved their marriage. Karen certainly didn't seem to be missing him tonight.

We ate on the old picnic table my dad had built on the back deck. Rhonda and Meg sat on one side of the table facing Karen and Chris on the other side. I pulled a deck chair over to the table and sat at the end. The oak planks were decorated with all sorts of drawings that Karen and I had carved as kids. The sketches of everything from daisies to mating horses quickly became the subject of dinner conversation. Rhonda pointed out a house that she'd carved and before I knew it, Chris had pulled out a knife and was trying to convince Meg to carve two stick figure girls holding hands in a small blank area of the wood near the horses.

Rhonda shot a smug "I knew it" look at me when Chris mentioned this. I shrugged. Maybe the story about her boyfriend was just a cover. After we finished with our burgers, Rhonda and Meg volunteered to help clean up while Chris and I went to feed the horses. Karen didn't seem to mind hanging out with Rhonda so I left her up at the house. The longer we delayed our finance meeting, the happier I was. She'd already sucked down two beers and was starting on her third. Drinking made her sleepy and I was hoping she'd be too drowsy to lecture me on cutting costs. She didn't seem to realize that Chris was newly hired and an expense we didn't really need.

Chris had flirted with me all through dinner. I tried not to think of it as flirting, except it was hard to ignore when she'd jumped up to take my plate when I'd finished and then refilled my drink. She stared at me too long and went on about how much she liked the ranch and how she could tell it was doing so well because a woman was running it. When I'd mentioned that I needed to go give the horses their evening meal, she was on her feet in seconds, offering to help. She waited by the door so she could open it for me. Karen rolled her eyes at this and even Rhonda smiled. I tried to convince myself that maybe she was just kissing up because she wanted to keep her job.

"So, how long have Meg and Rhonda been dating?" Chris asked, cutting the line on a bale of alfalfa.

"They're not dating." I took a flake of the alfalfa and tossed it into the trough for Jack-Be-Nimble, one of the retired racers. He was a handsome black thoroughbred that had won several races but had to be retired when he chipped his coffin bone five years ago. Now he rarely limped and I had a good feeling the old injury had healed but Jack, as we called him, seemed to enjoy his retirement and wasn't looking for any new reasons to race. His owner, Bill Koslovac, had moved all of his horses to the ranch the past winter. He had six horses in all, each with stellar pedigrees and good showings on the track. Bill had requested our best stalls for his horses. I made space for them in the main barn. Each stall had a small outdoor paddock allowing them space to walk around but not enough to run. Bill paid me nicely to make sure all six were well taken care of and exercised daily. I'd seen him only once since his thoroughbreds were unloaded from the trailer but his checks came on time every month and I didn't ask questions.

"Oh, my mistake." Chris brought a flake over for Attila, one of the other thoroughbreds and then looked at me closely. "You sure they're not dating?"

I could guess by the tone of her voice she was thinking that I'd been duped by my friends. "Well, if you're asking, they are both lesbians. But Rhonda insists they aren't dating yet."

"Hell, two lesbians that hang out together . . . it's only a matter of time before they move in to the same apartment and start thinking about raising a kid together."

"Is that a fact?"

Chris smiled. "Seems that way."

"You know enough about lesbians. I thought you mentioned you had a boyfriend in Nevada." I grabbed another flake and made my way down to the next stall. Another racer named Kujo was impatiently stomping his feet. I tried tossing the flake into his feed trough but he yanked it out of my hands and the alfalfa spread out over the stall. Kujo was a thorn in my side. I wouldn't have minded if Bill had decided to send this horse back to the racetrack.

Chris was already feeding the next horse in the line. She didn't look up when she answered. "Well, I had a boyfriend. For a while."

"And?"

"I dumped him for a cute girl I met at a casino."

She'd told me that her boyfriend lived in Nevada and that's where she'd come from. She hadn't told me how recently she'd left

Nevada and thinking back, I realized I hadn't caught her lying. "Why'd you mention the boyfriend at all? Why the story about Nevada?"

"I don't know. Figured you'd want a story. It won't help you get hired if you tell someone you've been looking for a job for the past two months and haven't had any good offers. And if I came right out and said I was a lesbian I didn't think that'd improve my chances."

"You told me you'd been working at the Sutherland's. Was that a lie too?" The Sutherlands had a ranch a few miles from here with a big sign out front that said GOOD HELP WANTED. I knew they used up ranch hands like an ordinary ranch went through grain bags.

She shrugged. "I worked there for a bit. Shoveled out stalls for a couple weeks and then quit. It wasn't the type of place with a lot of upward mobility."

"You know, I don't give a damn who you lick."

Chris blushed. So much for bravado. She stammered out, "Well . . . I just . . . you know . . ."

I shrugged. "It's all the same to me. As long as you do your job, I won't ask who you're planning to take to bed."

"Gabe told me you're divorced."

"Yep. I don't take anyone to bed anymore," I sighed.

"You date much? Ever go out with a girl?"

"No girls. And don't even think about asking."

Chris reddened again. "I never said I was thinking of asking you out."

"You didn't have to." I handed her the next flake from the bale and winked. "I just want to make sure we all know the ground rules. No dating at the ranch." We finished feeding all of the horses in the barn and then made our way to the pasture. The horses were lined up at individual feeding troughs waiting for their allotment of grain. I fed the pastured horses only one morning feeding of hay since they could graze all day. In the evening, they each received a half coffee can of grain. After all the horses had received their share, we headed back up to the house. Chris had kept silent since I'd embarrassed her. The day had seemed particularly busy and noisy and I appreciated the quiet of dusk.

Just before we reached the house, Chris said, "So, I guess I'll see you in the morning."

"Seven a.m."

She nodded and headed toward the front driveway. I watched her kick off her boots and climb barefoot through the open window of her truck. She drove an old Ford that didn't look like it would last another ten miles on the highway. The roof was splotched with sun bleached designs as was the hood and more than a few dings dotted the doors. The bumper was missing altogether. She got the engine started after a few unsuccessful attempts and waved as she turned onto the main road.

Meg was seated on the front stairs of the porch. She was playing a song on a harmonica and stopped as soon as I approached. Her legs were stretched out and she'd changed her boots for the flip-flops. I wondered where Rhonda was and then heard her voice come from inside the house. She and Karen were arguing about a TV beauty contest. They could both watch anything on TV and be perfectly content for hours on end. I didn't have their patience.

"So, how long you think that thing is gonna hold up?" Meg asked with a nod at the direction of Chris's Ford.

"I hope long enough to get her back to the ranch in the morning." I sat down on the step just below Meg, conscious of the distance between us. "I don't even know where she's spending the night. Maybe in the truck. Come to think of it, I guess I could have offered her the room over the barn."

"She doesn't live around here?"

"No. I think she's from Nevada originally. She came by the other day and asked for a short-term position."

"You hire anyone that walks by?"

"Not usually. I just got this sense she needed the job pretty bad and was willing to take the chance." I glanced at her harmonica. "I wouldn't have guessed you play the harmonica."

"I had a partner for a few years who taught me how to play. An

46

EMT partner, that is." She played the beginning notes of the Pink Panther song, then paused. "Joe taught me how to play on our slow nights. He used to sing along while I played. Our buddies nicknamed our ambulance 'The Duet.' Then he got hit by a stray bullet when we were working a call. Some gang kids were nailing each other and Joe got in the middle of things."

"That's awful. I'm so sorry."

"Joe's lucky, in a way. He survived the bullet wound and still plays the harmonica. He claims he likes spending more time with his family." She sighed. "But he can't work anymore."

I realized that Meg probably had quite a few stories. "I've never really thought of paramedics as having dangerous jobs but people call you out for all types of emergencies."

She nodded. "Most of the time there's no danger other than spraining your back trying to carry some patient down a flight of stairs. But I'm starting to feel a little too old for the gunshot calls."

"Can you play something I might know?"

Meg started up with a rendition of "Me and Bobby McGee" that was close to perfect, then played a few blues tunes that I recognized but couldn't name. She took a break. "Requests?"

I thought for a moment. "Do you know the song 'Crazy?'"

"Patsy Cline's 'Crazy?' Good choice but I don't know it." She played another song and then pocketed the harmonica. We sat together for a while not saying anything, just listening to the sounds of crickets and the television. The door was open and through the screen door you could hear the sound of a baseball game announcer. Apparently they had grown tired of the beauty contest and changed the channel. Or Rhonda had remembered the baseball game. Karen liked to see the guys in their tight white pants. Rhonda really liked the game.

"Sixth inning. It just doesn't seem right to drag out a game for nine innings," Meg said. She looked over at me. "Hope you're not a big baseball fan. I didn't just say the wrong thing, did I?"

"What, you don't like baseball? I thought all lesbians were into sports."

"Just a stereotype." She laughed. "Before I came here, Rhonda always referred to you as her cowgirl friend. I thought all cowgirls had cows and tough boyfriends that chew tobacco."

"No, I just wear the boots. No cows, no tobacco."

"No boyfriends?"

I shifted on the porch step and didn't answer. Something made me uncomfortable saying yes or no to her question. I didn't have a current boyfriend. But I felt like that wasn't all she'd been asking about. I changed the subject. "I used to like playing softball. But I can't sit through a televised game no matter what the sport is. You know, I think Rhonda would tear herself away from the TV set if we asked. Doesn't seem right that she's leaving you alone."

"I'm not alone." Meg skillfully looked away as soon as she said this. "Besides, I never get between a lesbian and a televised game of one of her favorite teams. Rhonda mentioned earlier that the Giants were playing and she was hoping to see the game."

"Karen will watch anything. But, Rhonda doesn't like to miss the Giants." Still, it was unlike Rhonda to not think of her date's interests. "She could leave the room and still know when one of the teams had scored as soon as the crowed cheered. She invited you here."

"I'm glad she did." Meg shrugged. "And I think it's nice to watch a game every once in a while. But I'm not in the mood tonight."

"Oh." I realized she was preferring my company to Rhonda's. Instead of being upset, I felt something inside me flicker like a slow switch. I crossed my arms, suddenly conscious of how close Meg was sitting to me and cleared my throat to break our silence. "My ex-husband used to watch basketball games obsessively. He was a fanatic. The games started to drive me crazy and I'd just have to leave the house when one was on." I'd brought up Greg on purpose. I needed to reiterate that I dated men.

Meg responded coolly, as if nothing had passed between us. "Really? One of my exes was obsessed with basketball too. I couldn't believe how she'd remember every player's height, what teams they'd played for, the year they started, their rankings but have no ability to remember to bring home peanut butter when she went to the store."

I smiled. "Exactly."

"How long have you been divorced? Hope you don't mind me asking. Rhonda said you were only married for a few years."

"I was married for three years." I purposefully avoided her first question, though I wasn't sure exactly why. "Greg, my ex, lives in Sacramento now."

She was waiting for me to answer the first question but when I didn't say anything more, she continued, "Are you still on good terms with him?"

"We aren't really on any terms at all. I asked him to leave, he did, we signed the papers and that was it. We didn't have anything to split up—you know, no kids, no credit cards. I haven't talked to him in ages."

"Ages?"

"A long-ass time."

She smiled. "Okay, I'll stop prying."

"Play another song."

She did and I relaxed back, closing my eyes and letting the music drift in and out with the sound of the ball game. We stayed on the porch after she stopped playing, not saying anything but just staring up at the stars together. I found myself hoping she wouldn't leave too soon. "How'd you like the ride this afternoon?"

"It was nice. I can't seem to get enough of the scenery here." She paused, grinning at me before she continued, "Of course, I would have liked the scenery better if . . ." She didn't finish the sentence but the intent was clear. I didn't think of Rhonda pining after Meg. Instead, I was thinking how much I'd wanted to go on their ride the minute they'd left the barn.

"Don Juan's a sweetheart," she continued. "I'd like to ride again but I think I might need a real lesson. I was going to talk to Rhonda about that." Meg turned the harmonica in her hands then played a few notes, "Take Me Out to the Ball Game." The game was in the last inning. She paused, "I figured maybe I could use a few pointers in the arena. I know Don Juan is a calm horse but you never know. Something unexpected could set him off."

A lesson was a good idea and I'd thought of suggesting it to Rhonda earlier. But now I wanted to volunteer. Rhonda was too busy to take on a new project anyway. "Why don't you come by later this week and I'll give you a lesson. Rhonda's got herself stretched thin for the next couple weeks. She's filling in for one of the other nurses out on maternity leave."

"You wouldn't mind?"

"No, not at all. I teach group lessons for some of the boarders on Monday and Wednesday at five o'clock. You can come either night, if you'd like."

"I work on those nights. And I was thinking more along the lines of a private lesson, if that's an option."

Meg probably wouldn't fit in well with the group class I had going now anyway. My other students were all more experienced riders. "Friday afternoon is open."

"Perfect. This Friday? Or is that too soon?"

"This Friday. Come by after lunch."

She stood to leave then, holding out her hand to shake mine. I watched her make her way over to her Jeep and waved when she glanced back at me. I knew by that look back that she liked me. The problem was, I had no idea what to do about it.

Karen set up her bed in the spare room. I lent Rhonda an extra blanket and she curled up at her usual place on the couch. Meg had left not long after her last harmonica song ended. After she left, I tried not to think of our conversation and didn't mention anything to Rhonda. I couldn't help but wonder if Meg had been waiting out on the porch because she didn't want to watch TV or because she wanted to catch me alone. With Chris, it was obvious when she had flirted with me. But with Meg, I wasn't sure if she was flirting or just being nice.

≈∾

Chris met me in the barn in the morning, right on time. We skipped the six a.m. breakfast meeting on Sundays. With the extra pair of hands we finished the pasture feedings a half hour sooner than I'd expected. "Have you eaten yet?"

"No, ma'am. I'm half starved too, so if you're offering anything . . ."

I wasn't entirely sure she'd slept much either. She was still dressed in the same clothes she'd worn the day before and her short hair was tucked under a blue bandana.

"Come on up to the house and I'll make breakfast. I've got two guests who I'm hoping to rouse with some loud pots and kick them out before they start complaining about hangovers. We've got an hour or so before the horses in the barn will want to be turned out."

"You all had a party last night?"

"No. I went to bed early. My sister and Rhonda stayed up late drinking and watching TV."

"Meg didn't stay?"

"No."

She mulled this over for a while, then said, "You know, the Giants won last night. I think Rhonda was hoping to catch the game."

"Yeah, she was cheering loud enough that they probably heard her in the stadium." The game had gone into extra innings and when the Giants finally won, Rhonda and Karen started yelling as if the players could actually hear. "Did you watch the game?"

"No, I listened to it on the radio."

I guessed from this that my earlier suspicion was probably true. "Chris, are you sleeping in your car?"

"No." She paused for a moment. "I picked up a tent at the Salvation Army. I'm staying at a campsite for the time being."

"You know, there's an apartment above the barn with a shower and a little kitchenette. I'll rent it to you, if you'd like. Cheap."

She hesitated then asked, "How much? The tent's fine but I wouldn't mind a bathroom."

I pointed back at the barn. "Climb the ladder on the right hand side, just to the left of Jack's stall. Have a look at the room and use the shower if you'd like, then meet me back up at the house. We'll figure out rent later." I knew I'd have to charge her or risk Karen's wrath but I wasn't sure how much would be reasonable. She'd need enough money to pay for food and I guessed she was probably saving up for something. Maybe a new car.

Karen and Rhonda were smoking on the porch. "Good morning." They both nodded, but didn't make any reply. Neither of them was very talkative before noon. I thought they looked like two morning-after lovers, both with messed hair and reddened eyes but I didn't say anything. Rhonda would have laughed if I'd said it. Karen would have killed me for the comment. Rhonda came into the kitchen after a while, hoping for breakfast. I made her a slice of toast while I was cooking the eggs and coffee. "So, what happened with you and Meg?"

She smeared butter on the toast, looking a little dejected as she examined my homemade jam collection. Peach and nectarine were the only fruits that we had an excess of each summer so that was the jam that my neighbor, Mrs. Hudson, made for me. "I don't know exactly. Maybe the chemistry isn't there."

I was glad she had come to this conclusion on her own. "So, you're just gonna be friends?"

"I guess so. We're probably going out to the club on Women's Night this week." She took a taste of the nectarine jam and murmured her approval. Our nectarine trees had a bumper crop last June and this year's harvest threatened to be almost as big. A row of empty jars were already lined up, waiting for the coming fruit. Rhonda continued, "You should come with us. It'd be good for you to get out and dance a little."

"You know I don't dance."

"You used to dance."

"There were a lot of things I used to do." Rhonda and I used to go out to the bar at least every week. We got drunk more than we danced but I wasn't going to bring that up. When my dad died and I took over managing the ranch, I'd given up a lot of things.

Rhonda said I'd become boring but that didn't seem to stop her from hanging out at the ranch. "Besides, I don't want to be a third wheel with you and Meg." I thought about Meg again, picturing her driving off last night in the Jeep and remembered how she'd looked back over her shoulder at the house before she turned onto the main road. "Maybe you two just need more time to get to know each other."

"Maybe. But I doubt it. I think she'd rather talk to you than me." Rhonda shrugged. "Course I already told her you prefer men. But come to the club with us. I don't really want to feel depressed when she asks some other girl to dance and I'm left alone at the bar."

"Who's gonna be alone at the bar?" Chris asked. She'd come into the kitchen in stocking feet and left her muddy boots at the doorway. Looking more presentable than a half hour ago, her wrinkled shirt was tied around her waist and her once shaggy brown hair, now wet, was neatly combed back behind her ears.

I pointed at Rhonda. "She's just feeling sorry for herself. You took a shower?"

"No. I just dunked my head under the faucet. A shower seemed like too much work when I knew I was just gonna get dirty later. But I'd like to take you up on your offer. How much is rent?"

"A hundred a month, meals included. And I'll be happy to have your help with the evening feedings."

She nodded. "Perfect."

Rhonda glanced from me to Chris. "You're renting the studio above the barn?"

"Yep."

"Starting when?"

"As soon as possible, I guess." Chris waited for my agreement and then continued to Rhonda, "So, why are you going alone to the bar?"

"I'm going with Meg. Women's Night is this Thursday. I'm trying to convince June, and possibly you, to come along."

Chris nodded immediately. "Sure, we'll be there. I haven't had any chance to get out to the clubs since I got here. We'll go together, right June?"

"I'll think about it." I dished up the eggs and set plates in front of Chris and Rhonda, ignoring both of their attempts to convince me about the club. I went outside to find Karen and call her in for breakfast. She'd taken a walk down to the barn and met me halfway coming up the path.

"The foals look good this year. Especially that black colt with the white star. I watched him run for a few minutes."

"That'd be Flash Dance. He's quick all right. And full of himself. I put his picture on the Internet and I think we already have a buyer for him." I was happy to hear Karen give me a compliment on the horses. The boarding horses were our bread and butter but the spring foals had always been our family pride.

"You know, we need to talk about finances."

"Of course." I knew I wasn't getting out of this lecture, though I had been hoping she'd forget.

"We've been getting raked by the cost of fuel. You need to cut down a little. And we already talked about cutting down on the grain rations but you didn't skim off any. The alfalfa you're getting is too expensive. And who's the new gal? I was hoping she was just a friend of Rhonda's but now I'm thinking you did something stupid like hire her."

I nodded, expecting this. "Our boarders pay an extra fee for the higher quality feed. And I hired Chris for next to nothing. She's just on a trial right now anyway. I'll fire her if we really can't afford it."

"We can't."

"You know the ins and outs always balance at the end of the year. I don't know why you make such a big deal about it."

"Because, June, we're supposed to be making money here, not breaking even. You know we can't afford another ranch hand. And why'd you hire a woman?"

Karen was one of those chauvinistic women who I've never understood. I didn't even want to tackle it now. "I've seen the bank records. We're doing better than ever. I know what I'm doing and we'll need the extra help this summer. I've got to get the two-year-olds started on their training and there are two geldings I've got buyers for already. There's a mare out of Jericho that we'll have a buyer for by the end of the month if I can get her trained by then."

Karen waved her hand to stop me. "What does this have to do with spending more money on an inexperienced young hand?"

"Chris knows how to handle horses and she's got a smoother hand than Shank." I hoped, anyway. Karen and Shank didn't get along and I figured that bringing up this sore subject would distract her.

"Fine. Keep the new hand. Obviously you like her well enough. But I'll tell you now, I think you made a bad decision hiring her." I wanted to argue but Karen wouldn't quit running her mouth. I knew her comment about Chris stung more than it should, in part because I'd second guessed myself already about keeping her on. Karen continued, "Just buy a cheaper grade of alfalfa and I'll stop nagging, okay? The bigger issue we need to talk about is water."

"Water? We're on a well." Of course she knew this. We had shared the well with the Hudsons for as long as either of us had been alive. As long as we were on good terms with the Hudsons, water wasn't an issue.

"You remember my friend, Tim?"

"Yeah, I remember that asshole." My attitude didn't surprise Karen. Tim was the developer who had nearly convinced Karen to divide the ranch land into little "estate" lots and sell them for development last year. Tim had been a football jock at our high school and was good friends with Ned. Karen thought Tim was "amazing." I'd never liked his arrogance.

"After his company gave up trying to buy our place, I guess they started working on the Hudsons. Tim called me up last week saying his company finalized the deal with Mr. Hudson. That old geezer's gonna retire with millions."

"And our well?"

"That's the problem." Karen nearly tripped over Mac, who was sunning his fat orange backside in the middle of the pathway. Mac felt Karen's kick, and hissed, scaring the hell out of her. Fortunately, Mac was quick when he needed to be and he was up and out from under her feet just as I caught Karen's arm. She swore at him, regained her balance and then we both started laughing as he jiggled down the path. "That cat is about the fattest thing I've seen on four legs. I can't believe he can even run. Maybe you should cut down on cat food too."

"He catches mice. Besides, do you want to make a cat the size of Mac angry?"

She continued, "So, I asked Tim about the water issue and mentioned that Dad and Mr. Hudson had made an arrangement about our well. He said he didn't see how we had any legal rights to the water. I guess Mr. Hudson had sold water rights along with the land. The developers will own it all."

"I'm sure Dad must have had something in writing. Mr. Hudson can only sell his portion of the water."

Karen shrugged. "If you can find something in writing, let me know. I've looked into it and the county doesn't have any records about the well. Maybe there's something in Dad's files. Just so you know, it doesn't look good for us."

"Shit." I kicked a rock at the tractor parked next to the house and got a nice resounding clang as it hit. "Under other circumstances I'd be happy to hear that Mr. Hudson was selling his land. His goat and that blind Appaloosa of his have been wrecking our fence. But the last thing we need is to replace them with a bunch of rich retirees in golf carts." The idea of estate homes going up on the other side of our hill and snobby city slickers moving in next door wasn't something I wanted to imagine. "Is there any way to block the deal?"

"I don't think so. Tim waited to call me until he knew the deal was as good as done. Apparently everything's signed. The county already approved splitting up Mr. Hudson's parcel of a hundred acres into a hundred and fifty lots. Ned thinks we should sell. If we can find another developer—"

"Are you kidding?" I felt sick to my stomach thinking of all the land being cut up and the streets being set on the soil. It was hard enough to imagine the Hudson place being destroyed. I wouldn't let them touch ours. "They'll probably rip out Mrs. Hudson's orchard."

Karen nodded. "Oh, I'm sure all the trees will be cut down. First thing."

I could hardly believe Mrs. Hudson had agreed to the deal. Of course, she probably would have naively thought that the developers would save the orchard. Mrs. Hudson had the best apricot and cherry trees anywhere around. "Next you're gonna tell me they're putting in a golf course."

Karen didn't smile.

"Oh, hell."

"They held a public hearing about the development and no one showed up to fight it. We might as well buy golf clubs now. Ned is looking forward to it already."

"There's got to be something that Mr. Hudson and Dad signed about the water. We moved some of his old file boxes up to the attic. Maybe there's something in there. Or we could just forge something. Mr. Hudson is half senile. He probably won't remember whether or not he signed a paper about water rights forty years ago or not. I could draw something up."

"Absolutely not. We won't be forging anything. Don't even think about it, June," Karen said, wagging her finger to drive home the point. "Right now, I think we should just focus on selling. Ned is approaching a few investor friends about it."

"Tell him to go screw himself."

"Look, June, if you have a better solution, start working on it. This ranch is barely making us any money. Why not sell and live an easy life?"

"Breakfast anyone?" Rhonda called out the front door to us.

"We're coming." I turned back to Karen. "Dad wouldn't have wanted to sell the place to developers. He would have found another way to get water in and keep the ranch running, regardless of golf balls. And I know there's gotta be a way around this. I'll figure out the county record keeping system and go through Dad's stuff. I'll just need a little time to make some calls about the water. Maybe you can sweet talk Tim into holding off on the Hudson deal."

"Look, it's not that I like the idea of giving this place up. I miss living here in a lot of ways. I miss watching the sunsets up at the summit. I miss waking up on spring mornings and running out to the barn to see if any babies had been born overnight. I miss not having any worries." Karen glanced at the house and waved to Rhonda then took one long look out over the pasture below us. I wondered what she could be thinking. "You know, I haven't had fresh ranch eggs and bacon in months. Maybe years."

"Give me some time, Karen. Don't bring the investors over here yet."

"We'll see." She headed inside without meeting my eyes.

Chris and Rhonda were at the table nursing mugs of coffee. Chris stood up when I entered, looking guilty. I was used to my employees sitting down on the job and almost told her to relax. But the look on Karen's face, with her lips pinched and her jaw muscles tightened, made me realize I needed to at least give the appearance of commanding a tight ship. "Break's over in five minutes, Chris."

"Sure, boss." Chris took her mug over to the sink to rinse it, wiping her wet hands on her jeans. She fished a pack of cigarettes out of her shirt pocket and headed outside, winking at Rhonda as she passed.

As soon as Chris was out of the room, Karen started in. "As if we needed one more problem around here, you hire some girl who looks like she's trying to be a man. Does she even know how to ride a horse?"

"I'll let you know when I need your advice on ranch hands, Karen."

She scowled but dropped the argument as I handed her a plate of eggs and biscuits. Rhonda was doing her best to stay out of our fight. She sipped her coffee with her gaze focused on the newspaper. I wondered what Chris and Rhonda had been discussing and why Chris had winked at her. The last thing I needed was to have Rhonda dating one of the ranch hands. Just as Karen started to eat, she made a scene of clanging her fork on the plate and stomping over to slam the front windows closed. "God, I hate the stench of cigarette smoke." She glared at me as if I was the one who had taken up the habit.

"Karen, what about just digging another well?" I asked, trying to change the subject. "Dad always talked about the underground stream running through the west pasture." A strip of land in a gully cutting through the west pasture stayed green even in the hottest months of summer. "It wouldn't be impossible to find a good place to tap our own water."

"Too expensive. And then we'd still have the golf course next door and the traffic. The land is worth more than you realize, June." She pointed at the bacon still on the grill. "I'll take a few slices of that."

She could walk over and get it as easily as I could but Karen preferred ordering other people around. I forked the bacon out of the pan and then glanced at the clock. Nearly half the morning was gone and I didn't want to spend any more time arguing with Karen. Anyway, I needed time to think about everything she'd told me to form a proper rebuttal. I didn't mind the idea of a golf course or traffic so much as I minded the idea of giving up the ranch. I wondered which horses I'd have to sell first. I could find a smaller place and just keep a couple of my favorites . . . but I knew I couldn't part with dad's favorites either, nor the retired brood mares.

Karen took a bite of the bacon and then wiped her fingers on her napkin. She made me keep white cloth napkins on hand for her and had told me numerous times just how uncivilized it was to wipe your hands on your jeans. Karen patted her lips with her napkin and then refolded it and placed it back in her lap, just like always. I never understood why she put on such airs. She saw me heading for the door. "I take it our conversation is finished?"

"For now. With both you and Ned against me, I need some ammunition."

"I'm not against you." Her tone was condescending. "We just need to be practical. We don't have to keep up our parents' dream forever. This place isn't a moneymaker. They would probably have decided to sell too. Live an easy life in their retirement, like the Hudsons." Rhonda's knife scraped against her plate as she cut a piece of toast.

"Who says everything has to be centered on profit?"

"The rest of the world," Karen replied.

I left then, knowing I was going to lose my temper, and the battle, if I tried arguing now. I got Chris started on cleaning stalls and then went to look after the retired racehorses. Water rights and Mr. Hudson's developer deal filled my head. It seemed strange that Mr. Hudson hadn't dropped any hints about selling his land yesterday. Maybe he hadn't even thought about our ranch and how we depended on sharing the well. Or maybe he had. I couldn't help but hate him more when I thought of the predicament he'd gotten us in. I needed to go search the files in the attic and hoped I'd come up with something. It seemed likely that forty years ago two neighboring ranchers might have thought to sign a deal about water sharing. Unfortunately, a handshake had always been Dad's way of business dealing.

I brought Jubilee, one of the prize thoroughbred mares, out to groom. She was in season and whinnied to the geldings as if they might be interested in helping her out. At nearly eighteen hands and well-muscled, she had enough strength to throw me off my feet just by tossing her head at the wrong moment. And she tried several times to find that wrong moment. I had a hard time keeping up with Chris's small talk while managing Jubilee. Chris asked me how long I had known Rhonda and I imagined red flags waving overhead. My best friend was notorious for this. I should have known better than to leave Rhonda alone with a single lesbian. "A long time," I answered. "Longer than you've been alive." This thought was a little unnerving, however true. I felt a surge of that *older and wiser* notion and had to stop myself from giving Chris a talk about finding someone her own age. She was old enough to make her own mistakes.

"I like her. I think she might be interested in me too."

"Oh, really?" I smiled, taunting her. "And yesterday she was flirting with Meg and as I recall, you were flirting with me."

"That was yesterday."

I noticed she wasn't blushing this time. "So, times change?"

She nodded. "Anyway, I heard a vicious rumor that you were straight . . . by the way, what do you think about Meg?"

"Hmm?" I'd heard her question perfectly well but the answer seemed to stall in my mind. I picked up Jubilee's foot and started cleaning the hoof. What did I think about Meg?

"Do you think Rhonda's really interested in her? I didn't get the sense that Meg was that into Rhonda."

"I don't think she's gonna be any competition if that's what you're asking. Rhonda and Meg aren't dating." I set Jubilee's hoof down and leaned against the horse, eyeing Chris. Chris was combing one of the gelding's tails, slowly. Her mind was obviously not on the task and the lower half of the tail was still caught in snarls. "Don't tell me you like her too?"

Chris smiled. "No. Meg's not my type. Too tough, too butch. And I'm too butch to go for a woman like Meg."

I didn't see Meg as all that tough. But I knew Rhonda had called her butch. Most of Rhonda's girlfriends were on the masculine side now that I thought about it. I bent to pick up Jubilee's back leg, examining this hoof. "So, Chris, what am I?"

"You?" She smiled. "Straight, I guess. I don't really put straight women in the butch or femme category. But Rhonda is more femme than you. Maybe you'd be somewhere in the middle. If you were a dyke, that is. Let me know if you change your mind and want to go there, okay?"

61

Before I had to answer, the sound of an engine interrupted us. Shank's truck was crunching down the gravel driveway, a cloud of dust following it. He parked up at the house and waved at us. He hollered something that we couldn't hear, probably an excuse about being late. I tossed the hoof pick in the tack box and slapped my hands on my jeans to shake off the dirt. I didn't want to answer Chris's question and bringing up Meg's name had somehow made me completely distracted. "I'm gonna have Shank take over here. I want to check on my sister. Make sure she hasn't decided to move into the spare room. Shank will show you the workout pattern for the old racers. All six of Bill Koslovac's horses have the same routine, excepting Atilla, who's happy to be pregnant. She gets a lighter workout. Shank will show you."

Shank had made his way over to the barn by then and nodded in agreement. He seemed surprised to see Chris back and joked that he thought I would have fired her for painting so slow. Chris colored at this and started to explain her theory about perfectionism. I left them to argue and walked up to the house, stopping to check on the pasture water troughs. All of the automatic watering lines were working and the troughs were full. Thinking about losing the well, I'd half expected to see the layer of green plant scum lining the base of a dry trough. But the water came through the lines, same as yesterday, despite my newfound knowledge of its worth.

Chapter 3

Meg

I forgot about most patients the moment their records were finished. Not June McCormick. But the idea of running into her
again . . . I'd dreamed up plenty of scenarios and none included
bumping into her under the auspices of being someone else's date.
I knew I had to tell Joe about it. It'd been a while since my last visit
and seeing June again was as good a reason as any.

"Remember that woman I kept talking about last summer, flew
off a horse and broke her tibia?" He shrugged. "Come on, you
remember. I talked about her for weeks."

"Nope, doesn't ring a bell. Was she after the go-go dancer?"

"Before. She owned a ranch up in El Dorado and got bucked
off some horse she was training. Remember, it was my first month
or so with Eddy." I kept going with a description of June, trying to
jostle his memory with the details.

"Why did you leave that go-go dancer anyway?" Joe never tired of my stories about Cheryl the go-go dancer. He must have noticed my look of frustration though because he followed up with, "Oh, wait, now I remember the cowgirl. Wasn't she straight, or at least married?"

"Divorced."

"Imagine that. You're interested in someone who's clearly unavailable. That never happens."

"Go to hell, Joe." I'd told Joe enough about my relationships over the past ten years. Now he knew too much about me.

Joe chuckled and wheeled himself out onto the back porch, motioning for me to follow. He had a way of moving in his chair that made you think legs were overrated. But Joe always had a talent for making any tough thing look easy. He got himself settled and pointed to the ice chest. I went over and got two beers for us.

The back of his head was sunburned at the edge of his receding hairline and he'd gained weight since I'd last seen him. Joe had been an EMT with me for eight years and was once an avid body-builder. Then one night we got a call that went bust. I was driving that night. Joe jumped out as soon as he saw our patient, a punk kid lying face down under the freeway ramp. Unfortunately, the kid's gang friends weren't finished with their argument. Three more shots were fired and one of the bullets lodged in Joe's spine.

"So, is the cowgirl the reason I haven't seen you lately? Don't tell me, you're gonna start listening to bad music and wearing a cowboy hat and tight jeans. I've got a pair of cowboy boots you can borrow."

"No, thanks. I already bought my own pair." I leaned against the porch railing and thought of June. I'd done a lot of thinking about her over the past week. Could hardly get her out of my head.

He took a sip of his beer. "So, she's pretty?"

"You'd whistle."

"Is this one better than the go-go dancer?" he asked, incredulous. Joe had never really forgiven me for breaking up with Cheryl before I'd brought her by his house.

"Maybe you'd have thought the dancer was prettier, but I like June more."

"June." He paused, as if turning the name on his tongue. "Sounds like a summer fling."

I didn't laugh at his bad joke, but he did.

"And what about Deanna the bartender? The one you're not really dating," he added.

"We're still not dating." I'd been seeing, or rather sleeping with, a bartender from the local gay club. Neither of us wanted a relationship. We were looking for company in bed with no strings attached. So far, it was a set-up that worked just fine.

"Well, damn, Meg, how am I supposed to judge who's the best woman for you if I never get to meet them? As your best friend I think I got a right to meet your girlfriends. You could bring all three over—the dancer, the bartender and the cowgirl. We'll have a party."

"I'm sure your wife won't mind." It was good to see him smile. The last time I'd dropped by he was too low to say much. That time I'd shown up after work and hadn't changed my clothes. I'd realized too late that he didn't want to see the paramedic uniform. Too many memories. "Besides, I don't think I want to see Deanna and Cheryl in the same room together and I haven't figured out yet if June is interested in me."

"What's she like?"

I paused, not knowing how to sum up a person like June. "She's nice."

"Nice? That's all I get? I sit around here all day and watch the flowers grow. Without hearing about your crazy life I'd be flat out bored. You can't come up with a better description than nice?" He slapped my knee and I caught the mischievous glint in his eye. He waited expectantly.

Several thoughts came at once. The problem with June was that I couldn't tell if she really liked me. I wasn't ready to explain my attraction more explicitly—as it was I had a feeling I might be sticking my neck out with her. "She's going to give me riding lessons."

"On a horse?"

"Yes, of course. And don't look at me like that." I suddenly didn't want to take the conversation any further with him.

Joe sighed after a minute and changed direction. "Fine. Keep your cowgirl a secret. Tell me about the bartender instead."

I didn't want to disappoint him but there wasn't much I could say about Deanna either. "She's good in bed. We get along well but we don't talk much."

"And that's not enough, is it?"

"No. She's keeping me from getting too lonely. But sharing a bed with a stranger isn't enough." I tried smiling but suddenly felt more depressed after admitting my loneliness. "I'd sing the blues but you'd probably tell me to shut the hell up."

"Please God, don't let her start singing." Joe made a sign of the cross on his chest. "Where's that harmonica when we need it?"

I fished mine out of my pocket and played a few notes, getting a laugh out of Joe. Then he started singing. He had a deep bass voice and a knack for making any song sound more bluesy. Hard as I tried, I couldn't carry a tune. Joe had suffered through my attempts at singing along with the radio on many long shifts. At first he'd encouraged me to practice. One day, he finally realized I was hopeless as a singer and gave me the harmonica. He was one of those annoying people blessed with perfect pitch and never could understand why I couldn't. "Anyway, Deanna and I just have a good time together, you know. Nothing serious."

"Oh, I see." He lit a cigarette and took a drag. "So, you gave up a go-go dancer to fuck a bartender and are still waiting for the straight cowgirl. You think she'll chase you down on her horse?"

"I'm not waiting for anyone to chase me down."

"Could happen. I've heard of stranger things."

Joe had this theory that if you thought about someone for long enough, you'd eventually bump into them. Sort of like ESP or quantum physics. I'd already told him I thought his "bump" theory was bunk. I knew he was thinking now that my running into June was a perfect example of his theory. "Yes, but you still believe in extraterrestrial life, alien encounters . . ."

"And Spiderman too. Yeah, I believe in all of it." He dismissed the subject with a wave. "Sit down and enjoy the view. I hate to have people standing around. Makes me nervous."

I took the bench near Joe's wheelchair and was suddenly eye level with the sunflowers. Rows of yellow sunflowers filled the yard. The blooms were all pointed west toward the setting sun. "Whose crazy idea was it to plant so many damn flowers, anyway? What happened to your amazing view?"

He scowled, halfheartedly. "Take it up with the women in my life." The sunflowers were as tall as his head.

Joe used to be a compulsive sunflower seed eater and he'd leave the shells on the floorboards of the truck. I'd given him hell about not cleaning up the mess too many times. After the accident I missed seeing the little seed husks in the truck and decided to fill Joe's yard with sunflower seedlings. He was pissed when he realized what I'd done and went on and on about how the flowers would block his view. Before the flowers, the only thing you could see from his back porch was a half-dead lawn and cinder blocks from the buildings that bordered his property. His wife Toni had added little purple petunias under the sunflowers.

"I have to admit I think it's pretty. Just don't start thinking I want these flowers messing up my view every year." He faked a scowl. "So, how's work? Anything new at the station?"

I didn't think it was a good idea to bring up work. Usually I skirted around the subject when he brought it up, hoping to protect him. Now I didn't want to talk about it myself. "Nothing new. It's a job, you know."

He pressed for more, "What about your partner? Are you still riding that boy about everything he does wrong?"

"Eddy's a slacker. Shows up late for shifts all the time and just wants to talk all the time. Drives me crazy with these stories of his. It's been over a year now and he still can't seem to find the gas pedal when we need it." I glanced over at Joe. His hands rested on the wheels like he was about to push them into motion. The old rage I'd felt at the kid who'd fired the gun suddenly welled up in me like acid. I swallowed and looked back at the garden. The rage was always replaced by my own guilt. I'd asked to drive that night, even though Joe was always our driver. For some reason, we'd switched places. "Man, I miss having you in the truck. It just isn't the same job."

He sighed. "You aren't still thinking about quitting, are you?"

I didn't answer. Joe's look made it painfully clear that the truth would be letting him down. After Joe's accident I took some time off. I'd been in and out of the hospital visiting Joe then took a trip down to Palm Springs to see my parents and another trip to see my little brother in LA. I'd used every excuse I knew of to keep from going back. It took me a full month before I was ready to work a shift and when I did, I couldn't get used to the idea of not having Joe around. I blew through a series of partners before I ended up with Eddy. He wasn't the worst of the bunch but he wasn't an EMT that I could depend on like Joe. "I feel like I'm just putting in my time, you know? I clock in at the station, go out on the calls, write up the records and go home."

"Give yourself some time. Give Eddy a few breaks." He snubbed out his cigarette after taking only a few drags and wheeled over to the cooler. He got out two more beers and tossed me one. "This is the good kind. Don't bother with that other beer. I only keep it around for guests."

"What am I?"

"Family." He smiled. "And the top paramedic on the service right now. Dispatch knows to call you when they get their doomsday disaster. You can't just walk away from everyone and take a desk job."

"Why not?"

"Why not?" His voice was raised. We'd landed on a sore subject. "Because, what else would you do? Answer emergency lines? Right. I can just imagine you at some dispatch desk. You'd be going bananas, jumping out of your seat 'cause the medics on call were all sleeping when you sent out your number one emergency page."

"There's always teaching." I'd been offered a job training paramedics but Joe had already shot that idea down. He wanted me on the front lines where the action was. I didn't tell him the nightmares I'd had after his accident or how many times I'd asked to be rerouted when a gunshot victim call came in.

"Teaching?" He snorted. "You'll be giving it all up. Someone else will be out there saving lives and not doing as good a job as you."

"Maybe I'm done." I met Joe's eyes. He wasn't smiling. I tried to lighten the mood, joking, "You know, I can't be the one to have all the fun. Gotta let the new kids try some time."

"Whose life are you gonna leave in Eddy's hands?"

"Hey, that's not a fair shot. There are other paramedics who will team up with Eddy. It's not like he'd be going out to a cardiac arrest on his own."

He shrugged. "Look, I know why I'm still alive today, even with a damn bullet in my back. I don't think that the person who pulled me out of the middle of a gang gunfight should be able to just quit EMS."

Joe still maintained that I'd saved his life. I'd recalled that night a half a dozen different ways and none of them involved me saving Joe. Truth was, the whole thing was a blur now. The nightmares had distorted the reality. "I'm tired, Joe."

"So go take a nap. You can snuggle with Sammy. You'll find him sleeping with Spiderman." Sammy was Joe's son. I'd given Sammy a three-foot stuffed Spiderman to keep him company when Joe was in the hospital. Now the toddler insisted on taking Spiderman with him everywhere and Joe had given me an earful about why I should have bought a smaller version. "After the nap, maybe you can take Spiderman for an ambulance ride. Never know when you'll need a superhero's help."

There was no use arguing. Joe wanted his job back maybe even more than he wanted to walk again. He couldn't understand why I'd want out. "Have you ever wanted a change, maybe just for the sake of change? I can't keep doing this forever. There's only so much blood-covered asphalt that a person really needs to see."

Joe didn't respond for a moment. He seemed to be lost in his own thoughts. His voice surprised me when he finally spoke. "You know what, Meg, maybe you're right. Who am I to talk? I won't ever know what it's like to burn out." Joe wheeled himself over to me and clinked his bottle against mine. "Hell, I don't care what you do so long as you come over and have a beer with me once in a while. Cheers."

I wished I hadn't complained about work. "Yeah, cheers."

"Give it some more time—wait a few months and we'll have this conversation again. If you still feel like you're just punching a time card then . . . well, I'll let you spend your days planting sunflowers in my yard instead of saving lives. I won't understand it though."

I took a sip, not feeling cheerful at all. Joe usually drank cheap ale but this wasn't half bad. I checked the label and realized it was the same brand that I'd brought over after he got home from the hospital. He grinned when I noticed this. "Just returning a favor. I owed you." Joe had a way of making his point, loud and clear. The last time we'd drank this he'd been ready to give up on life. The thought of spending the rest of his days in a wheelchair had been a hard pill for him to swallow and maybe he was still living his EMT life through me.

I finished my shift on Thursday morning exhausted and not completely sure I'd be awake enough for the twenty minute drive home. Busy shifts always seemed to come in threes but I'd had a run of four that week and enough overtime in the past two weeks to make my unflappable night supervisor shake his head. Eddy and I had recently been reassigned from the weekend schedule to weeknights. We rode together three or four shifts a week and then had the next few nights off. People were notoriously stupid on Friday and Saturday nights and Eddy kept saying how happy he was to be off weekend duty. I quickly convinced him that our clientele could be just as stupid in the middle of the week.

The past night we'd answered calls for everything from a kid with a cervical spine dislocation caused by an ill-fated bungee jump into a dry river bed to a mentally disturbed woman who called 911 saying she was being eaten alive. Turned out she had an ant problem in her house. Much to Eddy's dismay, I took us on a detour to the drugstore and bought the woman a can of insect repellant. She was so happy to see us again that she tried to kiss Eddy when we returned to spray the insects.

Throughout the last hour of work, Eddy described all the ways he was gonna spend the fat paycheck we were expecting from all the overtime. A vacation was number one. "Our next call is at a long, sandy beach with cold drinks, girls in bikinis and no EDPs." He'd said this line so many times I was at the point of hoping he really would go on a vacation. The number of EDPs, emotionally disturbed persons, had been dragging me down as well. Five out of six of our last calls were for EDPs. I was reeling from the two liters of Diet Coke I'd sucked down for the past eight hours and couldn't concentrate on anything beyond writing up my records for the night. "Eighty-year-old caucasian male, smoker, primary complaint of chest pain. Normal cardiac rhythm." We'd transferred the guy to the ER but I had a pretty good feeling he was just going to get a shower and a hot meal. His ECG looked perfect and his blood pressure was better than mine, thanks to the caffeine coursing through my veins.

Eddy and I parted ways at the EMS center. He gave me the same salute at the end of every week, "I'm going on vacation for the next six months. Don't spend all your money on one girl while I'm gone." Eddy and I were both single but I doubted if he ever dated. The only women he ever talked about were the ones on his video games. I started up the Jeep and gripped the steering wheel, trying to will the pounding in my head to stop. Shivering, I blasted the heat and wrapped my blue jacket tighter around me. Sleeplessness had a way of confusing your internal thermostat. I passed the bank clock tower and couldn't believe the thermometer reading of seventy-five degrees. It felt more like fifty degrees and I kept my jacket on and cursed the Jeep's lack of windows. I made my way onto the freeway, driving as slowly as I decided was safely possible and ignoring the honks from morning commuters. My only goal that day was to get home to my own bed and sleep a full eight hours.

A message from Rhonda was on the answering machine. She wanted to know if I was still going out that evening. It was Women's Night at the club. I called her and left a message on her cell phone, knowing she was already at the hospital. "Maybe. I'm beat. Call me before you go out tonight." Rhonda had been the nurse to admit my patient with chest pain that morning. We didn't have any chance to talk then but I hadn't forgotten about our plans that evening. I put a frozen pizza in the oven and collapsed on the couch, waiting for my cheese-and-pepperoni alternative breakfast.

I shared the two-bedroom condo with a university student named Clyde but almost never saw the guy. I could have afforded the place without Clyde but I'd never liked the idea of living alone. Splitting the rent also meant I could save money for a down payment on a house. I was stuck in the city until I had a good reason to get out. For now, my nest egg at the savings and loan could just keep growing.

Our condo was north of downtown, otherwise known as the sketchy part of Sacramento. A minimart that catered to the late-night drinkers was next door to our building and the commuter train passed directly under my bedroom window. During the day I had to sleep with earplugs. We'd had two fatal shootings on our block earlier that month and car windows were smashed on a regular basis but other than that, I liked the place all right.

Originally I'd rented the condo with Liz. She worked as a dental hygienist and we were introduced through a mutual friend. After the first month of dating, we'd made the bad decision to move in together. A month later, I'd come to the conclusion that Liz and I had nothing in common, except that if we broke up, we'd both be single lesbians. This fact, along with our healthy sex drives, meant that we broke up several times and always made up after. We were better lovers than friends and finally figured that out. We stuck it out until our living situation got too complicated. She had issues about monogamy—mainly, she didn't do it. I grew tired of the string of women that passed through our living room and asked Liz to leave. A big fight followed. Finally she moved in with another girlfriend. Her new girlfriend's name was Cheryl. Cheryl worked as a go-go dancer. I had no idea that a month later I'd be dating the same go-go dancer. Dyke karma worked in mysterious ways.

Clyde moved in before Liz had officially left. He answered my ad for a housemate just before Christmas. I was battling a rough bout of loneliness then and Clyde was a good distraction. He was loud, woke up too early and was as dirty as I remembered my younger brother being. Shortly after he moved in, Clyde met a girl and I could count on one hand the number of nights when we'd both been home in the past month. He had moved most of his stuff to his girlfriend's apartment on the other side of town last month. I couldn't figure out why he was keeping his room here. As long as he paid his share of rent, I didn't mind the occasional mess he made on the random nights he dropped in. By the sorry state of our kitchen with counters piled with dishes and the empty beer bottles cluttering the coffee table and the top of the TV, I guessed that Clyde had hosted his usual Wednesday night poker party at our place last night. I was too tired to clean up and hoped he might still intend to pick up the mess himself.

I turned on the TV and watched the morning news. I was already feeling sleepy and the newscasters didn't try to liven the morning up much. The phone rang when the oven timer went off. I turned off the oven and grabbed the phone with a pot holder. "Hello?"

"It's Rhonda. So, I've got good news and bad news. You know

that old guy with chest pain? He slugged the ER doctor in the face when he found out that he didn't have a heart attack and was going to be released. Now they've got the guy on an EDP hold."

Another EDP. I'd have to remember to tell Eddy about that. I'd had a hunch about the old guy and probably should have warned Rhonda. "So, what's the good news?"

"I think I've talked Chris and June into coming out with us tonight. I figured you'd be more inclined to go out if you knew we'd have company . . ."

Rhonda let her voice drop off and I wondered what else she was thinking. Maybe she had guessed my attraction to her friend June. It was a sticky situation since Rhonda had been the one to initially ask me out on a date and I hadn't yet broached the let's-just-be-friends subject. Maybe now I wouldn't have to. "Okay."

"You're still up for going?" There was some distraction in the background. Something about a case coming into ICU. Rhonda came back on the line, "I gotta go. One of your EMT friends just wheeled in some kid that got nailed by a truck. Get some sleep. I'll call you tonight to make sure you're awake."

The club was five blocks from my house and I walked there, enjoying the cool evening. The day had turned unseasonably warm and I'd had trouble sleeping. Our condo lacked an air conditioner which was a fatal flaw for a rental in Sacramento. The only way to cool the place was to open all the windows—we got a nice breeze but also heard every screech of brakes on the busy city streets and the commuter tram's bell. It was only May and the problem would just get worse. I'd suffered through it last summer and wasn't looking forward to another round.

I found Rhonda at the bar with Chris. June wasn't with them. I tried to ignore my disappointment but Rhonda immediately saw it. After our hellos, she piped up with, "So, she gave me some excuse about having to meet with her sister."

Chris nodded. "She came to the ranch this evening. They've been arguing about what to do without the well."

"The well?"

Rhonda elaborated. "The neighboring ranch is being sold, along with the water for the McCormick ranch. Karen wants to sell and she's been fighting with June over money. June's been tearing up the house looking for her dad's files and hoping to find something about the well."

I felt bad for June, already sensing at the barbecue that she and her sister had a strained relationship. It seemed that June's life was the ranch and I couldn't imagine what she'd do otherwise.

Chris interrupted Rhonda, "I told her she needed a night off work but I don't think June takes nights off."

"She doesn't." Rhonda agreed. She pulled a bar stool out for me and patted it. "Have a seat. We're drinking Coronas on account of Cinco de Mayo. You want to join us in our second round?"

"But it's May tenth." I had a hard time keeping up with the date but I knew for a fact Cinco de Mayo had come and gone. Eddy and I had worked that night and we'd had a horrible round of car accidents. I wanted to know more about June and was wishing for a good way to direct the conversation back to her. Deanna, the bartender, appeared and gave me a big smile.

"You know, the date's just a technicality. How's your night going, Meg? Planning on introducing your two new friends?" Deanna asked, pulling three bottles of Corona out of the ice bucket. She popped the three lids, one after the other, and jammed in lime slices. I liked to watch her work and think of all the women here who'd imagined taking Deanna home. Saying she was good looking was an understatement. She didn't have any flaws and the type of features that models have—high cheekbones and full lips, eyes lined in dark black lashes and an olive complexion. When she wore one of her tight tank tops, her breasts pressed toward you and she didn't try to hide the large nipples. She had an armband tattoo that looked like a rose vine, plenty of thorns but no roses. Most women pretended to look at the tattoo when it was perfectly obvious they were really thinking about how her breasts would feel in their hands. And most women were too uncomfortable to ever try asking for her number so they just sat at the bar, sneaking sideways looks at her.

I made the introductions as Deanna set the bottles down in front of us, still keeping her eyes on me. "Nice meeting you, Chris, Rhonda." She turned to leave and then glanced over her shoulder and added, "By the way, watch out for Meg. She never leaves here alone." She winked at me and I felt my cheeks burn.

Deanna moved to the other end of the counter to take an order from a young couple. The women had trouble taking a break from kissing to explain the drinks they wanted. I avoided Rhonda's and Chris's gaze.

"So you know the bartender?" Chris finally asked.

"Vaguely. We've shared a bed."

Chris laughed a little too loudly. "Vaguely?"

Rhonda only shook her head. I watched Deanna pour the drinks for the couple and then turn to help the single woman seated on the last bar stool nearest the door. The woman was pretty and Deanna didn't hesitate to flirt with her. The music changed from a techno dance beat to a Top Ten favorite.

"Oh, I love dancing to this song." Chris gazed longingly at the dance floor. There were two couples dancing and a half dozen single women milling around the edges, looking somewhere between hopeful and bored. "Wanna dance, Rhonda?" She had a pleading look and I was expecting a whine to come out of her if Rhonda said no.

Rhonda was reluctant to leave me alone but Chris was already tugging her onto the dance floor. I watched them dance, Chris pulling Rhonda a little too close to be thinking about just a friendship. I didn't mind being a third wheel but seeing Chris and Rhonda made me long for June. Deanna placed her hand on my shoulder and leaned over the bar. "You know, I can get off in an hour."

"An hour, huh? I don't remember it ever taking you that long."
She winked. "It will if you're lucky."

Deanna had come home with me more than a few times. In fact, I never came to the club on Women's Night if I wasn't looking to take her home. I'd been a little worried about seeing her here with June and had to admit it was probably best that June had canceled. Deanna and I had this weekly thing going for the past six months but neither of us had brought up the subject of dating. It was easier that way.

The first time I met her I was completely smitten. She was beautiful and hard to ignore. With a bartender like her, you'd spend half your paycheck on tips and not think twice about watered-down drinks. She told me on our first night together that she was French but then she admitted she'd never learned how to say anything except "will you go to bed with me," courtesy of Lady Marmalade. I'd laughed and asked her the same thing, in English.

With Deanna, I didn't think about long term. I just enjoyed the immediate pleasure of her body and our mutual attraction kept us both satisfied. She had the softest skin and a curvy figure—I could rub her back for hours and still feel like I hadn't gotten enough of her. She liked to wear tight jeans and the tank tops that made her customers pay attention. I also figured out early on that she liked uncomplicated sex without any toys and rarely took longer than a few minutes to climax. Beyond that, I didn't know much about her. Although she might have her pick of one-night stands, the bouncer had told me I was the only one she'd gone home with lately. I didn't ask Deanna if this was true. It wasn't my business but I did wonder why she was still single. Maybe she preferred it that way. She definitely got better tips if customers didn't think there was another woman waiting in the wings.

Chris and Rhonda danced for longer than I expected. I saw a couple of friends, barflies I knew well, and invited myself to join their game of pool. I lost my first game and got bored waiting for another chance to play. Chris and Rhonda were back at the bar and I joined them. We chatted for a bit about the ranch. Chris had moved into a room above the barn and was happily calling this home, at least for the rest of summer. I noticed Rhonda's attention drift when Chris started to explain how she'd like to live all over the world, for a few months at a time. I guessed Rhonda was in her mid-thirties and Chris looked at least ten years younger. It wasn't just their age, though. Rhonda looked settled just sitting on the bar stool. Chris, on the other hand, had that nervous muscle twitch that made you shift your feet and watch the door.

Chris had nothing but praise for June. "She's taught me more about working horses in the past week than I learned in a year working at the Nevada ranch. June can get a sense of their personality just by watching them out in the pasture for a bit, you know. She sees how they interact with each other and then trains them differently because of it. She knows exactly who tries to bite who at feeding time, who gets chased away from the water trough. She knows everything, really, about those horses."

"Chris, I think you'd better be careful what you say about June or we might start teasing you about the crush you've got on her." Rhonda turned to me and added in a loud whisper so Chris would hear, "Teacher's pet."

Apparently I wasn't the only one to pick up on this. Chris didn't try to deny it but she colored as red as her T-shirt. "Yeah. It's a good thing she's straight."

Rhonda just smiled. She didn't seem bothered that Chris was interested in her best friend. "You have no idea how many women have wanted to ask Mrs. McCormick out on a date. And men, for that matter."

"She still goes by Mrs. McCormick? I thought she was divorced."

"They signed all the papers but her ex never turned anything in. I think he still wanted the tax deduction. June doesn't care. To her, if two people have made an agreement, it's as good as done." Rhonda motioned to get Deanna's attention. Our bottles were empty but I didn't feel like hanging around here with Chris and

Rhonda for another round. Rhonda continued, "Honestly, I have no idea why June ever married Greg. He was about as interesting as, well, a guy."

Chris snorted. Deanna came by to collect our empties and Chris and Rhonda ordered another round. I glanced at my watch, wondering if I'd have time for another before Deanna finished her shift. "Five minutes, if you're wondering," Deanna said, handing Chris and Rhonda their Coronas. "You want another anyway?"

I shook my head.

"Five minutes till what?" Chris asked. "That was totally cryptic." She settled her hand on Rhonda's thigh, acting nonchalant about it.

I glanced up from Rhonda's leg, thinking that this night hadn't turned out as I'd expected. Instead of being upset at me, Rhonda was happily enjoying Chris's attention. And meanwhile, Chris was talking about June as if she'd like to kneel down and wait for her to come around to lesbianism. Deanna hadn't realized that I'd originally been invited here by Rhonda and now she was hinting about me taking her home. And the person I was really thinking about was on a ranch an hour away from here—and apparently straight.

"I have to go in five minutes. I asked the bartender to remind me."

"Where are you going?" Rhonda asked, glancing at her own watch. "You don't have to go to work tonight, do you?"

"No. It's a long story." I could feel both Chris and Rhonda staring at me, waiting for the long story. They weren't getting it. "So, Rhonda, when are you going out to the ranch next?"

She sighed. "I'm picking up a few extra shifts this week so probably not until next week. But if you want to go out and ride Don Juan, knock yourself out. He could use the exercise."

"Really? You wouldn't mind?"

"Not at all. Just do me a favor and don't get yourself hurt. June would kill me if I let you take Don Juan out alone and then you got bucked off."

"Why would she care?" Chris wondered.

I was wondering the same thing. Rhonda just repeated herself. "Just be careful. Don't get yourself hurt."

"Actually, June offered me riding lessons. I was wondering if I could use Don Juan for the lesson."

"Yeah, sure." Rhonda didn't hide her surprise. "June offered? Huh, go figure."

"What do you mean?"

She waved off my concern. "It's just not like June. But forget about it. Enjoy yourself. And if Don Juan acts up, don't be afraid to give him a good kick. He's a little lazy in the arena."

"Thanks for the warning." I said good night then and both of them seemed a little relieved to watch me go. Brakes screeched and a man's angry voice pierced the air as I stepped outside. Two cars had nearly collided at the intersection in front of the bar. One of the drivers jumped out of his car and started cussing at the other driver. "Temper, temper" the bouncer said, taking a drag on her cigarette. "At least we've got the paramedic on hand, in case these boys start fighting."

"No. I'm busy tonight."

"Mm-hmm." The bouncer gave me a knowing nod as I turned down the alleyway and headed toward the rear entrance of the bar.

The back door was poorly lit and littered with buckets of empty beer bottles and black garbage bags lined up near an overflowing Dumpster. Presents for the morning trash collector. I found a clearing several feet away from the Dumpster and leaned against the cold brick building. The stench of the club's backside was overwhelming at first but I knew in a moment the breeze would come and blend this smell into the city's general odor.

Deanna came out sooner than I expected. She kissed me on the cheek and hooked her thin arm with mine. She smelled faintly of alcohol and cologne. "Your place?"

We'd never gone anywhere but my place. I nodded. "It's a shorter walk." Actually, I had no idea how far away she lived. For all I knew, we might have been neighbors.

◈❧◈

Deanna left my house Friday morning sometime after the noise of the trash collector woke us. I pulled my pillow over my head and tried to ignore the beeping back-up alarm on the trash truck. I guessed it was around six a.m. and was surprised when Deanna climbed out of bed. I offered to make breakfast but she wasn't interested. "You know, we've never had a meal together." I'd spent half an hour last night, trying to fall asleep and counting up all the normal things that Deanna and I had never done. I'd forgotten to add meals to that list. Deanna had asked if that bothered me and I had to admit that it did for some reason. She offered to stay next time. This morning she had to go to yoga. I didn't know she took yoga but could have guessed that. The sex last night had been better than we'd had in a while. Both of us had been hungry for it. I didn't ask if there was someone else she was thinking about. She didn't ask me either.

I drove out to the ranch the next day, worrying for most of the drive that I should have called first to confirm the lesson. I didn't have the number though and it seemed unlikely someone would be in the house to pick up the phone anyway. As soon as I parked the Jeep, I gave up worrying—June was on the patio swing. Chris and Gabe were seated on the porch steps enjoying the shade. All three of them looked up at me. I swallowed my nervousness and pulled on my boots before heading over.

Gabe welcomed me with a big wave. "Hey Meg, you're just in time for siesta. Pull up a chair."

June smiled at me and I felt myself relax. "It's our lemonade break. You want a glass?" She had already stood up from her place on the porch swing and was going for the pitcher. She filled her glass. "You don't mind sharing glasses, do you?"

I took her glass without answering, then added "thank you" a few seconds too late. The glass was wet with condensation. I took a sip, letting the cool, tart flavor fill my mouth. She stared at me for a moment, then headed back up the steps to the swing. I sat down by Gabe, glancing over my shoulder and seeing June's eyes on me still.

"How was your night?" Chris asked.

I swallowed. "Good. And yours?"

"Not bad."

I was waiting for her to say more but that seemed to be the end of our discussion. I gathered from her tone that the night hadn't been bad at all, which meant Chris hadn't gone home alone. I wondered if Rhonda had enjoyed the evening as well.

"So, you're going for a ride?" Gabe asked. He had a way of talking while still smiling that put me completely at ease. "Rhonda called up earlier to say you might be coming. That's real nice of you to give Don Juan a little exercise. Rhonda doesn't get out here enough and that horse gets itchy for the trails. Don Juan is the type of horse who would take himself on a walk up to the summit, if we let him." He added, "And be home in time for dinner without missing any green grass along the way."

"Well, I think we're just sticking to the arena today. I've got a lesson."

Gabe glanced at June. "You're giving private lessons now?" June shrugged but didn't answer him. "Huh, go figure."

Chris and I both looked at each other when Gabe said that but neither of us spoke up. It was obvious that something had passed between June and Gabe because he stood up then, too quickly, and said, "Well, there's work to be done. Break time was over a while ago." He tapped Chris's shoulder. "Come on, we've got stalls to clean. Enjoy your lesson, Meg. You're in good hands."

Chris took a minute to finish her drink and then stood and stretched. Gabe was already halfway down the path to the barn. "Guess it's back to work for me. I'd rather take one of the racehorses out for some exercise than clean stalls."

"I bet you would. Unfortunately, Gabe's your boss today. I don't have any say in the work schedule. Friday's my day off."

I was surprised June gave herself a day off. Apparently she didn't consider that giving me a lesson was work.

"Well, I figured asking you was worth a try." Chris laughed. "There's nothing I hate more than shoveling shit. I think I'd rather do anything else."

"Careful what you wish for," June warned. "Gabe could easily find a job you'd hate worse."

Chris looked doubtful but wasn't ready to chance it. She jogged down the path after Gabe without glancing back at us. As soon as she was out of earshot, June said, "She's been in too good of a mood today. It's driving me crazy. She came in for breakfast whistling."

"Yeah, I hate being around happy people."

"That's not what I meant . . . I think she slept at Rhonda's last night."

"I wouldn't doubt it. They seemed pretty friendly at the bar. Does that bother you?" I could tell June was jealous. But who was she jealous of—Rhonda or Chris?

"Maybe a little. Chris is too young for Rhonda. I can't believe that it would work out. I know I can't tell Rhonda who to sleep with. I've tried before and she never listens. I don't usually listen to her recommendations either." She smiled. "But it just doesn't seem like she'll ever find the woman she's looking for the way she goes around."

"Not every girl you sleep with has to be *the one*. Sometimes they just have to be the one for the night. Doesn't mean you won't meet the right woman later. I sure as hell know that." I regretted my words as soon as I'd spoken them, knowing I'd just ended our conversation. By June's closed lip reaction I knew she was the type to fall for just one love. And here I was suggesting that I'd go to bed with any girl that seemed ready. I tried backpedaling. "That didn't come out the way I meant it."

"I won't ask what you really meant." June smiled but her expression seemed strained. She reached for my empty glass. "Come on, let's get you on a horse. Our afternoon's almost gone."

I caught Don Juan easily with a handful of carrots. He let me halter him and followed me over to the barn acting perfectly

83

docile. June handed me a brush and a hoof pick and then leaned against the tie railings to oversee me. Unlike Rhonda, she didn't seem interested in talking through this process and the only time I heard her speak up was to say something to the horses.

I went for the saddle that she'd pointed out. It was heavier than it looked and awkward to lift with straps and buckles clanking everywhere. As soon as I approached Don Juan with the saddle, he stepped away from me. I tried lifting it up slower but each time I got close, he sidestepped just out of reach. June noticed my frustration but gave me another couple minutes at it before she finally spoke up. "Do you mind if I give you a hand?"

"I don't mind at all. For some reason, I'm getting the impression he doesn't want me to ride him." I'd been scared to get on him the first time but I'd grown used to him on the trail ride and had felt comfortable by the end of it. Now my fear had unexpectedly returned. I stared at the horse, thinking I might just take him out for a walk on a nice long leash, like a dog, if June wasn't here.

"He's just feeling you out. It's his way of testing you." June took the saddle out of my hands and tossed it on the horse as quick as you'd flip an omelet. He didn't move a muscle.

"And obviously I failed his test." Don Juan bent his neck to look back at me. He sniffed my hands, pushing his muzzle as if searching for a treat.

"You didn't fail." As soon as June tightened the girth strap, he flicked his ears back and swished his tail, displeased to have lost his little game. June checked the stirrup lengths and then slapped the saddle. "All set here. Now you just need to get the bridle on him." She must have noticed my doubtful look because she continued with, "And relax, he hasn't even bucked you off yet."

"Is that likely? Does he usually buck?" My legs felt weak. I imagined Don Juan turning into a bucking bronco and couldn't shake the thought of flying off him. "He's a tall horse. It'd be a long way to fall."

"Tall? He's barely sixteen hands. Get the bridle and stop worrying. City folk spend too much time worrying." She grinned and slapped my shoulder. The motion was so friendly and natural that it took me completely by surprise. She continued, "Really, you'll be fine."

"You know, I knew someone that got bucked off once and broke their leg. She was knocked unconscious from the force of the fall. Luckily, she was found by this rock star paramedic, and . . ." I stammered as soon as she looked at me. All I could think about was the place where her palm had hit my shoulder. It was a simple move on her part. One touch that didn't mean anything to her. "Well, the woman's leg healed and then she met up with the paramedic a year later. Needless to say, the story has a happy ending."

"Oh, does it?" She laughed, shaking her head at me. "You're stalling."

I was completely distracted now. I mumbled, "You know, they're not like cars. They don't always stop when you hit the brakes. And steering isn't as easy as turning the wheel. And what if a wasp came along and stung them?"

"That's why you have me to show you what to do." She handed me the bridle and folded her arms against her chest. "Ready when you are."

Don Juan was unwilling to open his mouth for the bit and once I'd finally gotten him to take the metal, the latches and straps that connected to it were suddenly a mysterious tangle of leather in my hands. "You know, I once had to help a friend out of something that looked a lot like this."

"Oh, really? How friendly of you." June sighed and stepped next to me. "Watch me do it once, okay? It's easy if you just start up at the top of his head." She set her hand on Don Juan's head, right between his ears and the horse lowered his head, his muzzle sniffing her palm where the bit was. I tried to concentrate but I found myself staring at her hands, then her arms and shoulders. Her hair was pulled back in a ponytail but more than a few strands had slipped loose to frame her face. I wanted to brush the loose strands behind her ears and turn her chin toward me and kiss her . . . I nearly jumped when she spoke. "Okay, your turn."

She'd taken the bridle off and set the leather straps back in my hands. I fumbled with everything, knowing my cheeks were colored with a blush and that she was staring at me still. She didn't make me flounder for long. Her fingers brushed against mine and guided my hands. Don Juan waited patiently for us to slip the straps in place and latch the leather under his neck.

I stepped back from him before June did. She had craned her neck to the other side and was adjusting one of the straps. "You know, Rhonda tried to teach me the idiosyncrasies of all of the tack last time we went out on ride." I tried to steady my voice. "And I thought I'd been paying attention but apparently not well enough."

"It just takes practice, like most things."

June led the way over to the arena and waited for me to climb up in the saddle. I was still feeling unfocused and Don Juan took note of this, sidestepping every time I tried to get in the saddle. I pulled at his reins and he tossed his head, acting suddenly much younger and more frisky than I wanted him to be. "I don't know if he's up for a riding lesson today."

"He'll be fine. Meg, isn't it more likely that you'll get killed driving home tonight in that Jeep than by sitting in that saddle?"

"You're right. Maybe I ought to stay the night." The words slipped out before I could stop them. June's eyes dropped to the ground and the only sound was my heartbeat in my ears, the wind rustling through the trees and a horse whinnying somewhere off in one of the pastures. "I have no idea why I just said that out loud." I knew I had to say something quick to backtrack us but nothing was coming to mind.

She cleared her throat. "Maybe you ought to just wear your seatbelt and drive the speed limit. Get on."

I placed a hand on the saddle horn and tried not to think about my sweating palms or weak knees. After a couple more false starts, I finally got myself in the saddle. Don Juan tossed his head and took a few steps, ready to be going. June grabbed his reins and he stood motionless, waiting for me to get settled. I shifted my weight, got both feet in place in the stirrups and then glanced over at June. Her face was full of concern for me. I couldn't help but laugh then.

"Why are you laughing?"

"I was really hoping you'd agree to give me lessons. I thought if we had a chance to be alone I might be able to impress you."

"Well, you're certainly making an impression."

I would have given a hundred dollars to see her face as she'd said that but she'd already turned to open the arena gate. I wasn't sure if she'd been interested before. Now I was certain she was. But something still held her back.

I passed the next week thinking only of the coming Friday and my lesson with June. I considered going up to the ranch just to ride by myself but I chickened out. I wanted June to invite me and had a good feeling she wasn't going to make that step. She didn't. Deanna called instead, asking if I was avoiding her, or the club. I told her I'd been overworked and I was avoiding everyone, nothing personal. I was just exhausted. It wasn't entirely untrue. Eddy and I had worked a full extra shift filling in for a team that had called in sick. It was nearing the end of May and we'd had an early heat wave that was testing everyone's patience. With the extra heat, Eddy had come up with more reasons than ever for an oceanside vacation. By her tone, I thought Deanna may have sensed my interests were wandering but she let me off the hook without any more questions.

When I pulled in at the ranch, June met me in the driveway. She took off her straw cowboy hat and wiped a red bandana across her brow. "I've decided it's too hot for a lesson."

My heart sank. "Oh, I guess it is pretty warm." I shifted my position and felt my shirt sticking to the seat with my sweat.

"Ninety-seven degrees, according to Gabe's thermometer. I've already sent Shank home. He was working so slow it wasn't worth my money keeping him here. Gabe and Chris are taking a break and waiting for the sun to set. If it was August, they'd just expect this heat, but in May no one wants to work when it's like this. Anyway, how about a trail ride? There's a shady route we can take."

"Perfect." I jumped out of the Jeep and followed her down to the barn. We passed Gabe snoozing under a tree by the shed. Chris was watering the wilted garden that had been planted alongside the shed. She waved and halfheartedly threatened to spray us with the hose. Instead, she sprayed the chickens that had wandered over to peck at the moistened dirt between the rows of green sprouts.

"I'm thinking of taking one of the mares out on her first trail ride."

"Don't tell me you're taking Cassidy out." Gabe called over to us, apparently not as sound asleep as he appeared. He shifted to his side so he could see us better. "Which mare are you taking out?"

"You guessed it." June said with no apology in her voice.

Gabe shook his finger at her. "You know she's not safe in the arena yet. She nearly stampeded Shank and Chris yesterday. Why the heck are you gonna take her out on the trails? To get your neck broken?" Gabe acted more like an infuriated parent than a sleepy ranch hand now.

Under her breath, June said, "Cassidy's not real fond of Shank." She hollered over to Gabe, "Relax, I'm taking the paramedic along."

I had to stifle my laughter.

"June, why do you go out of your way looking for trouble? Do you want to give me an early heart attack?"

"Gabe, if you have a heart attack I'm gonna blame it on all the butter you put on your biscuits and the extra slices of bacon you eat every morning." She grinned, obviously unperturbed. "Besides Cassidy gets along well with Don Juan. It'll be perfect. Don Juan will lead the way. If Meg's okay with that—that all right with you?"

Her expression made it obvious I had no real choice in the matter. I wanted to agree with Gabe but looking at June I knew I couldn't. She wasn't waiting for anyone's permission anyway.

Chris spoke up before I had to answer. "Cassidy's come a long way, Gabe. We've been riding her a little every day and she's getting some nice manners. I think she'll be fine on the trail." She squirted the dog, edging his way over to the garden. He shook his wet coat and the chickens scrambled to get out of his spray.

Gabe stood up, took a long look at June and shook his head. "I'll say I told you so later." He stomped up the path to the house, muttering to himself.

Chris laughed. "You'd better get back in one piece or we're all gonna get a hell of a lecture from that man."

It took us a while to find Cassidy. She was in a thicket of birch trees that camouflaged her and two other horses. June tried approaching the horses, holding a carrot out like a sacrifice. The mare stood still until June was within a few feet of her and then reared and bolted past her like a deer. The other two took off as well. The sight of the three of them weaving through the trees was something. June was pissed though, so I didn't bring up the beauty of it.

After another failed attempt, June got out a lasso. I didn't mind watching the lassoing. She had a beautiful way of making the rope look like a living thing. The line circled over her head a few times then slipped out of her hands. It arced over us with a whoosh and dropped down on the mare's neck. Feeling the nylon, the horse reared up. June's arms tightened, ready for her. Her stance was as taut as the young horse. After a moment, both of them relaxed. June approached the mare, calming her with soft rumbling sounds. I wasn't sure if she was just making noises or actually saying something in particular and then realized she was cussing and nearly burst out laughing to hear her swear in such a tender way. But the horse bought into the sweet talking and finally lowered her head enough for June to halter her.

It wasn't until we'd led the mare out of the pasture that we noticed she was lame in her hind leg. June found a laceration above the hoof. She swore, this time not so softly. Her jaw was set and I could see the muscles grinding. We dressed the wound and then let the mare go. I didn't admit I was a little relieved when she said we'd have to put Cassidy's trail ride off for another day. In this case, I thought Gabe was right. The young mare was too wild.

We set off to another pasture and June picked out an older gelding she called Tanner. I noticed he was the same horse she'd taken on our first ride. His chestnut coat shimmered in the sun and the blaze on his head looked like a perfect stripe of white paint. The horses in this pasture recognized June right off and trotted up to the gate. Don Juan was in this pasture along with Tanner and both of the geldings came right up to us. I had to push Tanner back from the gate to get to Don Juan. It was obvious he wanted June's attention. "I think the boys like you. Which one's your favorite?"

June shrugged. "Haven't ever really thought about it. I trained Don Juan but he belongs to Rhonda now. Tanner belonged to my dad. I think he was one of my father's favorite. Whiskey was definitely first in my dad's heart. That horse doesn't like anyone else really." She pointed out Whiskey from the other horses in the herd. This one was a skinny bay gelding. He hung back from the fence a ways, warily watching us.

After the mare's fiery display I was ready to sprint for the fence at the slightest indication of trouble. Neither the horses nor June seemed to notice my discomfort. June dropped Don Juan's lead line into my hands and turned to head out of the pasture. Don Juan rubbed his head against me in greeting. I immediately forgot about being uneasy around him. "What do you think happened to the other mare? How'd she get that cut?"

"Who knows? Cassidy does stupid things all the time. Young horses always do. They'll spook when a tree branch falls and trip over their own feet."

"The cut won't need to be sutured?"

June smiled. "Well, you're the paramedic. What do you think?"

"If it was a person, I'd say they would need a tetanus shot and a couple stitches. Or skin glue. But I don't know much about horses and wound care."

"I don't think she'll need stitches. Most little things heal as long as you can keep the flies off the wound."

We tied the horses at the barn and I brushed them down while June got out our tack. I managed to clean all four of Don Juan's hooves, saddle and bridle him without any help. June didn't seem to notice my success. She was already waiting by the gate with Tanner long before I'd finished. I could tell she was distracted. "Is something wrong?"

"I was just thinking . . ." She sighed. Her voice sounded worn thin when she continued. "It's just some trouble here at the ranch. Little things that have to be taken care of and always one more glitch in the process, you know. I just get tired some times. No problems with you, though, so don't look so worried."

"Well, want to go for a ride and not think about responsibility for a while?" I couldn't decide if it was good or bad that her problems had nothing to do with me. In a way, I wished she'd at least consider us an issue.

"I'm ready when you are." She had already set her boot in the stirrup and her other foot swung over the saddle in one movement, just as easy as a person would sit down at the kitchen table. Tanner took a few steps and she pulled his reins, saying whoa in a low way that made him freeze. I got up in the saddle on the second try and patted Don Juan's neck as if he had something to do with my progress. June already had pointed Tanner to the trail Don Juan was quick to follow out the gate.

Before long I realized that I might as well be riding alone. June didn't seem to be paying any attention to the trail, the horses or me. Maybe she was waiting for me to take the first step past friendship but I was too guarded with her now. Last week had gone smoother. June relaxed into her role as my teacher and I'd learned more than expected. I'd spent most of the time after the lesson trying to figure out the right thing to say without scaring her off. Now I just wanted her to notice I was there.

We rode down a new trail this time, weaving through a valley scattered with dark green oak trees. In the few clearings we passed, orange poppies and purple lupine lined the sunny spaces just off the edge of the trail. June loosened up after a while, pointing out thickets of poison ivy when the path narrowed and a couple of her favorite trees. She missed two monarch butterflies and I finally convinced her to stop for a moment when a third butterfly darted past us. She smiled and mentioned that the sun was setting soon but I made her watch the butterfly for a bit anyway. She asked me two or three times if Don Juan was behaving himself and if I was doing all right. Don Juan was so easygoing I'd forgotten my earlier worries. The grasses were greener on this trail than around the ranch and June explained something about an underwater stream. The temperature here was also noticeably cooler. We reached the end of the valley floor and then zigzagged our way up a slope on the northern side. We turned west as if we were heading back to the barn.

"Do you mind a detour? I want to go check on our well. I collect a water sample from the source once a week for testing."

"I'm enjoying the ride. You can take me wherever you want to go."

"It'll mean a longer ride home."

"Fine by me." The more time I had with June, the more I wanted to spend with her. "I heard about this well. Rhonda mentioned that your neighbor was selling their land and your water might be part of the deal."

June sighed. "Looks that way. I've talked to the county and there seems to be no legal loophole that would let us keep the water. My dad didn't keep any records when he helped Mr. Hudson build the well. I think it might be easier to build our own well but Karen isn't sold on the idea."

It didn't take us long to reach the spot where the trail detoured from the valley floor. June pointed out the water tower, a big white balloon-shaped structure that seemed to have been planted in the middle of a fruit tree orchard. The well was a hundred yards or so from the tower. As soon as we had dismounted, June pointed at something over by the well. She tied her horse to a fence post and slipped between the barbed wire. June was halfway to the well before I realized what she'd seen. A man was lying face down in the clearing. It took me a little longer to tie Don Juan and I reached the man a moment after her.

"Is he dead?" Her voice cracked.

The man was gray-haired and overweight, probably in his late sixties. I watched his sides, looking for rib movement. No sign of breathing. I went over and felt his skin. He was still warm and I thought I felt a weak pulse at his neck. With a bit of grunting, I got him turned onto his back side and quickly checked for injuries. He was unresponsive but the pulse, however weak, encouraged me to try and rouse him. I yelled and rubbed my fist hard on his chest. There was a red mark on his cheek, possibly from where he'd hit the ground, but no other obvious injuries. I finally saw him take a shallow breath. I felt again at his neck and waited ten seconds before my fingers felt a swell of blood. "He's got a heartbeat but I think he's about to arrest."

June only stared at me, frozen.

"Arrest, as in, his heart is trying to stop." We needed to get him to the hospital but I was worried his heart would stop before then. My hands were already pounding on his chest. I took a deep breath and exhaled into the man's lips then continued chest compressions. I could tell by the look of shock on her face that June was going to need better directions if she was going to be of any use to me here. "June, where's the nearest phone?"

"Phone?" She came around then. "At his house. It's about a ten-minute walk from here."

"Can you make it there any quicker than that?"

"Tanner can. Are you sure I should leave you?"

I had no idea how long the man was going to stay with us. The chest compressions would probably do little good. "Yes. Go as fast as you can."

June ran over to the horses, slipping through the barbed wire again. She pulled a pair of wire cutters out of her saddle bag and cut an opening in the fence then jumped on Tanner. She rode over to me. "I'll be back in five minutes. You think you can keep him all right until then?"

I nodded. Of course, it depended on what you considered all right to be.

June gave Tanner a hard kick and whooped. The horse reared as soon as he felt the kick then took off at a full gallop. Don Juan danced around, whinnying as he realized he was being left behind. I turned my attention back to the unconscious man, giving him another breath. He wasn't breathing on his own. I felt his neck. Again, a weak pulse, so slow I wasn't sure the next beat would come. I went back to the chest compressions, taking occasional breaks to give him air, and quickly fell into a steady rhythm.

His chest rose suddenly without my help and I paused my compressions. Another ten seconds passed and he took another breath. I felt his neck and was surprised to feel a pulse of about fifty beats per minute. He wasn't out of danger yet but this was a good sign. I guessed he'd suffered a heart attack. It seemed odd that he'd be out here alone but then I decided he'd probably been on a ride and had fallen off.

I kept my eye on my watch. Ten minutes passed and June still hadn't returned. I started again on chest compressions when his pulse dropped to twenty. Fifteen minutes later and there was still no sign of June. I started worrying that his heart rate would stop completely and my old fashioned CPR might not work. I heard a rustling sound and Don Juan whinnied.

June appeared on the trail. An older woman was with her, riding another horse. The woman shrieked when she saw the man and jumped off her horse. She looked him over, keeping her hand over her mouth as she did. "He's alive still, isn't he?"

"He is, ma'am." In fact, his pulse was improving and he'd taken several breaths on his own.

"I'm his wife, Mrs. Hudson." She brushed her hand over his face tenderly. "Al, can you hear me? Al? I'm right here, Al." She repeated the man's name several times, shaking his arm as she did but got no response. Finally she stopped and gave me a pleading look. "You're sure he's alive?"

"Yes, but he's unconscious. I think he may have fallen off his horse."

"He's got a bad heart," Mrs. Hudson said. "He's supposed to take medications and not eat so much cholesterol. You know, he never listens to doctors."

June came over to my side after she'd tied the horses. "The ambulance is on the way. There's a cousin at the house waiting for the medics. The guy who answered the emergency call didn't have any idea how long it'd take and Mrs. Hudson didn't want to wait at the house in case . . ."

"He'll be all right, won't he? Unconscious, like a coma?" Mrs. Hudson was holding the man's hand now and pumping his fingers between her palms as if this might help wake him.

"Like a coma, ma'am." I didn't want to answer the first question. There wasn't any way of telling yet.

June sat down next to me with Mrs. Hudson opposite us and all of us stared at the old man. No one spoke. We each had a hand on one of his pulse points, mine on his neck, June's on his left wrist and Mrs. Hudson holding his right wrist. We assured each other with intermittent nods that there were still four living souls at the well. Twenty minutes passed before Don Juan whinnied again. He was as good as a watch dog. I heard the voices coming our way a minute later.

The old man's cousin was leading the way down the trail. I recognized the blue shirts that followed him as two of the day crew guys from my dispatch center, Harvey and Lincoln. I knew them both by sight but not much better than that. Harvey was a paramedic and a new transfer to Sacramento. I hadn't heard if he was good or bad so I guessed he was probably mediocre. Harvey knelt down to examine the patient and I stepped back, giving him space.

Lincoln was a basic EMT and a friend of Eddy's. He gave me a warm hello. Then added under his breath, "So, you trying to jump us for a job, Meg?"

"He nearly went into full cardiac arrest about a half hour ago. What took you boys so long?" I tried to temper my anger at their delay. I'd been on the other end of a first responder's wrath one too many times.

Lincoln shook his head. "It's been ten minutes since dispatch called us. We were the closest team to this place. You're lucky someone was in the area. It could have been even longer."

"If you'd stopped for lunch?" I knew I shouldn't have said this but the words came out anyway.

Lincoln looked like I'd just slapped him. "You can check the timer in our truck, ma'am."

I swallowed, knowing we should focus on the problem instead of argue. "Sorry I'm upset, we came close to losing him and believe it or not, this is my day off. We were out on a horse ride and found him here."

Lincoln glanced over at June. His eyes lingered on her longer than they should have. I guessed that Eddy had told him I was a lesbian and he was making the second step toward assuming we were a couple. Harvey distracted him, asking for a check on the heart leads. They had the heart monitor on the patient and cleared everyone back for a moment to check the signal.

Mrs. Hudson was decidedly calmer now that her husband seemed to be in good hands. She clung onto June's hand, not saying anything but watching carefully as Harvey checked the monitor. The pulse was up to seventy now and the ECG agreed with my suspicions about a possible heart attack. His heart had an abnormal fibrillation now and Harvey made the decision to try and correct the heart before moving the man. He looked at me for a sign of agreement.

I nodded. "It'll be safer to move him if you had venous access too. Maybe place a catheter and call in for the ER doctor at Sutter to give you permission to start giving drugs."

Ten minutes later we carried the old man on a stretcher up the trail and got him loaded in the ambulance. Lincoln helped Mrs. Hudson into the back of the truck and I gave her instructions on where to sit and what to do if a problem occurred, mainly to let the paramedic do his job. I waved good-bye to Harvey and Lincoln and breathed a sigh of relief when the ambulance took off. In a way, I was glad he was no longer my responsibility. It was unlikely that things would go well for the old man. The cousin thanked us profusely for our help. Apparently Mr. Hudson had said he wasn't feeling well that morning and mentioned something about a headache. He'd felt better later and had decided to go out on a ride to find a missing goat. His horse had come back without him so the cousin had gone out to look for him.

It was dark by the time we left the Hudson's place and I was glad June was leading the way. She stopped to fix the fence and then we rode back to the ranch in silence. The horses seemed to know their way in the dark and I just concentrated on staying on Don Juan. My butt was sore from the saddle and I let my feet hang out of the stirrups to ease the cramps in my knees. It'd been a longer ride than I had expected and I kept thinking about how nice a soak in a hot bath would be.

We were taking off the horses' tack when June finally spoke. "Do you have to work tomorrow?"

"No." I eyed her, hoping she was going to ask me to stay but not wanting to seem too hopeful. She had taken Tanner's saddle and was heading into the barn. I followed her to the tack room hefting Don Juan's saddle on my shoulder and wondering how June made the saddles look so light.

June set Tanner's saddle on a rack. "I told Chris that I'd make dinner tonight. It's a little late. She might have gotten desperate and gone for fast food but I doubt it. Chris is pretty near broke." She reached for the saddle that I was holding, meeting my eyes. "I was thinking of asking you to stay for dinner. I mean, do you want to stay—"

"I'd love to have dinner with you," I said, interrupting her. My heart was beating fast. I knew I sounded too eager. So much for playing it cool, I thought, feeling my cheeks warm. Fortunately the light in the tack room was dim and I doubted if she'd notice.

"Good. That's settled. I've been worrying about how I was going to ask you . . ." I could tell she was nervous and wished I could say something to relax her. She continued, "Just so you know, you might regret your decision after you taste my cooking but it's nice to have company." June took the saddle from me and tossed it on one of the high racks as if it were a sack of feathers. I considered myself strong and had the muscles to prove my gym membership wasn't wasted. But a lifetime of working on a ranch had given June a sinewy strength that won out. I followed her out of the tack room, wishing for another quiet moment to lock eyes with hers and hoping Chris had scraped together a few bucks and gone out for a burger.

Apparently Chris really was broke, or else lonely. She was waiting for us at the house and had started to chop up vegetables for a salad. June rehashed the story about Mr. Hudson, saying how lucky he'd been that a paramedic had happened to find him and waving me off when I tried to argue that it was nothing.

Chris didn't seem impressed anyway. "So, do you think the old guy's gonna make it? Wouldn't that be good luck if he died? You'd get your well back, June."

June glanced out of the dark window above the sink. She was washing a pile of mushrooms and red peppers. Her thoughts were clearly distracted from the task. Little bits of dirt still clung to the plump white mushroom caps after the rinse. "I think the land deal will go through regardless." She eyed me. "But do you think he still might die?"

"I don't know." I answered honestly. "It's too soon to tell."

We grilled marinated chicken with the mushrooms and red peppers on the barbecue. June called it shish kabobs but we stabbed the chicken, peppers and mushrooms onto roasting sticks only after everything had already cooked so it was more like a meal on a stick. I wasn't lying when I told her it was amazingly good, though I hadn't eaten since breakfast and thought I just might be starving. She said she'd take the compliment even so.

Chris was quiet during dinner. I assumed she was uncomfortable being the third wheel at a dinner date but she didn't give any indication that she was unhappy having me there. June finally asked if something was wrong. She hadn't finished her shish kabobs or her beer.

"I'm waiting for Rhonda to call me. I left a message on her machine this afternoon. Twice. She hasn't called back yet."

"Maybe she called and just didn't leave a message. You probably just missed her," June suggested.

Chris held up her cell phone. "I've been carrying it around all day."

"Well, the house gets terrible reception."

"It does?" Chris glanced at her phone and pressed a few buttons. A moment later she excitedly announced there was in fact a message waiting. This got her out of her seat in a hurry. "Thanks for dinner," she hollered as the screen door slammed behind her.

"Ah, young love."

"It's a little painful to watch, isn't it?" I took our dishes to the sink.

June followed me with the glasses. "Only because we've all been there." She leaned against the counter, her eyes fixed on the dark window above the sink. "So, Meg, why are you single?"

I squeezed soap onto the sponge and turned on the water, letting the spray rinse the plates. "The usual reasons I guess. Needed time between relationships . . . hadn't found anyone that I wanted to hold onto . . . or anyone that wanted to hold onto me."

"But you date regularly?"

"Not as often as I floss. I don't like going to the dentist so I try to keep my teeth clean." I smiled but she didn't smile back. Her eyes studied me and I realized too late that it wasn't time to joke around with her.

"It's important to go to the dentist." She said, as if we were two strangers discussing gingivitis.

The wall that had gone up at our riding lesson last week went up again. Whenever I felt we had broken down some little barrier between us I realized June was more closed off than anyone I'd ever tried to get to know. I thought of Deanna and wondered if I should tell June about her. But Deanna wasn't my girlfriend. We weren't dating. We were nothing, officially. "Actually, I enjoy most dates about as much as dentist visits." This much was true.

"I haven't dated anyone since I got divorced." She smiled now but her expression was strained. "But I like my dentist—twice a year and no cavities."

"When I was a kid I loved Bazooka bubblegum. You know the really sticky sweet kind? Six fillings later . . ." I opened my mouth, for no reason at all and pointed them out.

"Close your mouth, I get the idea." June laughed. "You want to borrow a toothbrush? I think I have an extra."

"Someone offers a toothbrush and usually that means they're asking me to stay the night." I swallowed hard and turned back to the dishwater.

"I'm nothing like your usual, Meg." She dropped a dish towel on the counter. "I'm just asking if you want to borrow a tooth-brush."

June left the kitchen and I heard the door into the family room open and close. I felt as if I'd been slapped on the face. I tried to finish the dishes without looking over at her. I knew the best thing to do would be to leave now. The phone rang and June answered it. "Hi Rhonda . . . Chris was waiting for your call . . . no, I think she went down to the barn . . ."

I finished the dishes and went to the family room. I'd left my car keys and wallet on the stand by the door and the jingle of the key ring brought June's attention to me. She held up one finger. I waited, wondering if there was any way I'd ever understand June. I wanted to ask her if I should keep trying.

"Rhonda, you've gotta make up your own mind on this one. I'm not even going to try and give you advice . . . All right, fine. Don't call her. But for the record, I think you should . . . No, I'm fine, just tired. Yeah, good night."

Her voice seemed tense. I guessed she would have said more to

Rhonda if I hadn't been in the room. June hung up the phone and came over to the door. "Where are you going?"

"Home." As if you care. I quickly silenced this line of thought. I didn't hold her gaze this time.

"You don't have to leave."

What the hell was she going to do now? Not ask me to stay again? I didn't want to wait around and have her kick me out later. I'd already been put in my place tonight. "Thanks for dinner, June."

"I didn't mean to chase you out."

"You didn't." Of course she had. I knew from her expression that she realized it too. "Are you saying I should stay?"

She nodded. "For a while, maybe."

"Maybe?"

She stepped closer and touched my hand. Her lips brushed mine. It happened so quickly I wasn't sure it had happened at all except for the light tingling sensation on my palm where her fingers still lingered. I leaned toward her and we kissed again, this time she let me guide her and our lips held together longer. Her lips had an urgency that I hadn't felt in years. She pressed into me exactly when I wanted her to. As soon as we parted she looked down, not wanting to meet my gaze. A moment later, her hand was on the door handle.

"Now you want me to go?" The last thing I wanted to do was leave. I reached for her hand instead. She let me hold it, not answering me. Her palms were roughly calloused but the backside was smooth. The contrast was strangely attractive. I didn't want to let go.

"Yeah, I think you should go." She opened the door.

"I'd wait for you to change your mind again but I have a feeling June McCormick isn't the type to go back on a decision more than once."

"You don't know me that well."

"I'm trying."

"Maybe you shouldn't." Her eyes were moist and I thought for a moment she was crying. She looked outside and the aloofness returned to her features. I left then, not looking back at the house until I'd climbed into the Jeep and clicked my seat belt. The porch light beckoned but the front door was already closed. I couldn't see June's shadow though I searched the backlit windows. My cell phone rang and I reached for it in the glove box. It was Deanna. She had only called me once before. That time she'd left her wallet in my bedroom and wanted to know if she could come back for it. This time she wanted to know if I wanted to have a drink, on the house. I could tell by her voice that she was bored. She said the bar crowd was sparse. Her manager had told her she could leave at eleven, an hour from now. I could use a beer and something else too. Without looking back at June's house, I turned on the engine and told Deanna I'd meet her in a half hour. I was almost certain June didn't watch me leave. She probably had already dismissed any thought of me. Her kiss was only a parting favor. She had no idea that the feel of her lips stuck with me.

Chapter 4
June

I kept my hand on the door, half thinking I might do something crazy like open it and call her back. Then I felt tired all over and let my hand drop down to my side. What the hell was I thinking? I pushed the curtain aside at the window by the door and glanced out at the Jeep. Meg had turned on her headlights but wasn't driving away yet. I thought at first she might come back and ask me to change my mind. I had a good feeling I would, if she did. Two minutes passed and then the Jeep's rear lights came on. I watched her pull out of the driveway and then dropped the edge of the curtain. I realized I'd been holding my breath and exhaled slowly. The phone rang. I didn't want to talk to anyone except Rhonda. Of course, no one else would call this late anyway.

"I don't know what to do about Chris. She's left me three messages now."

"Well, you could return her messages." I sank down on the couch and cradled the phone on my shoulder. My eyes stung.

"June, do you have to be so logical?"

"Yes."

Rhonda sighed. "I think I need to tell her how old I am. God, she's only twenty-three. Do you remember the shit we got into when we were that age?"

"No. I've always been perfect."

"Shut up, June. I'm serious. Do you think I should tell her my age?"

I'd already told Chris that Rhonda and I were the same age. It didn't seem like it was a big deal to admit to being thirty-four. "I don't think she cares how old you are."

Rhonda didn't say anything for a minute. We were used to thinking in silence and allowing the other to do that without making any judgments. Finally she said, "She's only been legally drinking for two years."

"What difference does that make?"

"It makes a huge difference. Bars, women. June, I'm too old for her."

I could have told Rhonda that a week ago and we would have skipped all this drama. I moved the phone to my other ear and settled lower on the couch, pulling an afghan over my knees. The draft from the window was cool and I was getting sleepy. I stifled a yawn. "I don't think Chris cares how old you are. She's just having a good time."

"I know. She's just playing around."

"Question is do you want to play?"

"No." Her answer was muffled and followed by, "Yes. I don't know, maybe. She's sweet. Kind of reminds me of my college ex."

"Because she's twenty-three?" It needed to be said.

"Jeez, what the hell am I doing? Am I completely crazy?"

"Not completely, hon." I promised her that Chris would be fine either way but that she should at least call her back and make some decision. Rhonda hemmed and hawed for the next five minutes and then finally agreed to call Chris. I told Rhonda about finding Mr. Hudson at the well. I wasn't ready to tell her about kissing Meg.

I fell asleep on the couch sometime after hanging up with Rhonda and was startled awake by a knock at the door. It was half past eleven by the clock on the wall. I rubbed my face and hollered that I was coming. When I opened the door, no one was there. I found Chris sitting on the porch swing, not swinging. She had her head in her hands. Though I wasn't the one that had just broken up with her, I felt a rush of guilt from the role I'd played. I sat down next to her and waited.

"I just got off the phone with Rhonda." She finally looked up at me. "She thinks she's too old for me. This is the first time I've been dumped after just two dates." She smiled meekly. "I feel a little stupid coming up here but I wanted to talk."

"I don't mind. I'm sorry about Rhonda."

"Whatever. I knew it wouldn't work. Anyway, she just had bad timing. I guess I just needed a friend tonight . . . needed to talk about some things." Her voice sounded as hollow as her words. "Didn't really expect her to just say adios and hang up." She looked away from me, down the hill toward the barn and then her gaze turned to the sky. There wasn't any moon tonight and the stars glowed brightly.

I stared up at the stars too, suddenly thinking about kissing Meg. It was the first time I'd kissed a woman. If I'd ever thought about it, which I couldn't really remember doing, I would have guessed it'd be just like kissing a guy. But it wasn't. Meg's lips were smoother than I'd expected and she'd let me push into her without taking over. Her hands had been on my hips when we'd kissed and I could still feel the place where her fingers had pressed into me. I'd had that strange sensation that she might have been holding me up. When she stepped away, I wanted her hands on me again. I had reached for the door still wishing we could kiss once more.

Chris cleared her throat, drawing my attention back to her. "Anyway, I want to talk to someone and the barn rats weren't interested."

"You should have tried the horses. They're better listeners."

"You got a Mr. Ed around here? 'Cause what I'd really like is a two-way conversation."

I smiled. "No Mr. Ed. But since I'm awake, you might as well try me."

She took her time, almost as if she was choosing her words one by one. "My dad called tonight, before Rhonda. I don't know how the bastard got my phone number."

"I take it you're not close."

Chris pushed her toe against the porch floorboards and set the swing moving. "We're about as distant as New York is to Hollywood. And I'd like to keep it that way, you know what I mean?"

"Where does he live?"

"Las Vegas."

"Along with your ex-boyfriend."

She nodded. "My dad and my ex-boyfriend's father were close. They used to go out to the shooting range together. There was a group of guys that would all go out on Sundays to shoot at targets. Then they'd come home and watch football. Male bonding. They even had a special handshake, no joke."

"Let me guess, your dad wants you to move back to Vegas and settle down with your ex?"

"Either that or go to hell."

"Well, that's a hard choice, isn't it?"

"Not at all." Chris smiled. "I'd go anywhere before going home to Vegas. To tell you the truth, I wouldn't mind never seeing my dad again."

"Not a nice guy?" I could tell there was something she needed to get out but didn't want to push her too hard.

Chris kept her gaze focused up at the dark sky as she answered. "My mom moved out when I was ten. I wanted to go with my mom but she didn't have anything at first and said I'd have to wait a while." She sighed. "Mom got a job dealing cards at a casino and shared a space in a single trailer with this guy who smoked like a chimney. I asked if I could move in with her but there wasn't room for me. She said I wouldn't have a good place to sleep. They had an extra twin bed but I couldn't fight it. A year after that, Mom moved to Texas. She went with the chimney smoker and said I could visit in the summers but I never did. I was too mad at her for leaving. That same year"—she paused, toeing the floorboard to get the swing in motion—"my dad started coming into my room at night. I never said anything about it. He finally stopped when I got a boyfriend."

I waited but Chris didn't say anything else. She kept her eyes focused on the sky. "I'm sorry, Chris." I wanted to say more but that was all I could think of. I wished I hadn't encouraged Rhonda to call things off with her. Not now.

She shrugged. "You don't need to be. Shit happens."

"Yeah, but it's still horrible. It isn't right that someone could hurt their daughter and get away with it."

"He'll be in hell, eventually. For the moment, he's in a trailer park an hour outside of Vegas. I'm not sure which is worse." Chris shifted on the swing and reached into her pocket for her cell phone. She took one look at it and then handed it to me. "Do you mind holding onto this for a while? I don't want to know if anyone's calling."

I took the phone and stood up. It was after midnight and Gabe would be here in six hours. Morning always came too soon. "Why don't you sleep on the couch tonight?"

Chris didn't argue. She followed me into the house and took the blue afghan I handed her. We said good night. Just as I turned to leave, she caught my arm.

"You won't say anything about tonight, will you? I know you and Rhonda are friends but I don't really want her to know that I came up here. Or about my dad and stuff, you know."

"I know." I reached out to embrace her and Chris clung to me tighter than I expected. She bent her head down to rest on my shoulder but didn't say anything. When she finally let go I brushed my hand across her cheek and felt the warm tears. She caught the rest on her shirt sleeve and then quietly lay down on the couch. She had to bend her knees because her lanky frame didn't quite fit and the afghan didn't cover her feet.

"You like Meg, don't you?" she asked just as I was leaving the room.

I paused in the hallway and glanced back at her. The room was full of shadows and I couldn't see her expression. "I don't know. Maybe."

"I'm not gonna say anything about it to Shank or Gabe but I was just thinking . . . she likes you a lot. Maybe you shouldn't tell her."

"Shouldn't tell her what?"

"That you're straight." She laughed softly. Even her voice seemed spent. "Besides, it isn't true, is it?"

I didn't answer her. She had her own problems to think about. "Get some sleep, Chris. We have a full day tomorrow. We need to go over to the Hudson ranch and see what we can help with over there."

"I thought we didn't like the Hudsons. They're selling to a golf course developer."

I didn't want to think about the golf course and I knew I should call Karen and talk to her about it. With Mr. Hudson in the hospital, I guessed Mrs. Hudson would want to get the land deal settled even quicker. There wouldn't be any time to build a case for our water rights. "They're still our neighbors and we don't know how long Mr. Hudson will be in the hospital. My dad used to say you helped neighbors even if they kept a rabid dog."

"Did you get along with your dad?"

"Sometimes."

She nodded. "It probably sounds crazy but I used to get along with my dad sometimes too. Before everything . . . I try not to think about things too much. I'm not going back. No way."

"You're welcome here as long as you want to stay—and work."

She murmured good night and I made my way down the dark hallway, more than ready for a chance to be alone. Sleep came easily.

I spent the next few days helping at the Hudson ranch. Chris came along the first day but I told her to stay at our ranch the next day. I gave her the time off, figuring she'd need to be by herself for a while. Rhonda was still on her mind and Chris wasn't good at keeping up with her work when she was distracted. Gabe and Shank managed our ranch well enough with just a little direction at our morning meetings. Rhonda was busy at the hospital and one of her college friends was in town visiting so I didn't hear much from her. Meg left a message on my answering machine which I didn't answer. She had called just to say hello. I wasn't ready to call her back. It was easy enough to stay busy now and not think about Meg.

Karen called on Thursday. She'd already heard about Mr. Hudson. She had an ear for gossip that astounded me. She was running between important business meetings and said she'd come to the ranch that evening to discuss our plan. I gathered that Ned was still out of town. Extended business was the explanation I got. I didn't ask if she thought he was having an affair. My sister was cantankerous enough as it was. Apparently, stock prices were in the dumps.

Rhonda called me after I'd hung up with Karen. Meg was coming that afternoon to ride Don Juan. They had worked out an agreement for a partial lease. I wasn't surprised. Rhonda rode infrequently and admitted she felt guilty for not giving her horse more attention. I didn't tell her that I thought it was a good idea. Instead, I told her I'd make sure Meg didn't do anything stupid with Don Juan.

Meg showed up after lunch. She looked like she'd just woken up. Apparently she'd worked the past four nights without much sleep in between. I thought she seemed a little distant and when I greeted her with a smile, she only nodded in return. I tried not to think about it. She was tired, after all.

"If you're interested in company, Cassidy's leg healed up and I was thinking of taking her out on the trail. I wouldn't mind having a seasoned horse for her to follow." I hoped Cassidy would look up to Don Juan and not try running him off the trail.

"If it's all the same to you, I think I'd like to go alone. I don't think I'm quite ready for that crazy mare of yours."

"Oh, yeah, of course." I stumbled over the words. Her response wasn't mean. She'd even smiled as she said it. But it still stung. I should have returned her call. I suddenly realized that I'd given her no reason to think I cared. She had to assume I didn't want anything to do with her.

"And I want to take some pictures of the sunset from the summit." She held up a camera. I could see she was trying to be apologetic about it. I was the one who should apologize. She continued, "Anyway, I don't want to slow you down. I'm sure you're busy here. It's okay for me to take Don Juan alone, right?"

I nodded. What could I say?

"Great. I'll see you later."

Karen came to the ranch with a bag of carrots, store bought potato salad and some steaks for the barbecue. She refused to cook and had an odd way of requesting to come over for dinner. Usually she just showed up at dinnertime with various items to contribute. I'd been expecting Meg to come back from her ride any time now but she still hadn't returned. I knew I couldn't go off searching for her and tried not to worry about it. Gabe offered to keep a look out for her and I realized how transparent I'd been, pacing around with one eye on the fence line leading up to the summit trail.

Karen was adamantly opposed to building a new well. I'd spoken with an engineer friend and crunched some numbers. The cost wasn't impossible but Karen refused to even look over the business plan I'd made. She'd talked to the developers that morning. They were still interested in our property, especially now.

"They're sweating over the Hudson deal now that Mr. Hudson's in the hospital. Tim's heard rumors that Mrs. Hudson had never liked the idea of the golf course or the tract homes and is thinking of reneging from the contract." Karen clicked through her cell phone messages while she spoke. She knew how much this annoyed me but persisted in the habit. She made a sour face and pressed a button on her phone, then slammed the cover on. "Ned left me a message. We're in a fight. Big-time fight."

"Can Mrs. Hudson get out of the contract? Isn't it too late?"

Karen nodded. "It's too late unless she finds some technicality."

"Like water rights?"

"Maybe." Karen reached over me and grabbed a baby carrot off the plate she'd set out. She chewed while she spoke, "The developers have doubled their initial offer for our land. They've decided that if Mrs. Hudson is going to make trouble, maybe it isn't worth it. Our land is more valuable anyway since it's closer to the highway."

"We don't have water."

"There's ways around that, for them. They have money."

"I don't care how much they are offering. We're not going to sell."

"Why do you always have to be so friggin' stubborn?" Karen crunched another carrot angrily. "Second piece of business. Bill Koslovac sent me an e-mail this morning. He's moving to Arizona and wants his horses transported there by the first of August. He's going to pay us to arrange for transport."

"What?" I didn't need this, not now. "The money he's paid for boarding and training his six horses have kept us out of the red for the past year."

"I know." Karen sighed. "Now do you want me to set up a meeting with Tim and his company?"

A knock came at the door at the same time Karen's cell phone rang. She glanced at the caller ID. "Oh, it's the hubby. Mind if I call him back from the phone in the spare bedroom? The reception is awful in this kitchen and I know this conversation isn't gonna be pretty." Karen was already halfway down the hall.

"Go ahead." I opened the front door. Meg stood on the porch in flip-flops. She'd already changed out of her dusty boots and looked like she was ready to leave with her car keys in hand.

"Hi. I'm on my way out—just wanted to let you know that part of your fence is down along the summit trail."

"Of course it is." I laughed, knowing my attitude would only make Meg more wary of me. "Thanks," I offered, too dully.

"Well, that's it." She smiled, somewhat forced, and turned to leave. "Have a good night."

"Meg, do you have a minute?" I stepped out to the porch and reached for her hand. It slipped out of my grasp as she turned toward me and I felt awkward for reaching for her. Her unwavering gaze was hard to bear, full on me and waiting. I cleared my throat and tried to stall, searching for a reason to have held her here a moment longer. "I'm sorry about not returning your call . . . I've been busy."

"I know. You're a busy woman."

"I mean, its not that I've been too busy to call. It's just that—" I paused, realizing the mistake of my words as her upturned lips moved downward. "It's just that I've been too busy to think of good things."

"Good things?"

"I liked that kiss the other night." There, I'd said it. I jammed my hands in my back pockets to hide the fact that they were shaking. "I want to get to know you. You just have bad timing."

"Wow, I've heard that before," Meg grinned. "But usually only after I've actually been dating someone."

I closed my eyes. God, how badly could I mess this up? "That came out completely wrong."

Meg reached for my hand and squeezed it. "I think we're both trying too hard with this. Maybe just give me a call when things are a little less hectic. We can try being friends then."

"But I'm not that busy."

Karen called from the kitchen. "June, where'd you put the potato salad? Is it in the fridge?" Apparently the conversation with Ned had been short.

I swore under my breath and Meg smiled but her expression was more sad than happy. "Sounds like you've got dinner plans. I won't keep you." She raised her hand in a halfhearted wave and took the steps down two at a time.

"June? Where's the salad? I can't find it anywhere—your refrigerator is a disaster."

"Check the middle shelf, behind the pickles," I answered Karen, still frozen in place at the front door. I didn't want Meg to leave but couldn't think of anything else to say to keep her. She jumped in the Jeep and looked back at me. I held her gaze for a long moment. The familiar sting of loneliness hit as soon as she turned on the engine. I didn't watch her drive away.

Chris hollered, "June, what time's dinner?" She was halfway up the path from the barn and carrying a bucket of grain in each hand.

"I don't know, when are you gonna get the grill going?" I poked my head in the house to show Karen where the potato salad had been placed and then went to the patio to check on Chris. A half a dozen times I nearly decided to call Meg and invite her back for dinner but I was too scared she'd say no. Maybe she was right. Maybe it wasn't just bad timing.

As soon as Shank and Gabe smelled the steak, they both decided to stay for dinner. I was glad to have the distraction of the ranch hands. The last thing I wanted was a quiet dinner with Karen. Unfortunately, Shank and Gabe left right after they ate. Chris volunteered to stay and help clean the dishes. Karen disappeared to the spare room to call Ned again. I didn't ask her if she was calling to check up on him but I had my suspicions.

I turned on the television and tried not to think about calling Meg. Chris took a seat next to me and called out half the answers to "Wheel of Fortune" before the contestants even bought a vowel. She swore her talent at game shows was something genetic.

Her cousin had been on a kid's version of "Jeopardy." He'd won a college scholarship and became the family's one claim to fame.

Karen finished her phone call in time to watch the finale with us. Before the next show came on, she made some comment about needing to discuss business matters. Chris took the hint and made an excuse of being tired. As soon as she'd left, Karen blindsided me.

"So, I'd just like to know how you rationalize messing around with a twenty-year-old woman when you're supposed to be running this ranch? It's no wonder were losing boarders."

"What?" Of course she was talking about Chris.

"Or is she even twenty? I saw you handed her a beer tonight so I'm guessing she's drinking age but the way she acts I'd guess she's still in high school."

"I handed you a beer too. What difference does that make?" I was pissed that she'd think I was interested in Chris and upset that she'd make an issue of it. "She's twenty-three. And, no, I'm not *messing around* with her."

"Right. Why don't you just admit you're a lesbian? It's not like I'd have a problem with that. But for God's sake, June. This one's too young for you." Karen gave me that coddling look I'd grown to hate when we were growing up. Her look made it plain that she was three years older and knew all the answers. "And, quite frankly, your timing sucks. You are supposed to be focusing on making this ranch profitable, not flirting with our staff."

I stared at Karen, debating whether I wanted to scream every obscenity I knew or simply kick her out. The last thing I wanted to do was debate my sexuality with her. "Unlike you, Karen, I'd never fuck my employees. Did Ned ever hear the truth about that?"

Karen whistled air through her teeth. "You really don't know what you're starting bringing that up, June. Do you really want to talk about my marriage? Let's start with all the affairs Ned's had."

"Let's not," I said and held up my hand. I knew I'd pissed her off and now I was the one regretting it. She'd had an affair last summer with some guy she'd hired as a receptionist. Just like

114

Karen, she told me all the gory details. Ned guessed that something was going on and Karen decided to fire the guy the next week. I knew she felt terrible about it. I went to the front door and held it open. "You know, I think you should leave. I don't want to spend the rest of the night fighting."

Karen didn't move for a moment. Finally she stood up and grabbed her purse. "I don't want to fight either. Look, this property is in both of our names. If I want to sell, that means we both sell to the developers or you buy me out. I'm done with all of the hassle of the ranch and barely breaking even every month." She stepped past me and paused on the porch. "Think about it. We could sell the land, you could buy a condo in the city and have enough left over to take a month off in Hawaii. You can even bring along your little girlfriend."

"Good night, Karen." I closed the door and turned the lock. I rarely locked the door and it seemed odd to hear the metal sliding against the latch.

I poured myself a drink and started dialing Rhonda's number. I hung up the phone before the first ring when I realized the only person I wanted to talk to was Meg. I knew she'd left her number on my machine but I'd never bothered to write it down. I'd erased her message without any intention of calling her. It took me a minute to remember I'd made her sign an insurance release before riding Don Juan. I knew her number was on that. Karen insisted on the release form and personal information for all riders. I thought it was a pointless excuse for more paperwork but had decided to make Karen happy anyway.

After a half hour of sorting through my file cabinet disaster, I finally found Meg's form. I stared at her neatly printed block letters. Meg Jeffers. I hadn't even realized that I didn't know her last name. I dialed the number and tried to ignore the moisture in my eyes when her answering machine picked up the call. Maybe she was at a friend's house. Maybe she was already sleeping. I couldn't leave a message. Instead, I hung up the moment after the line clicked.

I headed for the shower, not looking forward to a night of restless sleep. I decided to call my father's estate lawyer in the morning. First step, I needed to know what my options were for keeping the ranch on my own. Karen might have a point about selling out. I could use a month in Hawaii but selling the land wasn't something I wanted to consider. And the horses? I thought again about the Hudson well as hot water pounded my scalp. My other project was to see if I could get a loan for a new well. Without water, our ranch was worthless. I'd tried to explain that point to Karen but she didn't seem to listen. The developers would just build more wells, of course. I couldn't think about what my life would be like without the ranch.

Chapter 5

Meg

Randy at dispatch called me on Thursday night just after I'd left the ranch. Two men on the overnight crew were down with the flu and they were looking for a relief paramedic. Was I interested? He admitted I was the last one on his list and if I said no, he was gonna have to take the shift himself. I told Randy I'd need an hour. I stopped at my favorite downtown deli for a sandwich and an extra large Diet Coke then jetted to the station. A cop set up a speed trap on J Street and flashed his lights as I sped past. He gave me a knowing wave as soon as we recognized each other and let me off with a warning. I wondered if that was a good omen for how the rest of my night was going to go.

Randy had paired me up with some newbie EMT named Taylor who had a reputation for vomiting every time he saw blood. As it turned out, Taylor's reputation wasn't true. We worked three car accidents that night and answered a half dozen other calls, all minor, before Taylor really had a chance to prove himself. Our last call came in at a quarter after five. The sun had yet to rise and the sky had that surreal purplish blue that I'd grown to love. Dispatch sent us to the capitol building park grounds with the following cryptic message, "White teenage male found by pedestrian, epistaxis, unknown cause."

"You ready for this, Taylor?" Epistaxis meant the guy at the park had a nosebleed. If it was bad enough to get some passerby calling, I figured the blood would make Taylor sick as well.

It didn't take us long to find the kid with the nosebleed. He was on the west facing capitol steps and a trail of blood led up to him. Taylor grabbed a pair of gloves, bright white against his dark skin, and handed me a pair as well. "Ready?" he asked, snatching up the basic kit with his right hand and popping the door open with his left.

"I thought blood made you squeamish. What's your hurry? I can take care of this kid and you can wait in the truck."

He shook his head. "Vicious rumor. I started it myself, by accident."

We both jumped out of the truck and headed up the steps. I glanced around us, making sure the pedestrian who'd made the 911 call wasn't hanging around still. I'd walked into stranger ambushes. "So, why'd you start the rumor?"

"I lost my cookies on the first MVA I saw." MVA was a car accident with multiple vehicles involved. "I told my partner it was the sight of all the blood. Really, it was because I saw a baby smashed on the asphalt. Reminded me of my own little guy at home." Taylor was already kneeling by our patient, checking his pulse. "Looks like you might have a broken nose, my friend."

I agreed with Taylor.

"Really?" He seemed proud to hear something was broken.

"You run with a gang?"

The kid, who was probably closer to twenty than ten, shook his head. "No gangs. Some guy stole my wallet."

"Mm-hmm." Taylor and I both said in unison. We gave each other a knowing nod. The kid had a blue bandana in his hand, half covered with blood. There was more to the story but it was obvious that neither Taylor nor I would ever learn it.

"What's your name?" Taylor asked, scribbling notes on a pad of paper.

"Ben."

"And you guys got into a fight over the wallet?" I pressed.

He hung his head. "No. I tried running after him and tripped on the steps." He pointed to the bottom of the stairway where a circular red patch discolored the gray concrete. "It won't stop bleeding and I blacked out when I tried to stand up. Some jogger stopped here a while ago. He said he was gonna get help."

"You ever have a bleeding problem before?" I asked.

He nodded. Blood cascaded down from his nose to his chin with each move he made. "When I get scrapes they bleed for a long time. I take meds for it."

I stuffed cotton strips up his nose but he didn't flinch. "For hemophilia? Don't talk, just nod."

Another nod.

"Well, looks like you earned yourself a trip to the hospital," Taylor said, leaning over and lifting Ben up with one arm. The sky had started to lighten now and Ben looked paler as he leaned against Taylor's blue uniform. "You get to sit in the back and hang out with my partner here."

I went to open the back of the ambulance and helped Taylor lift Ben inside. "Ever ridden in an ambulance?"

He nodded. "Once, when I bled really bad. I don't remember the ambulance ride. Just the bad hospital food."

Taylor laughed. "Yeah, I hate the food too, kid."

I heard the gunshots just as Taylor started to close the back door. I shoved my foot in the door jamb and yanked Taylor into the truck. I gave him a once over and satisfied that he wasn't hit, finally took a breath. Taylor pulled the door closed with all three of us in the back. Ben's eyes were as big as saucers.

"Did you leave the front doors unlocked?"

Taylor nodded.

"Shit." I hoped the shots were just meant to scare us. The last thing we needed was one of the gang boys getting cocky and getting the brilliant idea of carjacking the ambulance. Maybe this was just Ben's friends playing a prank. Two more shots sounded, then silence. I made my way to the front of the truck and pressed the lock button, keeping my head down and away from the windows. I couldn't see anyone nearby. Maybe the shots were farther away. I radioed dispatch to let them know we were in a holding pattern. Ann was working the phone lines and she kept her surprise in check when I told her about the gunfire. A patrol car was on the way to the scene. I slid back to my seat next to Ben. "So, what should we know about this gang your not in?"

Ben shifted the bloody wrap on his nose, not looking at me. "I'm not in a gang."

"We're not gonna tell the cops." Taylor offered. "We just want to know whether or not the guys shooting out there are aiming for you or just having a good time."

Ben wasn't going to talk. I tried to ignore the growing fear that we were sitting ducks the longer we waited. Another round of shots came at us and I gripped the side rails of the truck, trying to keep my thoughts under control. Taylor glanced at the front seat like he had an idea to go up there and try driving us out of here. I wouldn't let him. As soon as someone appeared in the driver's seat, the gunmen would have a target. "So, since when did ambulance hunting become a sport, anyway? And when exactly is the season for that?"

Taylor smiled at me. "Year-round. Hell, you don't even need a license."

"They're probably only aiming at me. I don't think they care about the ambulance."

"You wanna tell us why?" Taylor asked.

Ben shook his head. We all waited for another round of shots but nothing came. A minute later, a cop's siren sounded.

"Damn, I hate to say this but I'm really happy to hear that sound." Taylor craned his neck around the front seat and gave us a report. "No one in sight yet. Okay, here comes the black-and-white. Two cops. They look tough." He smiled back at Ben and me. "I think we can all breathe a sigh of relief and get the hell out of here."

We got Ben to the hospital as soon as our next call came in. MVA on Highway 5. Highway patrol had already closed three lanes and another ambulance was en route. Unfortunately, the team in the other ambulance were both basic EMTs and there was no available paramedic except me. I apologized to Taylor, knowing this was going to put us into overtime. I still needed to give the cops a report on what had happened back at the capitol, though neither Taylor nor I knew much. Ben wouldn't talk, much as we pressed him. We arrived at the MVA and started triage. Four cars involved. Six patients total. One woman had significant head wounds and I started on her first. Judging from her injuries and the cracked windshield, I guessed her forehead had taken the brunt of things. Her husband only had a split upper lip. He asked me if she'd be all right and I couldn't respond. Taylor had to answer for me. I kept thinking how stupid it was to end up brain damaged just because the car in front of you stopped too quickly and you were tailgating at seventy miles an hour.

We finished paperwork at eight a.m. and Taylor offered to clean the truck himself. I'd owe him later for the favor but at the time, it was all I could do to thank him and drive in a sleepy daze to the police station. The cop who took my report wasn't much interested in the story and he let me go after five minutes of questioning. I got myself home, mostly awake, picked up the mail, took a hot shower and fell into bed. Sleep came in fitful bursts. My dreams were choked with the sound of gunfire, images of irate spouses of dead patients screaming at me and cracked windshields. Seven hours later the phone rang, jostling me awake. I stared at the number and realized after a minute that it was my mother. I picked up the phone but kept my eyes closed throughout our conversation.

"John and I are planning a trip to Seattle."

John was my father. They were retired now and one or both called my house nearly every day. "Seattle?"

"Yes. You know, the rainy city?"

"Yeah, I've heard of it." I stifled a yawn. "Why?"

She paused. "John wants to see the needle. I can't remember what it's called—you know the needle I'm talking about?"

I dated a woman who lived in Seattle for a year and a half before deciding I didn't like rain and I didn't do long distance relationships. "Yeah, I know the Space Needle. That's why you guys are going all the way up there? I thought you usually stopped in Oregon." They had moved to Palm Springs five years ago and now went north every summer. May was half over and I guessed their thermometers were pushing over eighty degrees on a daily basis.

"This year it's Seattle. We thought it'd be nice to visit you on our way through Sacramento. Unless, you're busy . . . haven't heard much from you lately. John and I decided there was probably a new woman in your life again." She paused here to laugh. My parents knew me well. "You'll be home on Sunday?"

"I'll be home."

"And any girlfriend you want to introduce us to? We'll be arriving at dinnertime."

My first thought was of June. Then I thought of Deanna from the club and decided against both. "No, Mom. Not this time. It'll just be the three of us for dinner." I hung up after she made an exaggerated smooch. She finished every phone call with either a "big hugs" or "toots."

I got out of bed feeling sticky from the day's warmth and opened the blinds. The sun flew in along with a wave of heat. I cracked the window to a rush of city noise. The commuter train rattled on the tracks and a car honked angrily in the intersection below. My fan only managed to beat the warm air about without cooling anything but I turned it on anyway. It was too hot for May and the thought of driving up to Seattle and a good dose of rain had a lot of appeal. Maybe my ex would put me up if she wasn't still married to that rich guy who hated my guts. The message light was beeping on the answering machine but there was no message—just dead air followed by a click. I blamed the phone solicitors and sat down at the kitchen table with a bowl of cereal. The mail pile that I hadn't sorted in a week glared at me. I tossed the junk mail and magazines.

A hand-addressed envelope from J.E. Hudson caught my eye and I ripped it open before the others.

To Ms. Meg Jeffers,

I hope you won't mind my writing you. Rhonda Stokes, who visited me today, provided your address. It seems the two of you are friends! How connected we all are. I wanted to invite you to my home for tea on Saturday. I'd like to properly thank you for your help with my husband Al. He is still in the hospital but the doctors say his condition is improving.

With many thanks,

Jan Hudson

I called the phone number under the signature and was greeted with the familiar warm voice of the old woman I remembered meeting at the well. I accepted her offer for tea the next day and apologized for responding so late. We settled on three o'clock and I hung up, wishing I'd gotten the invitation from her neighbor at the ranch next door instead. I finished sorting through the mail and headed off to the gym. Deanna had pinned a note on my front door saying she wanted me to stop by the bar that evening. I folded the note and tucked it in my pocket, not sure if I'd go or not. I didn't have plans but a night alone didn't sound bad either.

Jan Hudson met me at the door with a hug. The smell of her house reminded me of my grandmother's cabin in Oregon. Flour dusted her blue apron and she confessed to being in the middle of making cherry pies. When I volunteered to help, she set off to find me an apron. I was placed in charge of pitting the dark red cherries she'd picked that afternoon. She had brewed some ice tea and gave me a tall glass then went back to the business of rolling out pie dough. "We're making ten pies so pick those stems off as fast as you'd like," she said very matter-of-factly. "One for the church choir, one for the nurses on Al's ward at the hospital, one for his neurologist, one for the Clarks—do you know them? And one for my grandson's family, one for dinner tonight . . ." Her list went on.

"I think that makes eleven."

"Well, we don't really need a pie after dinner tonight, I suppose. I just made some oatmeal cinnamon cookies. Would you like one?"

I popped a ripe cherry in my mouth and shook my head. The sweet taste filled my mouth and I scraped the pit clean before spitting it out.

She laughed, pointing her roller at me. "Now the more you eat, the smaller the pies will be!"

"Have you tried these yet? The cherries are delicious." I took another and closed my eyes, savoring the taste. It seemed wrong to use such perfect cherries for a pie.

"Just go on and say it's the best cherry you've ever had." She laughed again, lifting a round of pie dough off a sheet of wax paper and fitting it into a pan. Her face clouded as she pinched the dough at the edges. "The fruit trees are what I'll miss here. Not this old house . . . I've heard from the real estate agent that they'll probably pull out all of the trees in the orchard to make an access road for the golf course. Breaks my heart thinking about it. So, I try not to!" She came over to the table and took two cherries out of the bucket and popped them in her mouth. "I decided I'll just have to gather every piece of fruit this season and enjoy it as much as I can. No use in crying over wasted fruit, now is there?"

I thought of the orchard and the well where we'd found Mr. Hudson. I'd only spent a half an hour there but it was clearly a special place. Under the thick cover of spring green leaves, the moist, dark dirt where I'd sat smelled so sweet. The trees had been full of unripe fruit, just waiting for the coming summer sun to change their colors. Even the wind had felt gentle there, whispering through the trees. "I think I might cry over it too. Especially, if I'd planted the trees."

"Ten peach, ten nectarine, ten apricot, ten cherry, ten pear, ten apple—all different varieties and then a few miscellaneous ones I've added over the years. There's two pomegranate trees that I use for my secret jam. I won first place for it in the El Dorado County Fair a few years back." She sighed. "I've been thinking of a way to repay you, for your help with Al. I don't think he would have made it if you hadn't been there." She dusted off her hands and stepped out of the kitchen. She returned with an envelope and handed it to me. "After the developer buys our land they're going to build a golf course and a bunch of cookie-cutter houses here, you know. It's all Al's idea. I'd stay here forever if I could but we've already bought a place down in Arizona. *An active retirement community.*" Her face lost the smile with the final words.

"My parents retired to one of those. They're in Palm Springs."

"Do they like it?"

"Not in the summer. In the winter they think it's fine." But my parents gave up an old tract house in the valley to move to Palm Springs, not a beautiful ranch."

She sighed. "Open the envelope."

I did. There was a check inside and I had to set it down when I realized how many zeros came after the five. "I can't take this." I immediately replaced the check in the envelope and handed it back to Mrs. Hudson.

"I can't imagine how awful I'd have felt if Al had died out there alone. He spoke for the first time three days ago. Saw me there and said hello. Then he kissed me." She sighed. "Well, it's probably better that we move now. He'll need to have doctors and a hospital close by. The place in Arizona is right by a hospital. They say he'll need surgery to help open his clogged arteries. Dr. Evans kept saying Al's cholesterol was too high. Last year he said Al was at risk for a stroke if he didn't change his ways. I should have made him low fat pies and rolls without all that extra butter . . ."

"Mrs. Hudson, I can't take this check." My mind was spinning.

"We don't have any children. We bought the place in Arizona free and clear. What else are we going to do with all the money? I guess I'll have to buy pies when I move there. I figured a young person with a good heart would put the money to good use."

"I just can't take the money." I set the envelope down, not wanting to look at the amount. If thought about it too much, I might lose my conviction and take the check and cash it. "Mrs. Hudson, you have to understand, I was just doing my job."

"On your day off."

I wouldn't budge. Finally Mrs. Hudson picked up the envelope and set it on the rolltop desk in the corner of the kitchen. She smiled and told me I was being silly. I did my best not to take another look at that envelope. In the end, she promised she'd find another way to repay me that I couldn't give back. The glint in her eye made me wonder what she was scheming.

When I left Mrs. Hudson's, four pies were in the oven. My fingernails were stained red and I guessed my lips and tongue were the same color. I thought about going home but turned down the gravel road to the McCormick Ranch instead. Gabe and the other ranch hand whose name I always forgot were leaving for the evening just as I pulled in.

Gabe waved when he saw me. "June's down in the arena lunging Cassidy. I'm guessing you came to see her and not Don Juan." He winked and jumped in his truck, not leaving me any time to argue.

I changed into my boots and grabbed the carrots I'd saved for Don Juan. I headed down to the pasture, shouting a hello to Chris who was painting little horse head profiles over the barn door. I didn't stop to ask her about it. Maybe she'd decided it was time for some home decorating. Don Juan was in the middle of a crowd of mares and it took me some time to get him haltered and out of the pasture. June had finished lunging Cassidy and was hosing the horse down by the time I had Don Juan tied by the tack room.

"Hello Meg."

Her greeting was lukewarm at best. At worst, it was politely formal. "How's Cassidy?" I didn't know what else would be safe to say. I wanted to ask if she was busy that evening.

"She's coming along. There's a man who's interested in buying her. He's coming out tomorrow." She sighed then combed some conditioner through Cassidy's mane and tail before rinsing the hair again.

"I thought you didn't sell the horses you got attached to."

She looked over at me, parted her lips like she was about to say something and then paused. After a moment of staring at me, she said, "You have a good memory. But I'm not that attached to this mare."

"Wanna go on a ride with me?" I wanted to beg but I tried to keep my voice measured.

"Let me put Cassidy back in the pasture. There's another gelding that needs some exercise. I've been meaning to take him out on a ride all week." June headed toward the pasture, the young horse in tow. I started brushing Don Juan and then went into the barn to gather his tack. I hadn't planned on her saying yes and I tried not to get too excited about it. She'd only agreed to a ride. And probably was planning on going for a ride—with or without me. To her, it probably didn't mean anything.

Chris met me as I was coming out. "Howdy."

"Done with painting?"

"Hopefully for a long time." She sighed, dropping the paint bucket in the utility room and dumping the used brushes in a can of paint thinner.

I found the saddle and bridle just as Chris was climbing the stairs up to the room above the barn. She mentioned something about needing a shower and then wished me a good ride. By the time I had Don Juan's saddle in place, I noticed Chris had come out of the barn and was staring at me. "Decided against the shower?"

"Can I ask you something?"

I nodded.

"Are you interested in June?" An unmistakable challenge tinged her voice.

I tightened Don Juan's girth and then checked the stirrup lengths. They were still adjusted for me and I guessed Rhonda, with her shorter legs, hadn't ridden since I'd been out last. Chris was still watching me. Every move I made was under close scrutiny. "Are you going to tell me she's straight? Or maybe taken?"

"I'm just asking."

Her tone grated on my nerves. Last I checked, she had no claim on June. Maybe things had changed. "Chris, I don't think you need to worry about it."

"Who said I was worried?" She pointed to Don Juan's saddle. "You might want to loosen that buck strap. And those stirrups are a little long for you."

Chris and I were almost the same height. I knew the stirrups were just right for me but didn't want to fight about it. Maybe the buck strap was a little snug. I clenched my teeth and adjusted it while Chris looked over my shoulder. "I'll double-check the stirrups before I get on."

"Suit yourself." She watched me place Don Juan's bridle and added, "You're going to get your finger bit if you stick it in the horse's mouth like that. He should just open his mouth and take the bit."

"Well, he doesn't, okay?" I slipped my thumb in the corner of his mouth, as I'd been about to do and Don Juan opened his mouth to take the bit. I fumbled getting the strap over his ears and almost swore when Chris stepped over and slipped it on.

"You know," she said, "I've been riding since before I could walk, practically. My mom taught me how to ride on this pony that hated my guts. I used to have to kick like hell to get him to trot."

"I wonder why he didn't like you," I said under my breath.

Chris didn't hear me. "I had my first pair of spurs when I was five." She nodded at my boots. "You could borrow a pair from the tack room. There's an extra pair that'll fit those boots. I always recommend inexperienced riders wear spurs."

"I'll keep that in mind." I planned on avoiding spurs at all costs now. I did my best to impress the point that our conversation was over by turning away from her and tending to Don Juan. The barn door finally slammed behind her and a few minutes later I heard the sound of a shower. I breathed a sigh of relief and even Don Juan seemed to relax.

Chapter 6

June

It took me a while to catch Whiskey. He yanked two carrots out of my hand before I had him haltered. Meg already had Don Juan saddled by the time I got back to the barn. She was waiting under the shade of the mulberry tree, drawing circles in the dirt with the toe of her boot. She looked up at me and smiled. It was good to see her looking so comfortable here. Every time I looked at her, I thought of kissing her again. I knew I had some fences to mend though. I tied Whiskey up alongside Don Juan.

"He's a cute horse." Meg nodded at Whiskey. "What do you call that color—beige?"

"Buckskin. He's half mustang and half quarter horse, or so we think." I brushed Whiskey quickly and then grabbed a hoof pick.

"You don't know?"

"No, we don't. He was abandoned at our ranch as a colt."

Whiskey pinned back his ears and threatened to bite my backside when I picked up his front foot to clean the hoof. I elbowed him hard in his side and waited a moment for him to give in. Meg was looking at me closely. "Whiskey is a pain in my ass, to tell you the truth."

"Why's that?"

"We have different ideas about who's the boss." I finished cleaning the first hoof and went on to the back ones, stepping quickly to the side when Whiskey kicked out at me.

"Maybe he just doesn't like his situation here. Maybe he doesn't like—"

"Me?" I smiled, catching Meg's blush. She was already shaking her head and trying to explain what she had meant to say. "You're right in a way. He isn't happy and hasn't been for a long time. He's suffering from chronic depression."

Meg laughed. Then when she realized I was serious, her expression changed to puzzlement. "Horses get that? Do they medicate them too?"

"I don't really know. He probably could use medication but I think he's morally opposed." I smiled. Truthfully, Whiskey had been a bad problem child ever since he showed up at the ranch. "It took my dad twice as long to train this horse as any of the others we've raised. Then we sold him to our neighbors, the Clarks. But Whiskey didn't adjust well to their barn and Dad had to take him back after he had kicked his way through two stalls. Whiskey was bonded to my father more than any horse I've seen. When he passed away, Whiskey dropped off on his feed. He lost weight and his ribs started to show." I pointed out the lines of his ribs that had started to fill in with muscle and fat, years later. "It got so bad you could make out his spine and the hip bones jutted out where his butt had once been round." Watching Whiskey waste away had been almost as painful as saying good-bye to my dad. I set a saddle pad on Whiskey and he shivered. I gingerly placed the saddle on his back and secured the girth.

"He seems to be in pretty good shape now."

I nodded. "It took several months of hand feeding to get him eating a full ration again and he'd almost regained all of the lost weight. He still misses my dad though."

"You'd think that a horse would eventually forget."

"Not Whiskey." I tried placing the bridle on Whiskey and as soon as he saw the bit, he opened his mouth and went for my hand. I yanked my fingers back, inches from his teeth and cussed softly. I couldn't yell at him. Our rapport was already stretched thin.

"Maybe he doesn't want to be ridden today. You could take a different horse out on the trail."

"Whiskey and I don't get along but he still needs exercise." I tried again and Whiskey bared his teeth. He tossed his head on my third attempt and came close to smashing my hand into the tie post. I tried not to let my anger show. It would only make Whiskey more nervous.

Meg shied back as Whiskey tossed his head again. I saw her cringe and wanted to apologize. "Careful June," she said quietly.

"I always am." I swore at Whiskey and tried again with the bridle.

Meg sighed. I didn't know what I'd said wrong but she'd turned away from me and went over to Don Juan. The gelding lowered his muzzle to sniff her open palm. She rubbed his head and kept her gaze on the far pasture, avoiding me.

I stepped back from Whiskey and tried to relax. I didn't want to fight with him in front of Meg. "I should apologize for what happened last time you were here."

"Don't worry about it." She rubbed Don Juan's head, not looking my way.

"I am sorry, just so you know."

"You don't need to be. I'm not upset anymore."

"Sure. I can tell." Just then Whiskey lowered his head. I slipped the bit in Whiskey's mouth as the noise of a slamming door distracted him. Chris came out of the barn and nodded at us. Her hair was wet and she'd changed out of the painting clothes into a pair of cutoffs and a T-shirt that looked vaguely familiar. It took me a while before I placed it as one of Greg's old shirts. A few of his things were still kicking around and I remembered tossing the clothes I'd found in the give-away box in the barn. It was strange to see Chris wearing it now. She headed up to the house and I guessed she was planning on sacking out on my sofa and spending the evening watching TV. She'd spent every night in my living room for the past few days. I didn't discourage it. Chris was good company. I fastened Whiskey's bridle neck strap and then glanced over at Meg. How did everything get so complicated? "All set."

She didn't move to get on Don Juan. Instead, she watched Chris make her way up the path. Chris passed beyond the hen-house before Meg looked over at me.

"You wanna ride off into the sunset with me or not?" I smiled, hoping a joke would break the strangeness that had settled between us. Whiskey was stomping his feet and unhappily grinding his teeth on the bit. Meg watched him for a moment and then came over and held out a baby carrot. She rubbed his head as he chomped on the carrot and just like Don Juan, Whiskey eased with her. Of course he likes her, I thought. "He hates everyone. Shank and Gabe can't even touch him. He chased Chris out of the pasture yesterday." I laughed, recalling the scene of Chris leaping over the pasture fence as Whiskey came at her with his teeth bared. Whiskey sniffed Meg's shirt and then her pocket. She fished out another baby carrot and he chomped on it immediately. "I'm not surprised that he likes you, though."

"Why's that?"

"You're easy to like." I could feel my cheeks blush and glanced away from Meg. I went over to check Whiskey's girth, avoiding Meg's eyes. "Ready?"

"Not quite. I think we should get something settled."

My grip on Whiskey's girth tightened. "What?"

"I don't really want to make a fool of myself." She paused a moment and looked over at me. "Are you interested in women or not?"

I nodded, not trusting myself to speak.

133

"And what about Chris? Is something going on between you guys?"

"She's got a crush on me." I felt my control wavering. I wasn't used to having someone grill me so closely, especially with all of my emotions caught up in my throat. "But it's all one-sided."

"What about you and me?"

"What about us?" I knew exactly what she meant. A half dozen things came to mind that I should have said to explain myself but nothing sounded right. "Well, I hope we're friends. Or getting to be. I know I screwed up before, but it looks like you might have forgiven me." Meg didn't say anything for a while. She stared at me long enough to make me almost certain I wasn't being honest with her.

"Friends. Okay."

I unclipped Whiskey's line, trying not to think about all the other things that I suddenly wanted to tell Meg. "Let's take the oak ravine trail. It's a hard climb and I think it'll tire Whiskey out before he tries to give me any trouble."

Meg mounted Don Juan easily, having gotten the knack of it now, and waited as I got on Whiskey. Don Juan followed Whiskey out the ranch boundary gate and I tried to focus on the trail, ignoring the impulse to look over my shoulder at Meg every few steps. I wanted to tell her that I thought I might be interested in being more than friends. It was hard to explain and too late now anyway.

We'd rode for a half hour or so before I finally let myself steal a glance back at her. "You doing okay?"

She nodded. Don Juan was reaching for grass along the edges of the trail and she did little to correct him. I couldn't help but smile.

A few minutes later, the path steepened. Don Juan pushed a little on Whiskey's butt and the buckskin's ears flattened back. He swished his tail and I warned Meg he might kick if Don Juan nudged his ass again. She promised to hold him back but he'd found a sudden boost of energy and kept pressing forward. Finally Whiskey had enough of it. He pinned his ears back and threatened a kick. At the same moment, a pheasant lurched out of the brush on the side of the path. Don Juan reared up and started at a gallop. I had Whiskey's reins pulled tight and got him under control quickly, but not before noticing Don Juan flying past us with Meg. Her reins were flapping loose and she didn't seem to hear me as I hollered for her to pull back. I felt sick thinking of how I'd promised to give her a lesson to prevent this very thing.

The path narrowed to edge up the ravine between the hillsides and the going was tight. The last thing I wanted was for Don Juan to slip. I had to get Whiskey into a fast lope just to keep sight of them. Finally Don Juan slowed down to a jog, and Meg soon managed to pull him to a stop. "You okay up there?" I slowed Whiskey to a jog as we caught up.

Meg looked pale and her hands were tightly clutching Don Juan's mane. "Damn pheasants. And Whiskey trying to kick didn't help." Meg didn't say anything. She looked about ready to jump off and walk. The oaks were thick on both sides of the path and the going was rocky. "Can you keep going? It's not much farther now."

"My fingers feel like popsicle sticks and my feet won't stop shaking but I'm still on the horse."

"Nice riding."

"Didn't you say you'd send a baby out on Don Juan?"

"Well, I'd expect the baby to hold onto his reins."

Meg glanced up the hillside and then eyed the portion we'd already climbed. "Would you think I was a chicken if I got off and walked?"

"Yeah, but I wouldn't hold it against you forever." I smiled. "Just keep a better hold on the reins and don't let Don Juan crowd Whiskey. Whiskey's got more attitude than my horse Tanner."

She stayed in the saddle and I promised to keep us at a slow pace for the rest of the climb. After a while the horses calmed down and the path leveled. I glanced over my shoulder at Meg and she pointed out a hawk that was circling us. "We have a lot of those up here. Don't worry, it's not a bad omen when they circle you." I paused, thinking of my mom who used to point out every bird we passed on a ride. "I ever tell you about my mother?" I knew full well I hadn't. I wiped my forehead with the back of my hand and dried the sweat on my jeans.

"No. I kind of gathered that she had passed away."

Even with my back to Meg, I could feel her gaze was on me now. I glanced over my shoulder just to see. Meg had a way of focusing on me that rattled me still. When she looked right at me I had the feeling I was between a pair of crosshairs rather than just being listened too. I cleared my throat and started again. "She did. Not long after Whiskey here was abandoned at our front door." I rubbed Whiskey's neck and he chewed on his bit. "She had cancer. Everything happened real quick. They diagnosed it late because she just kept thinking she had the flu . . . anyway, this was one of her favorite trails." I was usually careful to keep details of the past in the past but riding with Meg made me want to tell stories. She listened so damn well it just made me want to say something.

"My mom loved riding. She met my dad at a rodeo but always said she hated rodeo boys. She called them 'the bull riding idiots.' My dad had a few of his rodeo friends out one time and he was trying to train this young colt, Whiskey. Dad had gotten bucked off more times than his skinny ass wanted and one of his friends had this harebrained plan to get the colt drunk on skunk liquor and then ride him. Whiskey was whupped from all the bucking and he took the skunk lic without any complaints."

I leaned back and caught Meg's smile. "What happened then?"

"Well, my mom found out and she was pissed. She kept screaming about how the horse was gonna fall and break a leg. Or break my dad in the process. My dad jumped on Whiskey anyway. The colt stumbled around in a circle for a little bit. Not enough action for my dad's friend. He was nicknamed Billy the Kid for good reason. So, the friend decides to start hollering like they do to get the bulls excited, you know. Whiskey, poor son of a bitch, couldn't see straight and ran himself right through the old fence, right past my mom who was screaming bloody murder to get Billy the Kid to shut up and then directly into the damn henhouse. You never heard such a racket as a rooster makes when a horse tramples his hens. Mom threatened to shoot Billy the Kid then and there. She was so damn pissed."

"Was she worried more about your dad or about Whiskey?"

"Neither. She had a soft spot for the hens."

Meg laughed and I couldn't help but laugh too, remembering the scene. We reached the top of the east-facing slope and I pulled Whiskey to a halt and slipped one leg off the saddle. "We'll stop here for a minute to let the horses catch their breath." I loosened Whiskey's girth and leaned against him, watching Meg. My insides seemed to be all caught up in a slipknot, tightening the longer I spent wondering what I wanted to say to Meg.

Meg was still astride Don Juan, waiting at the crest of the hill and staring toward the west where the sun was working its way toward the far blue mountain range. An orange glow spread over her face. I turned away then and led Whiskey toward the two married oaks. The trees were joined at the hip and I'd always wondered if it was one tree that split or two that joined. The branches provided a semicircle of shade and the gold-colored grass underneath was pressed down in an oval the size of a fat cow's belly. Cattle and deer often bedded here for the night. They liked the cover of the trees. I slipped off Whiskey's bridle and tied his lead to the solitary fence post. The post remained here for travelers to tie up and camp, though no one knew anymore who had set the fence or who had ripped it out. Meg had jumped off Don Juan but hadn't moved far. She pointed toward the mountains and the setting sun and smiled, not saying how beautiful they were or anything. Just smiling.

I knew this place by what my mom called it. Pioneer's Prayer. I never asked why, never had a good idea until now. I wanted to tell Meg about this place, wanted to explain how I'd come here as a kid to whittle on a bit of wood while the horses grazed and dream about my tomorrows. I was staring at Meg, openly now, and when

Meg seemed to feel my gaze, she shifted and came toward the trees slowly, like you move when you know the trail but don't want to scare a doe that's watching you.

Meg tied Don Juan to the same post as Whiskey. The horses didn't bother each other now, dripping with the sweat of the climb and hanging their heads low as they sniffed at the dry oat weeds. I met Meg's gaze and felt her waiting. She took a step closer to me and I dropped my eyes. Our boots were only inches apart. We hadn't stood this close, not without a horse or a fence between us, since the night we kissed. I opened my mouth to speak but nothing came out. Meg pressed one finger to my lips then let it fall slow as honey, down my chin and throat. She paused just at the spot where my collarbones left a space, where they didn't quite meet.

My breath came quick and hungry. I stepped back and Meg's finger slipped off me. She closed her eyes and turned away from me. I felt as if I'd slapped her and wanted to apologize but didn't say anything. Meg went over to the married oaks then, her hand tracing the splitting trunk, her thoughts closed to me.

We finished our ride just after dusk and had to brush the horses down in near darkness. The light by the tie post had burned out and I added that to the list of things to pick up on the next trip into town. I found a note from Chris on the tack room door. She'd already done the evening feeding and was going to bed early. A light shined from the top barn window so I knew she was still awake, probably waiting for us to get in. After we put Don Juan and Whiskey back in the pasture I asked Meg to come up to the house. It was the first time either of us had spoken since our stop at Pioneer's Prayer. We'd watched the sun set there, the sky quietly changing from pale blue to orange and then to every shade of pink before we headed home.

We reached the front porch and I started wondering what I should offer for dinner. I had planned on eating leftovers but guessed Chris had eaten whatever was left in the fridge. "I'm running short on groceries. I do have a jar of spaghetti sauce and some pasta, if you're interested." My stomach was growling but I felt too uneasy to eat.

"How about cherry pie instead?"

"For dinner?" Pie was at the top of my dessert list but it didn't seem right eating it instead of dinner.

"It's okay to challenge social norms every once in a while. Besides, Mrs. Hudson made it for you with her fresh cherries. And fresh fruit is healthy."

"And so you're telling me that makes pie healthy? Right. And ketchup is a vegetable." I laughed when Meg nodded. I had to admit cherry pie did sound good. "How'd you get a pie from Mrs. Hudson?"

Meg arched her eyebrows. "I've got connections. I'll be right back." She jogged over to her Jeep and reappeared a minute later with a pie in hand. I got two forks and we sat down on the porch with the pie between us.

The night had finally cooled off and the breeze cut through my shirt. I glanced down at the fabric and realized how filthy the day's work had made me. Ordinarily, I never noticed but being with Meg made me look at myself differently. I tried not to stare at the smudges of dirt or think of how I must smell. "So, you're not going to tell me how you got this pie from Mrs. Hudson?"

"She gave it to me, in exchange for pitting cherries." Meg winked. "And on account of your helping her this past week. She wanted to say thank you."

"So, when did you become friends with Mrs. Hudson?"

"This afternoon."

I had a feeling that the more I pressed for answers, the less information I'd get out of Meg. I took a bite of the pie and murmured approval. "Amazing, as always."

"She says the secret is good fruit."

"Mm-hmm. You know her secrets too, huh?"

Meg grinned. "I know a lot of secrets."

"Try me."

"Rhonda slept with your sister, Karen. She's had a crush on her since you guys were kids. Chris wants to sleep with you. She won't get to though because you want to sleep with me. Whiskey likes me and I think the next time I come out you should let me try to ride him."

I'm sure my mouth dropped open and stayed open the entire time she spoke. "Karen and Rhonda? When? How'd you find that out?"

"Through a bartender I know. Rhonda spilled her guts to her after a few drinks. The bartender told me the story because she was worried about her and knew I was her friend. I don't know when it happened exactly." She paused. "You're not going to argue about the other things I said?"

"I've made it clear that I'm not interested in Chris. I also know that I didn't tell you I was interested in sleeping with you."

"You didn't have to." She grinned sheepishly.

How could Karen and Rhonda have hooked up without my knowing it. It must have happened the night they both spent at the ranch. But why hadn't my sister mentioned anything? I wasn't ready to analyze it too closely. "How do you know Whiskey will take to you? He doesn't like anybody. You gonna win him over with carrots?"

"A whole lot of carrots." She smiled. "And I have a few other tricks to get someone to like me."

I didn't miss her innuendo but said nothing. She might be right about Whiskey. He'd even come up to the gate after we'd let the horses out to the pasture just to sniff her outstretched hand. He'd never done that with me, regardless of carrots. "Next time, you can ride him as long as you promise never to drop the reins again. You scared the hell out of me."

She nodded. After a moment, she leaned over the pie to kiss me. Her lips roused my own and I wasn't ready for her to pull back when she did. "Will you send me home tonight if I kiss you again?"

"No." I couldn't remember how long it'd been since I'd asked someone to spend the night. "I'd like you to stay."

We showered, separately, to Meg's obvious disappointment. I sent her to the guest bathroom and then went to my own bathroom and undressed. The water refreshed me and the moment alone also left me feeling more nervous than I had with Meg at my side. I pulled a comb through my hair and avoided looking at the mirror. I dressed in a clean tank top and loose cotton pants before heading out to the family room where I knew she'd be waiting.

Meg was sitting cross-legged on the sofa. She had a green towel wrapped around her waist and wore nothing else. I stared at her, feeling suddenly awkward and unsure of myself. She waited, almost a full minute, before she stood up and came over to me. Her short dark hair was combed smoothly back behind her ears and she smelled like the lavender soap I bought for guests. I glanced down at her breasts and felt suddenly uncomfortable for doing so. She clasped my hand and then pressed it against her chest lightly. Her nipples were dark and her full breasts seemed to beg to be caressed. I'd never touched another woman's breasts and the sensation was strange. She moaned softly as my hands moved on her. She leaned forward to kiss me and I felt my muscles tighten and a warm wetness between my legs.

Meg's hands slipped under my tank top and rubbed my back. A moment later, she was helping me out of the top. She gazed at me, the only light in the room coming from the pale moonlight that slipped in through the open windows, then closed the distance between us, kissing me again. Our nipples brushed lightly against each other. I liked the sensation of it, strangely enticing and yet barely perceptible. She pulled me toward the couch. I hesitated for a moment, bringing a question to her lips. "You're beautiful," I whispered. I wasn't sure I wanted anything more—having her nearly naked, in my family room, the moonlight playing shadows on her taut muscles and desire in her eyes.

When she took another step toward the couch I followed her. She slipped off the green towel and covered the cushions, then sat down waiting for me. I sat down near her, our bodies barely touching, my hand in hers. I felt frozen in place, wished I could move toward her or that she might kiss me to break the tension. Her tan legs were stretched out and my eyes traced them up her thighs. "I feel as nervous as I did the first time I had sex." I'm sure I blushed. It had been a long time since I'd gone to bed with someone. I'd felt in control of the situation when I was with men but I felt completely at a loss with Meg.

"Nervous of me?" She grinned. "Relax, I'm just some girl who's madly attracted to you."

"I don't know why."

"I'll tell you all the reasons sometime." The back of her hand brushed against my cheek and she turned my head toward her, kissing me again. I let her push me back against the cushions, feeling the softness of her naked skin as she moved on top of me. She pulled my pants off slowly, inching them off my hips as she kissed my belly and then lower when she kissed where the hair began. I started to get nervous again and she came up to kiss my lips. Her hands moved over my body, exploring every curve. I stiffened when her hand slipped between my legs, unsure of what she'd do next. "I'm sorry."

"You want me to stop?"

I shook my head, wishing I could will away the nervousness. I wanted her to keep touching me but I didn't trust my voice to tell her as much. I reached for her shoulders and brought her close to me, feeling her breasts brush against mine. She kissed me again, murmuring for me to relax, and then rubbed her hands over my thighs.

I felt her lips brush down my neck and chest. She avoided the places where I tensed at her touch and shifted her body so her pelvis moved slowly between my spread legs. I closed my eyes and let my body move with hers. She rocked her hips into me and the rhythmic press awakened nerves I'd long forgotten I had. The sensation of her hair and her wetness rubbing against my center pushed me to the edge. I desperately wanted her to touch my clit but couldn't ask. I found her hand and slipped it between my legs. My voice wasn't my own when I called out to her. I saw her lips move upward with a smile. Her fingers traced around my folds, flicking my clit and then her head dropped and I felt the wetness of her tongue on me. Instead of pulling back, I pushed into her touch, crying out again as the orgasm raced through me.

Meg held me tight against her, letting my body tremble then slowly relax without a word. Her leg was pressed between mine and the weight of her body seemed to anchor us both. After a while, she pulled the afghan over us. I fell asleep with her on top of me. I woke only once, in the darkest hour. Meg slept soundly, her breath coming in even sighs. I tried to recall every place Meg had touched, tried to remember the way she'd teased my body and then gave in to pleasuring me. It was obvious she knew what she was doing. I was certain she'd had more experience than I wanted to know about. I wondered how I'd face the morning without blushing at the sound of my own voice, remembering how I'd called out to her.

Chapter 7

Meg

June didn't have much to say the next morning. She got up sometime around dawn and mentioned that Chris would be up soon for breakfast. I took the hint that I wasn't invited to sleep in. Without asking if I wanted it, she set out a clean shirt for me and left me to change. My dirty jeans would do without underwear—yesterday's were tucked in my back pocket. I wasn't ready to leave but I knew June wanted me out. She made me a piece of toast and offered a glass of orange juice for the drive home. I nodded, adding that I really did need to get on the road because my houseplants would be clamoring for our morning walk. I got a smile from her but nothing else. "What's wrong?"

"Nothing. I'm preoccupied I guess. An engineer is coming today to discuss sites for a well. I haven't figured out yet how I'm going to be able to afford it."

"So you're okay about what happened last night?"

She nodded. I had to guard myself from any hurt feelings. I should have known I couldn't expect much more from June. We said good-bye without a kiss and she waited at the front door while I put on my shoes. I took my time. "Can we talk later?"

"Sure. I'll call you."

She seemed to be saying the words only to be nice. I faked a smile and hoped I came off unfazed. "Okay. See ya." I headed for the Jeep and spotted Chris just coming up from the barn. I waved to her and she gave me a once-over that was clearly not congenial.

"How was your ride Meg?"

"Don Juan is a great horse. And the oak ravine trail is beautiful." I knew she wasn't interested in the trail but I wasn't about to discuss anything else with her. "You should take that ride sometime. Take a girl up there and watch the sunset. Perfect date spot." I was pushing her buttons and wondered why I wanted to make the situation worse. Her resentment toward me was painfully clear.

"Thanks, but I really don't need dating advice." Chris turned away before I caught her expression. She headed up the porch steps to the house.

"Just a suggestion." I watched her open the front door without knocking and tried to ignore the pang of jealousy. Chris was the one spending the day with June while I was being sent home. I half wondered if June was interested in Chris after all. Chris had a bravado and tomboyish look that I knew a lot of women liked. And June wasn't exactly stomping out the girl's crush.

Sunday afternoon passed without a word from June. I decided to head over to Joe's house before my parents came for dinner. It'd been a few weeks since I'd talked to him and I had a present for Sammy. Joe's wife was out grocery shopping and Sam and Joe greeted me at the door. Sam gave me a toothy smile and latched his small hand in mine.

Joe smiled as Sammy started tugging me inside. "He wants to show you the decorations."

"I'm four now." Sammy announced as soon as we reached the kitchen. Yellow streamers still hung from the window sills along with a red crepe paper number four taped to the fridge.

"Really?"

He nodded and held up three fingers. Joe reached over and plucked up Sammy's pinky. "Use all four fingers."

Sammy nodded. Clearly, they had gone through this before. I handed him the present. "Happy Birthday. Sorry I'm a few days late."

He glanced over at Joe, silently asking if it was okay to tear open the blue-and-yellow striped wrapping paper. Joe gave him a nod and the paper was soon flying off the box.

"Mini Spiderman!"

I nodded and helped him pry out the action figure from the plastic wrap. Within a few minutes, Sam had convinced us to go out to the patio and watch a cosmic battle of good and evil with Spiderman battling a snail. Fortunately, he lost interest in entertaining the adults and was soon playing by himself.

"You've been making yourself scarce lately." Joe began. "Cowgirl got her rope on you?"

"Something like that." I felt a swell of guilt not wanting to share my thoughts about June with him now. "The sunflowers are twice as high as I remember them."

"And I think you planted more this season than last. I was thinking of spraying weed killer on the whole yard but Toni would kill me. She goes on these rants about how I'm poisoning the family when I try to buy non-organic lettuce."

"She's a smart woman. I was hoping Toni would be here today. Haven't seen her in a while."

"She keeps herself busy working. Today she's running errands." Joe sighed. "I've finally decided to go back to work myself."

"Really?"

"What would you say if I was applying for the emergency dispatch position?"

I imagined Joe sitting in his wheelchair at the dispatch office, calming the frantic callers and sending ambulance crews out on wild goose chases just for fun on the slow nights. "I think you'd be good at it."

He looked over at Sam, keeping an eye on how far the boy wandered amongst the sunflowers. "I'll wait until Sam starts school in August. I've already talked to Randy about the position. He thinks I could handle it too. Randy mentioned you've had a few rough calls lately. He told me about the shooting at the capitol."

"News travels like wildfire at the station."

"I heard you were as cool as a cucumber. Apparently the EMT you were with told a bunch of guys how you saved his ass, pulling him into the truck as soon as the shooting started."

"Yeah, I pulled him into the truck all right." I stopped there, not wanting to remember all of the details. "I completely freaked out."

He shrugged. "That's not how the story on the grapevine goes. I heard that you were the one to hold everything together. You saved Taylor's ass and the patient you were transporting. You earned yourself another Cub Scout bravery patch, no doubt about it. Hell, maybe you'll beat out Jackson and get one every year in a row until they take away the honor."

I laughed. Joe loved to joke about the EMT achievement patches that the chief gave at the end of the year. The patches were designed to recognize EMTs who had gone above the call of duty to save a patient or help their partner. Jackson, one of our old EMT friends had gotten three patches—all due to saving people from burning vehicles three years in a row. I'd received my first patch for saving a toddler from his manic mother who had threatened to toss the child out the open window of her fourth-story apartment. The second patch I got was because of Joe's accident.

Unfortunately whoever designed the patches had picked a cute bear mascot and it was hard to take yourself seriously with a fuzzy orange bear sewn on the shoulders of your uniform. I didn't want another bear patch when I hadn't done anything brave. But there was more to it than that. "Joe, I don't want any more patches."

"But the bears are cute, don't you think?" Joe smiled but didn't look at me. His smile faded. He was watching Sam. Spiderman was inching his way up the length of a sunflower stalk while the enemy snail lurked in the petunias below. "You want to tell me you're ready to quit. We've been through this before."

"Randy's been talking to me about the teaching job again. You know, I'm not even really quitting EMS. I'll be taking shifts as they come up and going out with other paramedics for their training . . ." Joe clearly wasn't listening. He was tapping his hand on the wheelchair's armrest and humming a song. "I'm thinking about moving out of the city." For the first time in my life there was something I wanted to do more than ride in an ambulance and save lives. I wanted to live my own. But I couldn't tell Joe that. He'd give anything to be in the ambulance again. "I want to have more time to do things. And I'm getting too old for dodging bullets in gang fights."

"Too old? At thirty-four?" He chuckled. "Give me another line. You know, we used to say that teaching was the cop-out job."

"That's what you used to say." I didn't want to argue. "Remember the ranch I was telling you about?"

"Sure. The cowgirl's place. There's always a woman involved in your plans, Meg." Joe paused. "But with you the women come and go. You're gonna tell me you want to quit just to have a little more free time? Take some time off. You're too young to be done with the blues."

The EMT uniform blues. I gave Joe a look that told him to drop the subject. We chitchatted about Sammy and rising property values. Joe caught on that I was distracted and gave up on our conversation. We watched Sam silently. I remembered my parents' visit and gave this as the excuse for leaving early. Sam made me promise to visit again as soon as I could.

When I rose to leave, Joe followed me to the front door. He

caught my hand and gave it a firm squeeze, strong as ever. "I don't want to push you one way or the other. I know it's your decision to make. You'd make a great teacher."

"I think you're just saying that."

He nodded. "I am. And Meg, you look good in a uniform. How the heck do you think you're gonna catch all the girls without it?"

"I've got my ways." I smiled at him as he closed the door.

My parents only had time for a quick dinner. They were both looking forward to Seattle and I didn't have any big news I was ready to tell them. I'd been distracted all through dinner with thoughts of quitting my job and couldn't get Joe's look of disapproval out of my mind. I got home earlier than I'd planned on and was disappointed to find the place empty. Clyde was spending the night at his girlfriend's, Deanna wasn't working at the bar that night and I had no idea that if I did risk a phone call June would want to talk to me. I didn't fall asleep until well after midnight and woke up Monday feeling like I was coming down with a cold. I called Charley to ask if there was anyone scheduled for relief who would be willing to take my shift. Truth was, I just didn't want to go to work. I knew I wasn't that sick. Fortunately Charley owed me. I'd helped him out of more than a few jams. He was the one who had recommended me to Randy for the teaching job at the EMT training center in town.

Charley wanted to know if I'd given Randy my final answer on the teaching job. The hours would be better, as would the pay, but I knew I'd miss interacting with patients and the challenging cases—in short, everything that I liked about being a paramedic. I thought of Joe's disappointment. Charley promised he'd find someone to cover the shift. He mentioned that I needed to make up my mind on the teaching job soon. They needed to hire someone by next month and I was at the top of the list. I agreed to call Randy later that week with my decision.

I spent the morning running errands and when I got home

found a message from June. It lasted all of ten seconds. What I could understand was this: "I'm not sure what happened last night. Maybe it shouldn't have happened. I don't know. Call me when you get a chance." I tried calling her back but didn't leave a message. Frustrated, I started vacuuming and gave my house a much needed dusting. The phone rang just before five. It wasn't June calling to say she'd thought things over, changed her mind and was madly in love with me. In fact I didn't recognize the man's voice on the line and it took me a full minute to understand that I was speaking with Mrs. Hudson's lawyer.

"I pulled a few strings and twisted a few arms in order to get this worked out but the lawyers on their side just informed me they've accepted the newest addendum."

"Addendum? I don't know what you're talking about." I wondered if I was being sued and quickly sat down, trying to prepare myself for the worst. Maybe Mr. Hudson had died and I was somehow being implicated. I struggled to swallow. "Wait, whose lawyer are you?"

"My clients are Mr. and Mrs. Hudson. I'll need you to come down to my office some time this week so I can explain a few things. I'm afraid they're not making this an easy transaction." He paused. "Anyway, I'm calling to get your information—full name, social security number, birth date, that sort of thing."

"Am I being sued?"

He laughed. "No, no. It's good news. Mrs. Hudson wanted me to go through her letter with you in person though. She had some fears that you might not agree to her wishes unless I coerced you." He chuckled again.

"What exactly is this about?"

He sighed. "Fine, I'll tell you this much. Mrs. Hudson has arranged to transfer some of her land into your name. You're now the owner of five acres containing an orchard and a well."

"What?"

The lawyer continued as if he hadn't heard me. "The land borders another parcel and there is no developed road so you'll have to figure out some way of passing through the neighbor's parcel. Mrs. Hudson mentioned that you had some connections with the neighbors, the McCormick family. Is that right?"

"Mm-hmm."

"Good. Then you'll work something out with them, I'm sure."

I numbly agreed to meet with the lawyer the following day to discuss the details. I rattled off my personal information and hung up the phone still unsure of everything he'd told me. Five minutes later I called him back to make sure I'd understood him correctly. Yes, indeed, I now owned an orchard and a well. I needed to see the papers before I really believed it but the lawyer assured me I now owned a five-acre parcel in the middle of nowhere. No access roads. No structures on the land, excepting the water tower by the well and I'd have to sign some agreement to leave the trees in place. But the land wasn't in the middle of nowhere and that was just the point. Apparently, I'd traded the promise of fifty thousand dollars for sixty fruit trees and June's well.

I decided to call Mrs. Hudson then to thank her. She promptly insisted that it was nothing at all. "I admit, I think myself quite clever for this deal. The developers with their noisy golf carts are so angry with me." She laughed.

I promised to take care of the trees and send the fruit to Arizona next year. She happily accepted this plan and then started in on the details of the success of her cherry pies. "Everyone agreed they were the sweetest cherries. It was a hit at dinner last night. And Mr. Hudson is home from the hospital and recovering slowly." She'd decided that he was too crotchety to die from a little stroke. "He's planning on being a pest for at least the rest of my days here. And with my luck, he'll go on bugging me when we're buried too." She laughed again, her warm, infectious laughter that I didn't resist joining. I thought of Mrs. Hudson's trees and her cherries that had darkened my fingernails for days after our afternoon together. We hung up sounding more like giggling schoolgirls than two adults who had just completed a property transaction.

Clyde came home with his girlfriend as soon as I'd finished talking with Mrs. Hudson. He'd ordered a pizza and tried to get me to join in their evening plans of dinner and a movie. They'd rented some black-and-white romance from the Forties. Ordinarily I didn't mind hanging out with Clyde but his girlfriend got on my nerves with her nauseatingly sweet baby voice. Watching their date movie while they cuddled on our sofa was close to a night in purgatory. I didn't want them to ruin my good mood and badly wanted to tell June about the well. I knew I probably should wait for her to call but I was impatient and decided to drive out to the ranch. It was after dusk by the time I crossed the county line, catching commuter traffic on my way out of the city, and both Gabe's and Shank's trucks were already gone when I pulled up. I knocked on June's front door but she didn't answer. I sat down on the porch, intending to wait for her there but the porch light attracted every mosquito in the area and I got fed up beating off the bugs. I started down the path to the arena and heard June's voice just as I neared the barn. I paused to listen, knowing I should announce myself but not wanting to.

"I'm not gonna have this conversation with you," I heard June say.

"Just tell me, yes or no." Chris's voice was high. I thought she might have been crying. "If Meg wasn't in the picture, what then?"

"Meg has nothing to do with this." June didn't speak for a moment or if she did her voice was too quiet to carry. She continued, "I think you should make up your mind if you want to work for me or not."

Chris didn't answer. The barn door swung open and I made a quick move up the path toward the house, keeping to the shadowed edge. June came out, obviously upset. Chris followed her, grabbing her hand before she'd gotten far. June turned toward her and a sinking feeling in my stomach told me what would happen next. Their lips met. I closed my eyes, not wanting to watch.

I turned back in time to see June pull away from Chris, shaking her head. "Don't come up to the house tonight." Her voice was shaky. "If you show up for the morning meeting, I'll know you want to keep working here. Otherwise, you need to be gone by daybreak." Of all the strange things that had come to pass in the last week, this topped it all.

I jogged the remaining hundred yards toward the house, keeping to the soft grass so they wouldn't hear the gravel crunch under my shoes. June was only thirty yards or so behind me. There was no way to leave without her seeing me. She reached the top of the path just as I sat down on the porch steps. I watched her approach, knowing she wouldn't be able to see me until she'd turned past the bend in the driveway. I had a knack for bad timing and there was nothing to do now but wait for her to find me there. She crossed the upper lawn and paused, staring at my Jeep parked in the driveway. Her gaze moved to the house.

"Meg?"

"Over here." I stood up and moved out of the shadows.

She came toward me. "How long have you been here? You haven't been waiting long, have you?" Her eyes were red but her voice seemed as strong as ever. She'd recovered quickly.

"Not long."

"I'm glad to see you."

Her face was so sincere that I couldn't doubt her but the image of Chris kissing her wouldn't leave my mind. "Bad day?"

"Unbelievable." She clasped my hand momentarily then opened the front door. I followed her inside without being asked. "Karen called this morning. She's filing for a divorce from her husband and because of that, she's decided I need to buy her portion of the ranch. She needs the money. And she won't admit to sleeping with Rhonda but now I'm sure you were right." She paused. "Do you want to hear the rest? The day only got worse from there. The guy who was interested in buying Cassidy backed out of the deal. One of my best boarders confirmed with me that he's pulling out his horses a month early. The engineer gave me a quote that completely ruled out our building a well this year. I'll have to save for a full year and still take a second mortgage . . . so, I talked with

153

a lawyer at the county office hoping there was some loophole I hadn't found with the Hudson well. Found out there's no way in hell I'm getting water rights off their well unless I sue and then it'll be months and there's no guarantee. And"—I suppressed the urge to embrace her before she continued—"Chris is driving me up a wall. She won't work, claiming she can't think about anything else when she sees me and she's sick with jealousy over you. Rhonda warned me about lesbian melodrama but I thought it was just her." June pressed her hand against her head and laughed darkly. "Do you want to hear the last part? That involves you."

I nodded, swallowing hard.

"I didn't get any sleep last night. My mind was racing, thinking of everything I wanted to tell you . . . and I kept trying to decide if I'd gone completely crazy or if I was, in fact, a lesbian all along. I can't help but think that this explains a lot of things. And you've got me thinking all of these dirty thoughts." She smiled, not blushing.

"I guess I should say I'm sorry for keeping you up all night."

"But you're not."

I wasn't sorry that she was thinking of me all night, no. I didn't answer her directly. "So what did you decide? Have you gone completely crazy?"

She stared at me for a brief moment and then stood up and went to the kitchen. She opened the pantry door, closed it, then opened it again and grabbed a bottle of whiskey. "I didn't decide anything. All I've figured out is that my peaceful little ranch life has been completely upturned. And all I know right now is that I'd like to have a drink with you."

I'd never seen June so full of emotions and I couldn't help my attraction to her at that moment. She wasn't backing down, wasn't giving in despite everything piling up against her. She was just spending time in her corner and figuring out her fight plan. And what was more, she was willing to include me in it.

She poured two shots and handed me one of the glasses. "Just for the record, I don't think I should get drunk with you."

"I'll make sure nothing unforeseen happens."

"Can you make sure I don't lose the ranch while you're at it?"

I nodded. "I'm getting pretty good at handling horses. Maybe I could volunteer as a horse hand. Think that might help?"

She smiled. "I'll hire you over Chris any day."

"And I just inherited a really nice orchard with the sweetest cherry trees you've ever tasted. We could go pick some fruit and get sick on cherries, then fall asleep under my water tower. It might take your mind off other things."

"I do like cherry pie." She grinned. "Wait, what did you just say? You inherited an orchard?"

I hadn't wanted to tell her about the deal until I had all the details sorted out but I was terrible at keeping secrets. "Mrs. Hudson gave me her orchard, along with the surrounding land which happens to include a water tower and a well. Your well."

"Why did Mrs. Hudson do that?" June's expression betrayed her disbelief. "Are you sure?"

I continued, "The deal is I'll be harvesting her fruit next year and mailing it to Arizona. She heard about the trouble you were going through with the developers over water rights. Her lawyer told me that Mrs. Hudson had originally requested the well be excluded from the property sale but the developers wanted every inch they could get and Mr. Hudson caved. She decided to set things right after what happened."

"Now you own the well? Free and clear?"

"I don't know all the details yet but as I understand it, yes. I'll have the title to a five-acre parcel, bordering the McCormick Ranch—the parcel includes a well and an orchard. Water rights are split between my land and yours." June didn't say anything in response, maybe because she still didn't quite believe me. I hardly believed it myself. After a minute, I continued, "I don't have the papers yet but the lawyer is drawing everything up."

June stood up and went over to the kitchen sink. She turned on the water and sprayed a pile of dirty dishes then stared out the dark window. "I don't know what to say. Why did Mrs. Hudson give you her land?"

"She offered me money originally, for helping her husband. But

I turned her down. I didn't feel comfortable accepting money for that. Then I got a call from her lawyer. He said there's five acres in my name now and all I have to do is come by and sign some things. Apparently there's nothing I can do to stop it. The lawyer says the paperwork is finalized and he's adamant that Mrs. Hudson does not want me to return it." I waited but she didn't say anything more. I had expected her to be happy. "Is something wrong?"

"No. It's just I wasn't expecting this. Why didn't you just take her money? How much did she offer? And what are you going to do with five acres of land in the middle of nowhere?"

"It isn't in the middle of nowhere." I sighed. Maybe I should have waited to tell her. We still barely knew each other. She turned away from me. "June, I'm sorry if I've upset you." I stared at June's back, waiting for a response. "I thought you'd be happy about this. At least now you don't have to worry about the well."

After a long moment, she came back to the counter. She picked up the shot glass and downed the whiskey. "What do you want from me, Meg?"

"I don't want anything . . . well, I guess I'd like to know you a little better." I realized as soon as I'd spoke that I was trying too hard again. If June wanted a relationship with me, she would have asked me something about my life by now. Maybe she wasn't ready for a relationship with me. Not now, maybe not ever. "Are you always a pain in the ass to get to know or are you just being challenging for my benefit?"

"This is who I am." Her stone-faced expression was sobering. "I've made a business of keeping things to myself. And I don't like many people. You're the first person I've kissed in a long time. Three years. Rhonda even gave me the number of a relationship counselor." She laughed sarcastically. "She thinks I have trouble forming relationships. I didn't tell Rhonda why I refused to see some counselor. I'll tell you, though, if you want to know. I already figured out my problem. I'm not attracted to men. Go figure."

"Well, see, now that's a start at something positive, right?"

June stared at the shot glass, not answering.

"What happened three years ago?"

"Long story."

I reached over the counter between us and clasped her hand in mine. "Should I keep trying or are you telling me to leave now?"

She shrugged. Her moist eyes betrayed the indifference of her gesture.

"Why are you afraid to let someone get close to you?"

"I'm not up for psychoanalysis tonight but thank you for your concern. I've got a lot of other things on my mind to deal with. I'll go get a counselor when I retire." She pulled her hand out of mine and sighed. "I'm exhausted."

"We could go to bed early."

"I think maybe you should go."

I nodded, fighting a wave of frustration. "You mind if I ask why you want me to leave?"

She opened her lips but didn't speak for a moment. I could see her hesitation and wanted to jump on it. Under other circumstances, I would have. This was too important, though. I needed her to want me to stay. Finally, she answered and her voice wavered with the quiet words. "I need to think about things. I don't want this to get complicated." She cleared her throat and looked away from me. "You know, just because you own the well doesn't mean all my problems are solved and you're suddenly part of my life."

I gritted my teeth to keep from swearing. I'd never been more caught up with a woman and angry with myself at the same time. I set the shot glass down carefully, fighting the impulse to slam it on the counter. June didn't come to the door to kiss me good night and I was glad of it. I was too angry now anyway. She watched me leave and didn't say anything when I asked her to call me later, if she felt like talking. Maybe she didn't hear me, I thought halfheartedly.

I phoned Deanna as soon as I got to the Jeep. Her voice was soft and friendly. She said she was happy to hear from me and sounded as much. I tried not to look back at June's house or at the fading rays of the porch light as I pulled onto the main road. Deanna told me she'd be at my place, waiting. When I got home, she didn't ask where I'd been that evening and didn't question me if I seemed distracted. Instead, she kissed my cheek and slipped her arm through mine as if we'd been dating for months. Maybe it didn't matter that we knew little more than each other's phone number and what sounds we made during sex.

Two weeks passed without a word from June. I refused to go to the ranch, figuring I was hurting myself more than her. I missed the horses more than I thought I would. Deanna and I saw more of each other—I'd taken to visiting the bar more often than not. I knew when her shifts would be ending and the bouncer seemed to look for me every weekend night, complaining to Deanna on the nights that I didn't show. I was becoming a bit more of a barfly than I wanted to admit but Deanna didn't complain. She also didn't seem to care that my heart wasn't in it. Other parts of me were. Deanna was at my house the night Rhonda called. We'd gone to bed early that night, for us anyway, and when the phone rang at midnight, I had an unsettling feeling that it would be someone from work. I'd been dreaming about work. I was trying to place an IV catheter in a patient who was peppered with bullet wounds. The ambulance kept swerving and I'd been yelling at Eddy to not get us killed en route to the ER. Rhonda's voice surprised me and I had to ask her to repeat her first sentence, still filtering out the images of my dream.

"Sorry for calling this late. Something's happened to Chris. June just called. I didn't get all the details. I'm heading over to the ranch now. Can you come with me?"

Deanna was awake now and sleepily rubbing her eyes. She draped her arm over my chest and squeezed me against her naked body. "Tell whoever's calling that you only sleep with one girl per night. What time is it anyway? And who the hell calls you this late?"

"It's midnight." I gave Deanna an apologetic look and climbed out of bed, rummaging through my dresser for clean underwear and a T-shirt. I wondered why Rhonda wanted my company then hoped that it was June who had asked her to call me. "Where are you now?"

"I'm parked outside your apartment. How much time do you need?"

"I'll be down in two minutes." I glanced over at Deanna as I stepped into my jeans. "Three minutes." I leaned across the bed and kissed Deanna. She pulled me down to her and kissed my belly, then tried unzipping my jeans. I caught hold of her hands, just as she was reaching past my underwear. "I'm sorry. I have to go."

"Why?"

"I don't have time to explain." I knew she'd be upset that I'd leave her in my bed in the middle of the night. I considered lying and saying that I'd been called into work but knew it might backfire. Instead I only told her, "I'll tell you the whole story later. Get some sleep. I'll be home in a few hours."

Deanna nodded and rolled onto her side. I slipped out of the apartment and jogged down the stairs. Rhonda was parked in front of the building and gave me a nod as I climbed in.

"June just called back to give me more info. Apparently she heard a gunshot about an hour ago. She went down to the barn, thinking that maybe Chris had got herself drunk and was shooting at stars or something stupid. She couldn't find Chris anywhere." Rhonda turned on the car and made a U-turn in the middle of the street then headed toward the freeway. "There was this cryptic note on the barn door that Chris had left. Something about how life at the ranch was too painful and she knew it was time to move on. Chris's truck was still there but one of the retired racehorses that boards at the ranch is missing."

"Shit." I was fully awake now and thinking that we should probably be calling the cops soon to help us track Chris. "June's okay though?"

"As good as can be expected, I guess. She blames herself that she didn't resolve things with Chris sooner. What's worse, June went up to get her dad's gun after seeing the note and found an empty case. Not only did Chris steal one of the racehorses, June is worried about a sheriff getting involved because of the gun. If she got caught by the sheriff . . . I just hope we can find her before she does something stupid."

"Too late."

Rhonda nodded. "Thanks for agreeing to come tonight anyway." She leaned over and sniffed my shoulder. "I wouldn't have thought of you as someone who'd wear rose perfume. It smells nice though, don't get me wrong."

"I don't wear perfume." I realized the mistake I'd made as soon as I spoke. Of course I couldn't smell it on me but Deanna always wore rose perfume.

Rhonda arched her eyebrow at me. "So, who does?"

"Deanna. The bartender."

"Don't tell me you were with her tonight? Did you leave her in your bed?"

I nodded. "We just mess around. It isn't serious. We have an agreement."

"Uh-huh, I've heard of those sorts of agreements." Rhonda laughed. "Damn, girl, I'm a little jealous. I knew you'd slept with her but I didn't realize it was an ongoing thing. You know, half the lesbians in town have had a crush on Deanna."

I shrugged. "Well, they ought to ask her out. We're not exclusive."

"Speaking of which, June said she wanted to call you herself tonight but she thought you might not answer her call. She said you two got into a bit of an argument. Lover's quarrel?"

I guessed that June hadn't discussed much with Rhonda about our relationship or lack thereof. "I don't think you could call it a lover's quarrel. I think June would have to like me first."

"Oh, she likes you." Rhonda sighed. "She's been having trouble thinking of anything else except you. I talked to her the night after you slept over." Rhonda gave me a knowing wink when I arched my eyebrows. I hadn't thought that June would have told Rhonda that we'd slept together. Or maybe Rhonda had guessed as much on her own. Rhonda continued, "Don't let June fool you. She likes you all right. She just can't deal with getting close to anyone. I'm her only friend and I could count on one hand the number of times June has told me some intimate detail about herself. The rest I just have to figure out on my own. Fortunately, she gives me a lot of cues."

"Cues?"

"She sighs whenever anyone mentions your name." Rhonda grinned. "No kidding. She sighs first then gives me some generic answer that doesn't answer the question. And she's been a piece of work for the past few weeks."

"How does sighing mean that she likes me?"

"She sighs when she talks about Cassidy."

"The crazy mare?"

"Yeah, the crazy mare that she's not gonna sell no matter how many buyers come looking. She's already had three guys come to buy the horse and she's discouraged all three. I know she wants to keep that horse but God forbid she says something out loud like 'I want this.' It's against her moral fiber."

I thought of Cassidy and wondered how June could like the mare's wild nature and fierce attitude. Maybe she was drawn to the idea of taming the untouchable horse. "June likes things that are a challenge—that she can try to dominate, doesn't she?"

"She likes things she can't dominate."

"So, what does that have to with sighing?"

"Try listening to what she doesn't say. You'll understand what I mean."

I wondered if trying to figure June out was worth the effort. Being with Deanna was getting easier and easier. We exchanged simple pleasures and drifted off to sleep peacefully. I had an idea it wouldn't last long with Deanna. Both of us seemed to be waiting for something better to come along. But lately I was happier with Deanna than I was with anyone else.

"June is my best friend, you know. But sometimes I'm ready to disown her. She and Karen have spent the past week fighting about the ranch. Karen's ended most of their phone conversations crying. I'm caught somewhere in the middle of it all. By the way, is it true you got a land title from the Hudsons?"

I nodded. "Five acres and an orchard."

"And a well."

"The well's what made June suddenly want nothing to do with me."

"She just needs some time to accept things. Gabe said you haven't been coming to the ranch anymore. He thinks that's why June's been such a bear to deal with lately."

"I think she's been too occupied with other things to notice I haven't been around. Like Chris, for example."

"Don't be too sure."

My thoughts returned to Chris. Her crush on June had annoyed me at first and even sparked my jealousy but I only felt sorry for her now. "You think Chris is just doing this for attention? Would she actually do something to hurt herself?"

"I don't know. She's young and in love. I can remember doing a lot of things for attention when I was twenty-three."

I smiled, thinking that Rhonda probably had a few good stories to tell about her own youthful loves. "I was twenty-three when my first serious girlfriend left me for another girl. Broke my heart. I had this plan to key dirty words onto the new woman's car."

"Did you?"

I didn't answer. "Youth and unrequited love can be a bad combination."

"Exactly."

"Speaking of love . . . I heard through the grapevine that you slept with June's sister."

"Ah, the grapevine. I won't ask who told you. I don't really want to know how fast news travels in the Sacramento dyke scene." Rhonda sighed. "I've had a crush on Karen since I was a kid. But I never told her. Anyway, she was always into guys. After she got married I gave up hope." Rhonda glanced over at me. "Lesson learned: Never give up hoping a straight girl might change her mind. Even a married one."

"And be prepared for all hell to break loose when it happens."

"I guess you heard she's filing for a divorce."

I nodded. "And she wants June to buy her half of the ranch."

"June's pissed. I think she blames me." Rhonda shook her head. "But I have to admit I wouldn't have done anything differently. Karen is an amazing lover. She was at my house again tonight. She's thinking of moving in at the end of the month."

I didn't find Karen attractive and she seemed an unlikely match for Rhonda. Still, it was obvious Rhonda was happy. "Don't you think that's a little soon?"

"Maybe for her. But I've been waiting for the past twenty years."

I decided not to push any further. To me, the whole idea seemed crazy. Rebound warning signs flashed in neon but I wasn't going to be the naysayer this time. We drove the rest of the way to the ranch in silence. June was waiting for us in the driveway. Don Juan, Tanner and Whiskey were all saddled. Rhonda took Don Juan's reins and June handed me Whiskey's. Whiskey immediately brushed his muzzle across my hands, sniffing me. He didn't balk when I rubbed his head and I tried to swallow the fear that was building up in my chest. I'd never ridden at night and after seeing Whiskey rearing up with June on our last ride, I wasn't anxious to get on him.

"I think she probably headed south. I've already gone up to the summit and didn't see any sign of her on the north side. I called over to the Hudsons to let them know that we had a horse escape. Mrs. Hudson said she'd call me if she spotted any riders or horses on her side. There's a trail that we can follow along the southern ridge. I think we'll have enough moonlight to see the path. Then I thought we could separate when the trail splits. Rhonda, you can take the trail leading over to the Clarks' place." June's voice cracked, betraying the exhaustion and fear in her body. I noticed her eyes were red and she wore the same clothes I'd last seen her in—a pair of faded blue Levis and a button-down red collared shirt with the sleeves rolled up. She'd added a dark blue coat to the outfit and looked every bit the cowgirl with her black hat perched on her head. "At the split, Meg and I will head down to the riverbed. The going is a little rough there and I hope she didn't take Jack there. But that's the best way out of the valley and if she knew what she was doing and intended on stealing Jack, that would be the way she should go. There aren't any roads for miles in that direction and she could ride all day and not be noticed."

I doubted that Chris was doing all this just to steal a horse. Jack was one of the racehorses I remembered from the barn. Jack-Be-Nimble. He was jet black with one white blaze on his head. It was unlikely we'd be able to spot a black horse tonight, especially if Chris was intent on not being found. And who knew how much distance she had on us or which trail she had taken. Too many trails led out of the valley and I doubted we'd find her. If we did, it probably wouldn't be good news.

"Do you honestly think she wanted to steal Jack?" Rhonda asked as she adjusted Don Juan's stirrups and then mounted.

"I don't know what she wanted to do." June glanced over at me and then looked south toward the ridge we'd follow. "I only know what she did."

She jumped on Tanner and then turned in her saddle to watch me fumble with the girth. The saddle seemed a little loose but Whiskey wasn't happy with me trying to cinch it tighter. "You okay to ride Whiskey?"

I nodded. Rhonda and June were waiting for me. I grabbed a hold of Whiskey's mane and placed my toe in the stirrup. He took a few uneasy steps to the side before I managed to get into the saddle. We set off at a quick jog. The horses warmed up with the excitement of a night ride and I had to keep my focus on Whiskey.

He was ready to break into a run and only Tanner's wide rump seemed to deter him from tearing down the dark trail. After we'd gone a mile or so, the trail split. Don Juan tossed his head a few times, reluctant to separate from our group and Rhonda finally had to give him a hard kick in the side to get him moving. The night closed about them quickly as they disappeared down the dark path toward the neighboring ranch.

June pressed onward without a word. She kept her eyes focused on the trail ahead and motioned for me to keep a flank lookout. I tried to discern objects in the hazy darkness but all I could make out were rocks and oak trees. Too many shadows crowded about us. The trail split a second time and June hopped off Tanner and shined a flashlight down the two paths. I guessed she was looking for hoofprints. I couldn't make out distinct marks on either side.

"Looks like there are hoofprints on both paths. How do you feel about splitting up?" She came over to Whiskey and handed the flashlight to me then slung her canteen over my saddle horn. "There's water if you get thirsty. Stick to the trail. Whatever you do, don't get off the trail. If Whiskey gets antsy and tries balking at something, just keep telling him whoa and pull back on the bit like you mean it."

"I don't remember agreeing to separate." The last thing I wanted to do was ride alone on Whiskey in the dark down a path I'd never been.

"If we pick one path and she's taken the other . . . look, I'll understand if you don't want to go any further. You can go back to the ranch and wait there. But I'm really hoping you won't."

I gazed back at the trail toward the ranch and then at the split in front of us. June had already gone back to Tanner's side and had her foot in the stirrup, about to mount. She paused when our eyes met and took her foot out of the stirrup. "You really can head back, if you want."

"June, what's going on with us? You're so hot and cold, I can't even convince myself that you like me. Two weeks passed and I didn't hear a word from you. Where the hell are you?"

The sound of a branch cracking distracted both of us. June glanced at the trail back the way we'd come, then looked forward to where it split. She finally answered, her voice low and her eyes avoiding me. "I've missed you. I wanted to call, but . . . maybe we just need to be friends for a while and figure things out before—"

"Before what? Before you decide it's okay to kiss when we greet each other? Bullshit." I had to stop myself from raising my voice. I wanted to scream that of course something was going on between us. Anyone could see it. But maybe I was wrong. Biting back the words only made the hurt worse.

"I feel like I hardly know you."

"So ask me about my life. I'll tell you anything." I knew I should back down now but my desire for her was so much stronger after a few weeks of not seeing her. I couldn't understand why she was making this so hard. "June, you can decide if you want me in your life or not. But just so you know, I'm not going to settle for a friendship."

June turned away from me. She took a few steps toward the dark path on the right and kicked a felled log at the trail's edge. After a moment, she turned back to me. I couldn't see her face clearly in the darkness but her voice betrayed the tears. "I need some time to think."

"About what?" I sighed, unable to hold back the frustration. "I'm not asking you to marry me. I'm just asking you to act like you want to date me. Half the time I think maybe we're making progress and then I can't tell if you want me around you at all. And what the hell is going on with you and Chris?"

"Nothing. That much I can promise you." June didn't say anything more right off and I felt stupid and jealous for asking. Still, I didn't know if I completely trusted her that no feelings were involved between her and Chris. June fished through Tanner's saddlebags for a moment before finding some small object wrapped up in a handkerchief. She handed this to me and motioned for me to unwrap it. "I got this for you. I kept meaning to call and invite you out here for a ride but I thought I may have lost my chance with you."

A shiny silver buckle slipped out of the handkerchief. The words El Dorado County were printed on one side of the buckle with a sketch of a rearing horse. On the back side of the buckle someone had etched the words WELCOME HOME.

"I thought since you were going to be my neighbor . . . I need you to take things slow with me. But I'm happy you're going to be here in El Dorado, in my life." June rested her hand on my leg. It was the first time she'd touched me all night and the weight of her hand made my thoughts leap to other things. "Things have been crazy at the ranch. Karen and Chris are taking up all of my energy but I haven't stopped thinking about you. Every night I've picked up the phone to call but I hang up before I hear the first ring."

I stared at the buckle and curled my fingers over the cold metal. "You know, you may be the most challenging woman I've ever wanted to be with."

"Challenging, huh?" She smiled. "Thanks for not saying I'm difficult or truly disturbed. And by the way, yes."

"Yes what?"

"Yes, I'd like you to kiss me. Whenever you'd like." She mounted Tanner and sighed. "Don't ask me why you'd want to put up with me though." Pointing to the path on the right she continued, "Ride until you reach the creek. Don't cross the creek. The path on the far side isn't safe at night. And if Chris has gone that far, she was intending on leaving."

"You don't think she was?"

"I'm hoping she just wanted to pull a stunt to get my attention." June gathered up Tanner's reins and gave him a nudge down the path on the left. She glanced over her shoulder at me. "By the way, I appreciate your help tonight, whatever happens. It means a lot to me. I'll meet you back at the barn by daybreak. Will you stay for breakfast?"

"Maybe." Whiskey tossed his head and snorted when June got

Tanner into a jog. They disappeared down the dark trail leaving Whiskey and me to decide which direction we'd head. Part of me was strongly pushing to turn back and wait at the ranch. Maybe Chris had a change of heart and was back at the barn already. Another part of me wanted to take the trail June had chosen, though I guessed she wouldn't be happy to see me. A very small part of me knew I'd have to take the new trail. This won out, I think, mostly because of my damn ego.

I had to get off and lead Whiskey a few feet down the new trail before he decided it was a good option. He waited for me to climb back on and then we jogged for a half mile or so before I pulled him back to a walk when our path narrowed. Coyote bush bordered the path and scratched against my jeans. The thick trees overhead blocked whatever light the moon cast. The crickets were quieter here and I made myself believe that the scratching sound in the underbrush was only the scamper of mice or a bird stretching his wings. Whiskey slowed after a few paces through the narrow section. I turned on the flashlight and gave him the edge of my heel. He took a few steps and then raised his nose as if sniffing the wind.

"Go on, boy." I kicked harder and Whiskey finally agreed to move. Another ten paces and he stopped again. My mind was making up all sorts of shapes in the shadows now and I had to force back the swell of fear when a branch cracked or leaves rustled. The path split ahead and Whiskey paused, waiting for my direction. I chose the path on the left since the going seemed a little wider. We made good time on the wider trail and Whiskey seemed to have an idea of where he was going now. Every so often I thought I caught the sound of rushing water and wondered if we were close to the stream. It might have been ten feet away and I wouldn't have seen it with all the brush and tree cover.

After we'd gone about twenty minutes down the wide trail, Whiskey pulled up suddenly and stretched out his neck. His nose lifted to the wind and I wondered how adept he was at following a scent or if he was just pulling this trick as an excuse to stop. His ears perked forward and I let him jog a few steps before he abruptly stopped. On our left the path opened to a small clearing. He whinnied and a few seconds later, a soft nicker came in response to his call. I spun the light in a circle around us, straining to see something besides the grayish green leaves. A moment later, Jack-Be-Nimble was rubbing noses with Whiskey.

"Chris?"

"Hi, Meg." She was sitting on a rock slab at the edge of the clearing. I felt a rush of relief. Jack's long lead line was wrapped around her wrist. "I didn't expect you to come looking for me. What are you doing out here?"

"Well, I thought it'd be a nice night for a ride." I slipped off Whiskey and walked over to her. The relief I'd felt quickly disappeared when I saw the gun in her lap. I tried not to stare at it but she noticed where my eyes went.

She picked up the gun, resting her finger on the trigger then playing with the safety, shifting it back and forth. She set the gun in her lap again and looked up at me. "You're not out here alone, are you?"

"Rhonda and June are out here too, somewhere. We all took different trails."

"I can't believe I'm going to say this but I'm glad you found me instead of June." She stretched out her legs and leaned back. "You know, I had this crazy idea that she would eventually decide she liked me."

"I'm starting to think June likes to be single."

Chris nodded. "Could be. She's playing hardball with you too, huh? I noticed you've been too busy lately to come out to the ranch. Got burned by a girl?"

I nodded. "She bruised my pride a little."

Chris continued, "I had this idea that it'd be kind of like a game tonight. Where I'd keep riding until she found me. If she found me before I decided to use the gun, well then I'd talk things out. If she didn't find me, then . . ."

"Why not just keep riding? Maybe no one would ever find you."

"That was Plan B. But I figured June would call the cops.

Stealing a horse would be a stupid way to end up in jail. I've done things that deserved a night in jail . . . I don't want to go there again."

"Again?" She ignored my question and I didn't press for an answer. Right now wasn't the time to scratch old wounds. For the moment, Chris was open to me. I didn't want to blow our strange trust by talking too much. "So, what's your new plan?"

"Figured you were going to tell me."

I shook my head.

"I kind of already decided against using the gun."

"Kind of?" By the way she was acting I knew she'd made the decision to stay amongst the living. She had settled herself with this resolution and the gun's safety was set. I'd taken enough suicidal people to the hospital to know Chris was safe—for the moment. "If you could do anything, what would you do next?"

"I want to go see my mom." She answered immediately. "She lives in Texas. I haven't seen her since I was twelve. We've had . . . communication problems." She laughed sarcastically.

A rustling at the side of the clearing startled the horses and we all waited to see if anything would come out of the brush. After a while the horses started poking among the weeds again, chewing what they could find. Chris and I relaxed as well. "You want to patch things up with her?"

"Maybe. Mostly I just want to see her again. My mom and I have been on bad terms for a long time. I don't even know exactly where she's living anymore. I got letters from her for a while. She found out about my arrest and the letters stopped coming. That was years ago. I heard she was in a trailer park outside of Austin a year ago. I don't know if she's still there."

"I've got a friend in Dallas." Actually she was an ex but I wasn't going to bring that up. "She works for the phone company and has a knack for finding hard-to-find people. Her name's Alice. I can hook you up with her, if you'd like."

"Alice from Dallas. Okay, maybe." Chris picked up the gun

again, twirling it around in her hands. "I wonder what June would have said if she'd been the one to find me."

"There'd been a lot of cussing."

"She's mad?" Chris didn't need me to answer. She continued, "So, what do I do now? Can't just go back to the ranch. Can't keep going all the way to Texas on Jack . . ."

"We'll go back to the ranch together. Rhonda and June are both still out looking for your ass."

"Then what?"

"You'll put Jack back in his stall, get in your truck and start driving. I don't think that thing will make it all the way to Texas but it should make it into town. I can spot you the money for a Greyhound ticket to Dallas. I'll let Alice know you're coming and she'll start the search." I let her think for a minute and then reached out my hand, waiting for the gun.

She placed it in my palm without arguing. "Do you always have this effect on people? I don't feel half as angry as I was when you found me."

"I do. It's a skill I've picked up." I pocketed the gun with a wave of relief. I'd handled enough guns to be comfortable seeing them but I was still on edge when someone else had one.

"You get that skill from your job? I guess ambulance drivers have to be calm under pressure."

"No, the job is a piece of cake compared to some of the crazy women I've dated. Puts the EDPs to shame."

"EDPs. I've heard that before. Emotionally disturbed, right? That's me tonight."

"Chris, we all have our moments. Keeps life interesting."

"Maybe." She stood up and shouldered her backpack then went over to Jack. "Are you gonna keep trying with June? Think you'll ever end up with her?"

I shrugged. "That depends on June. I'm still not completely sure June actually likes anyone that isn't a horse."

"She likes that fat orange cat. You ever see that cat run?"

I laughed, remembering the scene of him chasing after a bug, rolls of fat rippling at his sides as he dashed ten feet and then had to stop in complete exhaustion. "Well, then, who knows . . . maybe there's a chance." We rode back to the ranch in silence. I think Chris was worried about making noise and getting June's attention. I hadn't told her which direction the others had taken and she kept looking back to make sure no one was riding up on us. Chris gave me Jack's reins when we reached the barn. I wrote down Alice's phone number and her address in Dallas.

"Can you write down your number too? I won't call unless I'm returning your favor. Thanks, by the way."

"Call if you need anything, Chris. Can't guarantee I'll be able to help but I'd like to hear from you anyhow." I gave her the money I had in my wallet. It only added up to sixty-eight bucks but she thought that'd be enough with the hundred she had on her. It figured she'd pick payday as the day to leave. "Good luck."

"Tell June I'm sorry, for everything."

"Write her a letter, or call, when you get to Dallas. She'll be missing you."

She took the path up to the house and paused for a moment, just staring at the house and at the barn below. I waved and she nodded at me. We'd become strangely linked and I had a feeling this wasn't the last time I'd see her. She got in her truck finally and the noise of the engine shattered the night's silence. I listened to it rumble down the road until the sound slowly merged with the breathing of the horses and the breeze coming through the valley.

Chapter 8
June

I guess I didn't expect to find her. The first shreds of daylight were brightening the eastern sky when I finally reached the ranch boundary gate. Don Juan was tied up at the barn and he gave Tanner a whinny. I noticed Whiskey was already in the pasture eating. Someone had already fed the pastured horses. I checked my watch. It was ten minutes to six and I knew better than to think that Gabe or Shank had shown up early. For a moment, my heart jumped at the thought that Chris had come home on her own and was waiting up at the house for me now.

As soon as I saw Meg bringing a flake of alfalfa over to the tie post I knew I was wrong. She'd fed the horses. I slid off Tanner and led him over to the tie post. Meg had a bucket of grain waiting for him. She took his reins and handed me a cup of coffee. I let her take off Tanner's tack and enjoyed the first sweet sip. I always drank mine black but this was sweetened and had a good amount of cream. I held the warm liquid in my mouth a moment before swallowing. I knew I should thank Meg but I was too exhausted to speak.

Rhonda came out of the barn, smiling. "You heard the news?"

I looked at Rhonda and then over at Meg. Meg grinned sheepishly. I waited, knowing Rhonda wouldn't keep a secret long.

"Jack-Be-Nimble is in his stall happily enjoying his breakfast," Rhonda announced. "And Chris is on her way to Texas. You can thank Meg."

Meg picked up my dad's gun from the planter box by the barn. Somehow I hadn't noticed it there earlier. "Chris wanted me to tell you that she was sorry."

I took the gun, hardly believing it was my dad's until I saw his initials etched on the handle. I stared at Meg not knowing what to say. She looked at me with an understanding in her eyes that almost made me break down and cry right there. I knew she didn't expect me to say anything yet.

The gun wasn't enough. I had to see Jack. I pushed open the barn door and moved down the aisle to his stall, half dazed. He poked his velvet black nose over the door as soon as I whistled. After giving my hand a good sniff and deciding I didn't have any treats, he returned to his breakfast. I listened to him eat for a few minutes and then went over to the stairs leading up to Chris's apartment. The door was closed and I imagined it might bust open at any minute. I'd spent the past few hours hating Chris for her stunt and now that she was gone I felt as hollow as an eggshell.

Rhonda came into the barn and stood at my side. She slipped her hand in mine. "You have to promise me one thing."

"What's that?" I asked, my voice weak and sounding barely like my own.

"Don't start missing that one."

I knew Rhonda was right. "My dad would say she came here to find her compass and we gave her one." In a way, I missed her already. After what happened last night though, we would never have been the same. I wouldn't have trusted her with anything. "I guess I expected it would happen all along."

"I'm gonna give Meg a ride home. I think you should talk to her before we go."

"I owe her breakfast." Add it to the list, I thought. She had a way of making me indebted to her. I wondered what she'd said to Chris and if I'd have had the same good luck getting Jack home.

"And I think you should tell her something else too."

I glanced over at Rhonda and knew what she was getting at without asking. "She knows I like her."

"You told her that?"

"Well . . . no. Yes. Sort of."

"June, she's not gonna wait around forever. I know you like her. Just tell her you're interested. Otherwise she's just gonna settle in with her bartender and you'll have lost your chance."

"What bartender?"

"The woman she's been sleeping with."

I felt my breath catch in my throat. "I thought she was single. I just assumed . . ."

Rhonda shrugged. "She assumed you liked her about as much as a doormat. Why shouldn't she date other people?"

Why not? I sank down on a bale of hay and closed my eyes. The sugared coffee had left my exhausted body jittery and now my nerves were pressed too far. I felt the moisture start in my eyes and didn't stop it. Rhonda hugged me and let my tears fall silently. I thought of how Meg had looked at me the day we first met and again the night we kissed. I'd felt like I might be the most important person in her world at that moment. And I'd run from that, too scared to accept that anything like that might be true. I'd pushed her as far away as I could stand, wanting at the same time to hold her so tightly she might not leave. "Every time she came to the ranch I hoped she might stay an hour longer, might stay the whole night and the next day too. But I wouldn't tell her that. Instead I guess I sent the opposite message. If she never came back here, I thought I'd forget about her eventually. Problem solved, you know?" I wiped my face on my sleeve and let go of Rhonda. "Can you thank her for me? Just tell her I'm not feeling well."

"Sorry, I can't do that," she said in a hoarse voice. Rubbing her throat she continued, "I'm coming down with laryngitis myself."

I smiled. "You're a worthless friend."

"Who's fucking your sister."

"Did you have to bring that up right now?"

"I thought we might as well get everything out on the table."

"Thanks, Karen already told me too many details. You know, I don't really want my sister explaining how hot she thinks my best friend looks in chaps."

Rhonda laughed. She was clearly pleased with this. "Yeah, you should see your sister in silk lingerie. With a whip."

"Okay, that's going too far." I couldn't keep a straight face and soon we were both laughing. It felt like it'd been months since I'd laughed that hard and my sides were hurting by the time I finally stopped.

Rhonda hugged my shoulders and then pointed me to the barn door. "All joking aside, someone's waiting for you."

I put my hand on the door and paused. Rhonda gave me a full minute before she opened the door instead. Her face was full of disappointment as she went outside. I didn't follow. My feet seemed to be nailed to the dusty barn planks. The door closed and I gazed through the cracks. Meg wasn't at the tie post. She'd gone up to the driveway and was waiting by Rhonda's car. Rhonda gave her a wave and went up the path to meet her. I stayed in the barn until they'd driven away.

By the time I reached the house, Shank and Gabe were just pulling up. Coffee was already made. I had a second cup, black. Three plates were set out and the morning eggs had been collected. Gabe came in with a basket of hot biscuits. Shank followed him. The kitchen was filled with their noisy banter and when they asked after Chris, neither seemed very surprised to hear she'd quit. She'd been with us for a month and that was all there was to it. We slipped back into our old rhythm without missing a beat.

I worked for a few hours and then told Gabe I wasn't feeling well. He let me off without any questions. I went to the house and slept fitfully until one, waking only to make lunch for the guys. Instead of going back to bed, I decided to take Cassidy out on a ride. I went over to the Clarks' place first to let them know the missing horse had been found, safe and sound. I told Mrs. Hudson more or less the same story. She asked me to stay for tea and we chatted a bit about Mr. Hudson's health and she ranted about hospitals. After a while she brought up Meg's name.

"Are you two special friends?"

I didn't know what to say but yes.

She blushed and patted my hand. "You know, I knew all along that June McCormick wouldn't bend her ways for a man. Even when you were a little girl I told your father that he'd never marry you off. 'And good for it,' he'd said. You know, he never liked your husband. He told me once that the man was as worthwhile as feathers in a henhouse. But he was rather handsome, wasn't he?" She patted my hand again and sighed. "Of course, I don't think your father would have guessed you'd be with a woman. But I think Meg is a wonderful girl—lady, I should say. And she's agreed to take care of my fruit trees. Did she tell you yet? I hope I'm not ruining the surprise."

I nodded. I guess I hadn't known what to expect but seeing Mrs. Hudson so pleased wasn't it. I wished I could have told her honestly that we were lovers. Now I wasn't even sure if we were friends. I thought of Greg and realized how incomparable Meg was to him. I had no idea now how I'd ever decided to marry him. Strangely, I'd always thought my dad had liked Greg.

Mrs. Hudson continued, "I have a feeling she agreed to the deal only for you but I know her heart was in it when she promised to care for my trees. You know, when your mother passed, I've always thought of you as a little lost lamb." She squeezed my hand. "I think now though, you've found your own way, haven't you? And you'll look after our well, as always. The horses and the trees must have their water."

Mrs. Hudson gave me a bucket of apricots before I left. She asked me to share one with Meg so she might know the fortune she'd inherited. I took Cassidy up to the summit and watched the sun set before riding home. She hadn't given me an ounce of trouble that afternoon and I let her munch on a few remaining bits of green grass, hiding under the shade of the trees while I sat on a rock and watched the sky fill with color. After a while, Cassidy came over and nudged my hand. I rubbed her head and she lowered her muzzle to my knees, enjoying the attention. I'd finally settled my heart on one thing. I wasn't selling Cassidy.

I called Meg four times over the next three days. Each time I hung up the line when the message machine answered. I spent more time than I ever remembered dusting and mopping the house, looking for any excuse to stay by the phone and hoping she'd call. I had too many thoughts of sexy bartenders waiting for Meg to come home and touch them the way she'd touched me. I went through phases of resenting myself and thinking that I didn't deserve someone like Meg to phases of intense anger thinking that she had no right to mess around with other women just because I wasn't ready for her when she wanted me. By Friday, I'd resigned myself to the fact that I'd have to leave a message. I did. It was this: "So I was wondering where you grew up. Who was the first person you kissed? Do you like your job? Do you like saving people all the time? I've got another question but I want to ask that in person."

She called back an hour later.

"I wanted to know if you were interested in having dinner with me." I paused. She didn't say anything so I said, "Or maybe just a drink sometime."

"Are you asking me out on a date, Ms. McCormick? You know what, don't answer that. I don't want to tempt fate." She laughed. "I'd love to. Do you mind if I pick the place? I know this amazing spot."

I'd figured we'd have dinner at the house. I hadn't even thought of what I'd cook though. Maybe it would be easier if we just went out to eat. Suddenly I was worried about what to wear and whether or not I should ask if it was a dressy place. "Okay."

"Great. Just so you know, the food's not all that but I think you'll love the atmosphere. I'll be at the ranch at six, if that's okay. I've got a few errands to run before then."

Meg showed up early. She had a picnic basket and a bottle of wine. She smiled when she saw me in a skirt and asked if I knew how to ride in it. I'm sure I turned every shade of red. Then I asked if she'd mind if I changed. I felt silly in the skirt anyway and happily picked a pair of jeans and my favorite blue tank top. She had Whiskey and Cassidy tied up and saddled by the time I met her down at the barn. I watched her load the contents of the picnic basket into Whiskey's saddlebags thinking of a thousand things I wanted to tell her and yet not wanting to do anything more than watch her.

"So where's this place with the amazing atmosphere?"

She smiled. "Some people call it Pioneer's Prayer."

"You have good taste." I hopped on Cassidy and waited as she mounted Whiskey. "Just so you know, we're celebrating tonight."

"Oh, really? Why's that?"

"Karen decided not to sell her part of the ranch. But she's decided she's tired of running the business part of things. She's leaving it up to me for the year." I'd just gotten the call from Rhonda that afternoon. I don't know how Rhonda convinced Karen but I wasn't going to ask questions.

"What happens at the end of the year?"

"I don't know. Hopefully she and Rhonda stay together that long and I won't have to worry about it. I know it's Rhonda I have to thank."

"Gotta love divorces."

I smiled. "You obviously haven't been through one."

"There's still a lot you don't know about me. But you're right. That's not one of my past secrets." She winked at me.

I wondered now what other secrets she had, thinking of the

bartender that Rhonda had mentioned and knowing there might be ten other women she'd dated in the past year. I didn't want to be just another date and felt a little foolish to even be trying with Meg. Yet every time she looked at me, my doubts slipped out of my mind. She took the lead heading out on the trail. Whiskey was clearly happy with his new rider. He didn't hesitate to follow her signals and I could see she was better suited for him as well. He was one of the taller horses on the ranch and her long legs didn't look at all out of proportion on him. We rode up the trail to Pioneer's Prayer and when we tied the horses, Meg brought out two buckets of grain for them.

"You know, you'll spoil them."

"There's nothing wrong with sweet oats every once in a while." She caught my hand and brought it up to her lips. I felt her skin brush the back of my hand. A moment later her lips were on mine. I had an idea I might never get enough of kissing her. She let me try five or six times and then stepped away. "Hungry?"

We didn't head back to the barn until dusk had set in and I was a little uneasy riding Cassidy through the shadowy parts of the trail. Fortunately, Whiskey led the way and Cassidy liked him well enough to follow. By the time we got to the ranch, Gabe and Shank were already gone. The other horses had been fed so all that was left to do was brush down Whiskey and Cassidy and give them their night's ration.

"Would you mind coming up to the house for a bit?" I asked, hoping Meg wouldn't hear the uncertainty in my voice.

"No, I wouldn't mind. But to tell you the truth, I was hoping you'd ask me to stay all night."

"I didn't want to seem too forward."

She grinned. "Well, then, I'll take that honor. June, can I spend the night, and while I'm at it, can I take a shower with you?"

I agreed, guessing that my blush was as red as Cassidy's lead line. We dropped by the barn to close up the place for the night and then headed up to the house, followed by three of the four ranch cats who were begging for their dinner. I made the cats wait at the front porch while I went inside for the cat food. Meg watched me fill the bowls. She seemed thoughtful and I wanted to ask what was on her mind but hesitated. I didn't have a right to ask personal questions when I'd hid my own emotions from her. After a while, she broke the silence.

"I'm thinking of taking a new job. There's an opening for a teaching post. I'd have a better schedule but there wouldn't be any patient care or . . ."

"Excitement?"

She nodded. "I'm a little worried about being bored. I feel like I'm ready for something new but I don't know if I'm cut out to be a teacher."

The phone rang, interrupting her.

"I don't really feel like talking to anyone but you," I admitted.

She smiled. "I was hoping you'd say that."

I offered Meg a drink and we tried to ignore the ringing. Finally the answering machine picked up. I poured two glasses of wine and handed Meg hers just as Chris's voice came over the line.

"Hi, it's me. In case you're listening, June, I don't blame you for not picking up. I really am sorry about everything that happened. Anyway, I just wanted to let you know I'm in Dallas. I'm staying with a friend of Meg's for the night. Tomorrow I'm going to see my mom." She paused and I had to fight the impulse to pick up the line. I stared at the phone, barely breathing and not quite certain why I wanted so badly to talk to her. Chris continued, "I miss you. Maybe someday I can get back to El Dorado for a visit. I'll wait a few years though so you'll forget how pissed you are at me." She chuckled. "Anyway, if you want to say hello, I'm gonna give you the number for where I'm staying—"

I pressed the mute button on the answering machine and looked over at Meg. Her arms were crossed on her chest.

"Why don't you just pick up the phone and talk to her." She was clearly upset.

I couldn't explain my feelings for Chris to Meg. I didn't completely understand it myself. She'd reminded me of a younger sister and something more too. "I don't want to talk to her."

"Nothing was going on between you and Chris?"

"Nothing." I felt like I was lying. Maybe I was.

She shook her head and turned away from me. I half expected her to leave but she didn't. She went over to the couch and sat down, not looking at me. "June, do you want to try opening up, just this once? I think it'd be a really good idea."

"It's not like I'm trying to hide anything. Unlike some people."

"What are you talking about?"

"Rhonda told me that you've been dating a bartender." I knew it was the wrong time to say it but I didn't stop myself. Before this got any further, I had to know what I was in for. The last thing I wanted to do was be someone's affair. "When were you going to tell me you were in a relationship?"

"I don't know, June, maybe after the birth of our first kid." She threw her hands up in the air. "I'm not dating anyone. Deanna and I are fuck-buddies, pardon my directness. I broke things off with her last week. You know, after what happened with Chris, I had this crazy idea that maybe you were interested in me."

I'd used the bartender as ammunition and the shot had found a mark—on me. I wished I hadn't brought it up at all. Why wouldn't Meg be having sex with someone else? I had no claim on her. "I kissed Chris once." I felt my knees weaken and wanted to sit down. Meg's eyes were on me. I stared at my hands instead of at her, wondering how they could be so still when the rest of me seemed to be shaking loose. "I felt close to her but I didn't want a relationship. I guess I liked her around because she seemed to need me. And, I know, she had a crush on me that I didn't do much to end. Just for the record, I didn't want to have sex with her. She reminded me a lot of myself at her age and I guess I wanted to help her. I wanted her to be happy."

"You could have slept with her. That would have made her happy."

"You're right, I could have. But I didn't. I didn't want her."

"But you miss her now."

I nodded. "A little." There was no use lying but I didn't want to fight about Chris. "She was just wandering through El Dorado." I looked over at Meg finally. "You're not just wandering through, are you?" She didn't say anything. Meg was waiting for me like I'd once waited for a stray cat to learn to trust me. I could feel her eyes on me and had an idea she might be able to see inside. Somehow she'd see my fear of letting her close and somehow she'd know the disappointment I'd be to her, like I'd been to my father, to Karen and to Greg. She stood up and came to me, holding my hands in hers and still not speaking. "I'd like you to stay around. Can we put Chris and your bartender in the past?" I didn't want to think about Meg making love to anyone but me now. I wanted her so badly that I couldn't speak when I thought of it.

She nodded.

"You'd be home nights if you took that teaching job, wouldn't you? And maybe you could come here after teaching."

"Maybe we could start seeing each other on a regular basis, is what you're saying, right?" She laughed. "June McCormick, are you asking me to go steady?"

"Well, I thought we could put you to work on the ranch for entertainment—to keep you from getting bored, I mean."

Her eyebrows arched at this and I tried to retract my words. She slipped her arm over my shoulder. "Hell, I'll take the job of entertaining you any time."

"What I meant was—" I paused and looked up at her. She was still grinning. I caught myself staring at her eyes, so blue and so transparent when it came to her every emotion. Her eyes somehow captured the joy in her spirit and I couldn't help but smile too. I liked the feel of her body close to mine and her arm holding me as if she had every right to do it. "Never mind."

"I almost forgot," she said, suddenly going to find the satchel she'd brought and fishing for something in the front pocket. She brought out her harmonica and directed me over to the sofa. I sat down on one end and she took the other. She sat cross-legged and stared at me for a moment. "So, you'll have to forgive me if I get a few notes wrong. I'm no Patsy Cline."

I closed my eyes when she started to play. I could hear my Mom singing right along with the harmonica's perfect notes. Then I found myself singing the chorus, like I used to with my Mom. "Crazy for trying, crazy for lying, Crazy for . . ." But I couldn't finish the words and as soon as I stopped singing, I felt Meg's gaze on me. I didn't explain the tears that had started.

She played another Patsy Cline song and then set the harmonica on the coffee table. She'd given me enough time to wipe away the tears and didn't ask why they'd sprung up. "You know, I'd love to help out at the ranch but I won't be able to for a while." She paused. "I have this crazy plan of building a little cabin in a clearing above the orchard. Something like an artist studio, you know? The land is so beautiful and I'm ready to ditch my apartment in the city. I think I need to feel more dirt under my shoes or something."

I'd barely let myself believe that Meg really owned the well and that our ranch wasn't going to lose the water. I'd never considered that she'd actually want to live on the property.

"And Mrs. Hudson gave me more land than I was expecting. The lawyer gave me a little map of my section of land. It's a strip right between your property and the new development. Two of the acres are covered by the well and the orchard and another two acres are a hillside that I won't be able to use but I think there's a flat acre that might be perfect for a little place." Her excitement was obvious. She continued, "If I take the teaching job, I'll have more free time to do a project like that. And I think I've got enough money saved up to build something halfway decent. Nothing big, you know. I'll only need a room for a bed, a little kitchen and a bathroom. And I want a bunch of windows everywhere so I can see all the trees. What do you think?"

"I think tomorrow we should go pick out a site for the cabin. I couldn't think of a better neighbor than you. And I've always wanted to be madly attracted to the girl next door."

"Really?"

I smiled. "Although Rhonda tried to set me up with every eligible woman she knew, I can honestly say until you came to the ranch, I never once considered falling in love with a woman."

"So that means you're considering it now?"

I kissed her instead of answering. "I think we should go take that shower, as promised."

Meg followed me into the bedroom. I apologized for the clothes strewn about and the unmade bed. She shrugged and slipped off her clothes. "I'm too exhausted to notice. Anyway, I kind of like a person who doesn't think keeping their room clean is the most important thing."

"Well, lucky you caught me on an off cleaning day. Otherwise, you might get ideas about my life priorities."

"Are we talking about life priorities already?"

I swatted her with a pillow and laughed as she ducked. "Well, you never know what a woman like you might get a person to start thinking about."

I hesitated to undress in front of her. She was naked by the time I'd started unbuttoning my jeans and I felt a little uneasy shedding my clothes as she watched. She stepped toward me, pulling my shirt over my head then working on the buttons of my jeans. I let her undress me and then stepped into the shower before she had a chance to do anything more. I was still uneasy with her touch, though I wished I wasn't, and wanted her to slow down a bit. The pleading look she gave me every time I pulled her hands away from my body was hard to take. I didn't know how to explain that although I was a thirty-four-year-old divorced woman, I still felt like a novice at sex.

The warm water relaxed me a little. I handed Meg the shampoo and let her lather her short hair first. She finished with her hair and I handed her the soap. She shook her head and put it back in my hand, along with a washcloth. I stared at her for a moment before it dawned on me what she wanted. Sheepishly I rubbed the soap on the washcloth and lathered her chest and arms. She stood still, watching me and murmuring as I rubbed from her shoulders down to the small of her back. I moved down the back of her legs with the soapy washcloth and then up her front, avoiding her private area. I loved the defined muscles on her arms and back and the soft curves of her breasts now dripping with warm water as she rinsed off. Her dark eyelashes were even darker and seemed longer now as the deep blue eyes sneaked a look over at me. I wished in some way she might not look so perfect. I couldn't help but compare the plainness of my body to her striking features.

She took the washcloth from me and lathered it with soap then took a step toward me, looking more serious now. "I'm not sure what you we're just thinking about, June, but I can tell you're unhappy about it, whatever it was. I hope you aren't wishing you were here with someone else, are you?" It was far from the truth. She seemed to realize I wasn't ready to talk and instead lifted my chin toward hers. Her kiss held me steady. I kept my eyes closed after she pulled away and felt her hands start working the washcloth over my body. "Whatever it was, we can save it for later, I guess. Right now, I just want to enjoy your body."

I nodded, wishing I could quiet my fears as easily as her voice made things seem. I didn't want to explain anyway. There would be time later to tell her I wasn't sure how, or what, I could do to please her. Her hands rubbed my back and then moved toward my front. She leaned her head down, kissing the space between my belly button and the rise of hair. Later, there would be time to tell her, I thought.

"I love how smooth you feel," she murmured. "The curve of your hips . . . and your breasts just fill my hands."

My nipples perked with the slightest brush of her finger over them and I felt a shiver race up my spine every time her lips touched my chest. She didn't allow any place to go untouched, working the washcloth down my legs and then up my inner thighs. I kept my eyes closed, feeling the water pelt my face and back and hearing only Meg's voice, half-whispering, as she described every inch of my body that she liked. I only opened my eyes when she'd turned off the water. I took the towel she handed me and stood in the shower stall dripping, feeling strangely numb as she stared at me.

"I think I might be falling for you."

"What would you do if I fell for you first?" For the first time in my life I was completely certain it could happen.

Meg took my hand and kissed it. She led me to the bed and pulled down the covers. The night had kept the day's warmth and we stretched out on our towels not saying anything. Meg lay on her side with one arm hugging me close to her. I closed my eyes some time after midnight but I didn't think I'd fall asleep. Most nights I slept without dreaming or forgot the images by morning. This night I remembered my dream. I was lying on the hillcrest of Pioneer's Prayer. Above me a hawk soared, sunlight tinging his dark wings in orange. I could smell the dried grasses and the adobe dirt and when the wind picked up, I could hear the oak leaves rustle. When I woke, I found Meg asleep with her arm still draped over my belly. I'd never felt more comfortable than I did in her embrace. It was nearing dawn and I worried that she might wake and shift away from me. But her breathing remained slow and even until the first bit of sunshine made its way through the windows to light her naked back.

OUT OF THE FIRE by Beth Moore. Author Ann Covington feels at the top of the world when told her book is being made into a movie. Then in walks Casey Duncan the actress who is playing the lead in her movie. Will Casey turn Ann's world upside down?
1-59493-088-0 $13.95

STAKE THROUGH THE HEART: NEW EXPLOITS OF TWILIGHT LESBIANS by Karin Kallmaker, Julia Watts, Barbara Johnson and Therese Szymanski. The playful quartet that penned the acclaimed *Once Upon A Dyke* are dimming the lights for journeys into worlds of breathless seduction.
1-59493-071-6 $15.95

THE HOUSE ON SANDSTONE by KG MacGregor. Carly Griffin returns home to Leland and finds that her old high school friend Justine is awakening more than just old memories.
1-59493-076-7 $13.95

WILD NIGHTS: MOSTLY TRUE STORIES OF WOMEN LOVING WOMEN edited by Therese Szymanski. 264 pp. 23 new stories from today's hottest erotic writers are sure to give you your wildest night ever!
1-59493-069-4 $15.95

COYOTE SKY by Gerri Hill. 248 pp. Sheriff Lee Foxx is trying to cope with the realization that she has fallen in love for the first time. And fallen for author Kate Winters, who is technically unavailable. Will Lee fight to keep Kate in Coyote?
1-59493-065-1 $13.95

VOICES OF THE HEART by Frankie J. Jones. 264 pp. A series of events force Erin to swear off love as she tries to break away from the woman of her dreams. Will Erin ever find the key to her future happiness?
1-59493-068-6 $13.95

SHELTER FROM THE STORM by Peggy J. Herring. 296 pp. A story about family and getting reacquainted with one's past that shows that sometimes you don't appreciate what you have until you almost lose it.
1-59493-064-3 $13.95

WRITING MY LOVE by Claire McNab. 192 pp. Romance writer Vonny Smith believes she will be able to woo her editor Diana through her writing . . .
1-59493-063-5 $13.95

PAID IN FULL by Ann Roberts. 200 pp. Ari Adams will need to choose between the debts of the past and the promise of a happy future.
1-59493-059-7 $13.95

ROMANCING THE ZONE by Kenna White. 272 pp. Liz's world begins to crumble when a secret from her past returns to Ashton . . .
1-59493-060-0 $13.95

SIGN ON THE LINE by Jaime Clevenger. 204 pp. Alexis Getty, a flirtatious delivery driver is committed to finding the rightful owner of a mysterious package.
1-59493-052-X $13.95

END OF WATCH by Clare Baxter. 256 pp. LAPD Lieutenant L.A Franco Frank follows the lone clue down the unlit steps of memory to a final, unthinkable resolution.
1-59493-064-4 $13.95

BEHIND THE PINE CURTAIN by Gerri Hill. 280 pp. Jacqueline returns home after her father's death and comes face-to-face with her first crush. 1-59493-057-0 $13.95

PIPELINE by Brenda Adcock. 240 pp. Joanna faces a lost love returning and pulling her into a seamy underground corporation that kills for money. 1-59493-062-7 $13.95

18TH & CASTRO by Karin Kallmaker. 200 pp. First-time couplings and couples who know how to mix lust and love make 18th & Castro the hottest address in the city by the bay.
1-59493-066-X $13.95

JUST THIS ONCE by KG MacGregor. 200 pp. Mindful of the obligations back home that she must honor, Wynne Connelly struggles to resist the fascination and allure that a particular woman she meets on her business trip represents. 1-59493-087-2 $13.95

ANTICIPATION by Terri Breneman. 240 pp. Two women struggle to remain professional as they work together to find a serial killer. 1-59493-055-4 $13.95

OBSESSION by Jackie Calhoun. 240 pp. Lindsey's life is turned upside down when Sarah comes into the family nursery in search of perennials. 1-59493-058-9 $13.95

BENEATH THE WILLOW by Kenna White. 240 pp. A torch that still burns brightly even after twenty-five years threatens to consume two childhood friends.
1-59493-053-8 $13.95

SISTER LOST, SISTER FOUND by Jeanne G'fellers. 224 pp. The highly anticipated sequel to No Sister of Mine. 1-59493-056-2 $13.95

THE WEEKEND VISITOR by Jessica Thomas. 240 pp. In this latest Alex Peres mystery, Alex is asked to investigate an assault on a local woman but finds that her client may have more secrets than she lets on. 1-59493-054-6 $13.95

THE KILLING ROOM by Gerri Hill. 392 pp. How can two women forget and go their separate ways? 1-59493-050-3 $12.95

PASSIONATE KISSES by Megan Carter. 240 pp. Will two old friends run from love?
1-59493-051-1 $12.95

ALWAYS AND FOREVER by Lyn Denison. 224 pp. The girl next door turns Shannon's world upside down. 1-59493-049-X $12.95

BACK TALK by Saxon Bennett. 200 pp. Can a talk show host find love after heartbreak?
1-59493-028-7 $12.95

THE PERFECT VALENTINE: EROTIC LESBIAN VALENTINE STORIES edited by Barbara Johnson and Therese Szymanski—from Bella After Dark. 328 pp. Stories from the hottest writers around. 1-59493-061-9 $14.95

MURDER AT RANDOM by Claire McNab. 200 pp. The Sixth Denise Cleever Thriller. Denise realizes the fate of thousands is in her hands. 1-59493-047-3 $12.95

THE TIDES OF PASSION by Diana Tremain Braund. 240 pp. Will Susan be able to hold it all together and find the one woman who touches her soul? 1-59493-048-1 $12.95

JUST LIKE THAT by Karin Kallmaker. 240 pp. Disliking each other—and everything they stand for—even before they meet, Toni and Syrah find feelings can change, just like that.
1-59493-025-2 $12.95

WHEN FIRST WE PRACTICE by Therese Szymanski. 200 pp. Brett and Allie are once again caught in the middle of murder and intrigue.   1-59493-045-7 $12.95

REUNION by Jane Frances. 240 pp. Cathy Braithwaite seems to have it all: good looks, money and a thriving accounting practice . . .   1-59493-046-5 $12.95

BELL, BOOK & DYKE: NEW EXPLOITS OF MAGICAL LESBIANS by Kallmaker, Watts, Johnson and Szymanski. 360 pp. Reluctant witches, tempting spells and skyclad beauties—delve into the mysteries of love, lust and power in this quartet of novellas.   1-59493-023-6 $14.95

ARTIST'S DREAM by Gerri Hill. 320 pp. When Cassie meets Luke Winston, she can no longer deny her attraction to women . . .   1-59493-042-2 $12.95

NO EVIDENCE by Nancy Sanra. 240 pp. Private Investigator Tally McGinnis once again returns to the horror-filled world of a serial killer.   1-59493-043-04 $12.95

WHEN LOVE FINDS A HOME by Megan Carter. 280 pp. What will it take for Anna and Rona to find their way back to each other again?   1-59493-041-4 $12.95

MEMORIES TO DIE FOR by Adrian Gold. 240 pp. Rachel attempts to avoid her attraction to the charms of Anna Sigurdson . . .   1-59493-038-4 $12.95

SILENT HEART by Claire McNab. 280 pp. Exotic lesbian romance.

1-59493-044-9 $12.95

MIDNIGHT RAIN by Peggy J. Herring. 240 pp. Bridget McBee is determined to find the woman who saved her life.   1-59493-021-X $12.95

THE MISSING PAGE A Brenda Strange Mystery by Patty G. Henderson. 240 pp. Brenda investigates her client's murder . . .   1-59493-004-X $12.95

WHISPERS ON THE WIND by Frankie J. Jones. 240 pp. Dixon thinks she and her best friend, Elizabeth Colter, would make the perfect couple . . .   1-59493-037-6 $12.95

CALL OF THE DARK: EROTIC LESBIAN TALES OF THE SUPERNATURAL edited by Therese Szymanski—from Bella After Dark. 320 pp.   1-59493-040-6 $14.95

A TIME TO CAST AWAY A Helen Black Mystery by Pat Welch. 240 pp. Helen stops by Alice's apartment—only to find the woman dead . . .   1-59493-036-8 $12.95

DESERT OF THE HEART by Jane Rule. 224 pp. The book that launched the most popular lesbian movie of all time is back.   1-1-59493-035-X $12.95

THE NEXT WORLD by Ursula Steck. 240 pp. Anna's friend Mido is threatened and eventually disappears . . .   1-59493-024-4 $12.95

CALL SHOTGUN by Jaime Clevenger. 240 pp. Kelly gets pulled back into the world of private investigation . . .   1-59493-016-3 $12.95

52 PICKUP by Bonnie J. Morris and E.B. Casey. 240 pp. 52 hot, romantic tales—one for every Saturday night of the year.   1-59493-026-0 $12.95

GOLD FEVER by Lyn Denison. 240 pp. Kate's first love, Ashley, returns to their home town, where Kate now lives . . .   1-1-59493-039-2 $12.95

RISKY INVESTMENT by Beth Moore. 240 pp. Lynn's best friend and roommate needs her to pretend Chris is his fiancé. But nothing is ever easy.   1-59493-019-8 $12.95

HUNTER'S WAY by Gerri Hill. 240 pp. Homicide detective Tori Hunter is forced to team up with the hot-tempered Samantha Kennedy.   1-59493-018-X $12.95

CAR POOL by Karin Kallmaker. 240 pp. Soft shoulders, merging traffic and slippery when wet . . . Anthea and Shay find love in the car pool.   1-59493-013-9 $12.95

NO SISTER OF MINE by Jeanne G'Fellers. 240 pp. Telepathic women fight to coexist with a patriarchal society that wishes their eradication.   ISBN 1-59493-017-1 $12.95

ON THE WINGS OF LOVE by Megan Carter. 240 pp. Stacie's reporting career is on the rocks. She has to interview bestselling author Cheryl, or else!   ISBN 1-59493-027-9 $12.95

WICKED GOOD TIME by Diana Tremain Braund. 224 pp. Does Christina need Miki as a protector . . . or want her as a lover?   ISBN 1-59493-031-7 $12.95

THOSE WHO WAIT by Peggy J. Herring. 240 pp. Two brilliant sisters—in love with the same woman!   ISBN 1-59493-032-5 $12.95

ABBY'S PASSION by Jackie Calhoun. 240 pp. Abby's bipolar sister helps turn her world upside down, so she must decide what's most important.   ISBN 1-59493-014-7 $12.95

PICTURE PERFECT by Jane Vollbrecht. 240 pp. Kate is reintroduced to Casey, the daughter of an old friend. Can they withstand Kate's career?   ISBN 1-59493-015-5 $12.95

PAPERBACK ROMANCE by Karin Kallmaker. 240 pp. Carolyn falls for tall, dark and . . . female . . . in this classic lesbian romance.   ISBN 1-59493-033-3 $12.95

DAWN OF CHANGE by Gerri Hill. 240 pp. Susan ran away to find peace in remote Kings Canyon—then she met Shawn . . .   ISBN 1-59493-011-2 $12.95

DOWN THE RABBIT HOLE by Lynne Jamneck. 240 pp. Is a killer holding a grudge against FBI Agent Samantha Skellar?   ISBN 1-59493-012-0 $12.95

SEASONS OF THE HEART by Jackie Calhoun. 240 pp. Overwhelmed, Sara saw only one way out—leaving . . .   ISBN 1-59493-030-9 $12.95

TURNING THE TABLES by Jessica Thomas. 240 pp. The 2nd Alex Peres Mystery. *From ghosties and ghoulies and long leggity beasties* . . .   ISBN 1-59493-009-0 $12.95

FOR EVERY SEASON by Frankie Jones. 240 pp. Andi, who is investigating a 65-year-old murder, meets Janice, a charming district attorney . . .   ISBN 1-59493-010-4 $12.95

LOVE ON THE LINE by Laura DeHart Young. 240 pp. Kay leaves a younger woman behind to go on a mission to Alaska . . . will she regret it?   ISBN 1-59493-008-2 $12.95

UNDER THE SOUTHERN CROSS by Claire McNab. 200 pp. Lee, an American travel agent, goes down under and meets Australian Alex, and the sparks fly under the Southern Cross.   ISBN 1-59493-029-5 $12.95

SUGAR by Karin Kallmaker. 240 pp. Three women want sugar from Sugar, who can't make up her mind.   ISBN 1-59493-001-5 $12.95

FALL GUY by Claire McNab. 200 pp. 16th Detective Inspector Carol Ashton Mystery.   ISBN 1-59493-000-7 $12.95

ONE SUMMER NIGHT by Gerri Hill. 232 pp. Johanna swore to never fall in love again—but then she met the charming Kelly . . .   ISBN 1-59493-007-4 $12.95

TALK OF THE TOWN TOO by Saxon Bennett. 181 pp. Second in the series about wild and fun loving friends.   ISBN 1-931513-77-5 $12.95

LOVE SPEAKS HER NAME by Laura DeHart Young. 170 pp. Love and friendship, desire and intrigue, spark this exciting sequel to *Forever and the Night*.
        ISBN 1-59493-002-3 $12.95

TO HAVE AND TO HOLD by Peggy J. Herring. 184 pp. By finally letting down her defenses, will Dorian be opening herself to a devastating betrayal?
ISBN 1-59493-005-8 $12.95

WILD THINGS by Karin Kallmaker. 228 pp. Dutiful daughter Faith has met the perfect man. There's just one problem: she's in love with his sister. ISBN 1-931513-64-3 $12.95

SHARED WINDS by Kenna White. 216 pp. Can Emma rebuild more than just Lanny's marina? ISBN 1-59493-006-6 $12.95

THE UNKNOWN MILE by Jaime Clevenger. 253 pp. Kelly's world is getting more and more complicated every moment. ISBN 1-931513-57-0 $12.95

TREASURED PAST by Linda Hill. 189 pp. A shared passion for antiques leads to love.
ISBN 1-59493-003-1 $12.95

SIERRA CITY by Gerri Hill. 284 pp. Chris and Jesse cannot deny their growing attraction . . . ISBN 1-931513-98-8 $12.95

ALL THE WRONG PLACES by Karin Kallmaker. 174 pp. Sex and the single girl—Brandy is looking for love and usually she finds it. Karin Kallmaker's first *After Dark* erotic novel.
ISBN 1-931513-76-7 $12.95

WHEN THE CORPSE LIES A Motor City Thriller by Therese Szymanski. 328 pp. Butch bad-girl Brett Higgins is used to waking up next to beautiful women she hardly knows. Problem is, this one's dead. ISBN 1-931513-74-0 $12.95

GUARDED HEARTS by Hannah Rickard. 240 pp. Someone's reminding Alyssa about her secret past, and then she becomes the suspect in a series of burglaries.
ISBN 1-931513-99-6 $12.95

ONCE MORE WITH FEELING by Peggy J. Herring. 184 pp. Lighthearted, loving, romantic adventure. ISBN 1-931513-60-0 $12.95

TANGLED AND DARK A Brenda Strange Mystery by Patty G. Henderson. 240 pp. When investigating a local death, Brenda finds two possible killers—one diagnosed with Multiple Personality Disorder. ISBN 1-931513-75-9 $12.95

WHITE LACE AND PROMISES by Peggy J. Herring. 240 pp. Maxine and Betina realize sex may not be the most important thing in their lives. ISBN 1-931513-73-2 $12.95

UNFORGETTABLE by Karin Kallmaker. 288 pp. Can Rett find love with the cheerleader who broke her heart so many years ago? ISBN 1-931513-63-5 $12.95

HIGHER GROUND by Saxon Bennett. 280 pp. A delightfully complex reflection of the successful, high society lives of a small group of women. ISBN 1-931513-69-4 $12.95

LAST CALL A Detective Franco Mystery by Baxter Clare. 240 pp. Frank overlooks all else to try to solve a cold case of two murdered children . . . ISBN 1-931513-70-8 $12.95

ONCE UPON A DYKE: NEW EXPLOITS OF FAIRY-TALE LESBIANS by Karin Kallmaker, Julia Watts, Barbara Johnson & Therese Szymanski. 320 pp. You've never read fairy tales like these before! From Bella After Dark. ISBN 1-931513-71-6 $14.95

FINEST KIND OF LOVE by Diana Tremain Braund. 224 pp. Can Molly and Carolyn stop clashing long enough to see beyond their differences? ISBN 1-931513-68-6 $12.95

DREAM LOVER by Lyn Denison. 188 pp. A soft, sensuous, romantic fantasy.
ISBN 1-931513-96-1 $12.95

NEVER SAY NEVER by Linda Hill. 224 pp. A classic love story . . . where rules aren't the only things broken. ISBN 1-931513-67-8 $12.95

PAINTED MOON by Karin Kallmaker. 214 pp. Stranded together in a snowbound cabin, Jackie and Leah's lives will never be the same. ISBN 1-931513-53-8 $12.95

WIZARD OF ISIS by Jean Stewart. 240 pp. Fifth in the exciting Isis series. ISBN 1-931513-71-4 $12.95

WOMAN IN THE MIRROR by Jackie Calhoun. 216 pp. Josey learns to love again, while her niece is learning to love women for the first time. ISBN 1-931513-78-3 $12.95

SUBSTITUTE FOR LOVE by Karin Kallmaker. 200 pp. When Holly and Reyna meet the combination adds up to pure passion. But what about tomorrow? ISBN 1-931513-62-7 $12.95

GULF BREEZE by Gerri Hill. 288 pp. Could Carly really be the woman Pat has always been searching for? ISBN 1-931513-97-X $12.95

THE TOMSTOWN INCIDENT by Penny Hayes. 184 pp. Caught between two worlds, Eloise must make a decision that will change her life forever. ISBN 1-931513-56-2 $12.95

MAKING UP FOR LOST TIME by Karin Kallmaker. 240 pp. Discover delicious recipes for romance by the undisputed mistress. ISBN 1-931513-61-9 $12.95

THE WAY LIFE SHOULD BE by Diana Tremain Braund. 173 pp. With which woman will Jennifer find the true meaning of love? ISBN 1-931513-66-X $12.95

BACK TO BASICS: A BUTCH/FEMME ANTHOLOGY edited by Therese Szymanski—from Bella After Dark. 324 pp. ISBN 1-931513-35-X $14.95

SURVIVAL OF LOVE by Frankie J. Jones. 236 pp. What will Jody do when she falls in love with her best friend's daughter? ISBN 1-931513-55-4 $12.95

LESSONS IN MURDER by Claire McNab. 184 pp. 1st Detective Inspector Carol Ashton Mystery. ISBN 1-931513-65-1 $12.95

DEATH BY DEATH by Claire McNab. 167 pp. 5th Denise Cleever Thriller. ISBN 1-931513-34-1 $12.95

CAUGHT IN THE NET by Jessica Thomas. 188 pp. A wickedly observant story of mystery, danger, and love in Provincetown. ISBN 1-931513-54-6 $12.95

DREAMS FOUND by Lyn Denison. Australian Riley embarks on a journey to meet her birth mother . . . and gains not just a family, but the love of her life. ISBN 1-931513-58-9 $12.95

A MOMENT'S INDISCRETION by Peggy J. Herring. 154 pp. Jackie is torn between her better judgment and the overwhelming attraction she feels for Valerie. ISBN 1-931513-59-7 $12.95

IN EVERY PORT by Karin Kallmaker. 224 pp. Jessica has a woman in every port. Will meeting Cat change all that? ISBN 1-931513-36-8 $12.95

TOUCHWOOD by Karin Kallmaker. 240 pp. Rayann loves Louisa. Louisa loves Rayann. Can the decades between their ages keep them apart? ISBN 1-931513-37-6 $12.95

WATERMARK by Karin Kallmaker. 248 pp. Teresa wants a future with a woman whose heart has been frozen by loss. Sequel to *Touchwood*. ISBN 1-931513-38-4 $12.95

EMBRACE IN MOTION by Karin Kallmaker. 240 pp. Has Sarah found lust or love? ISBN 1-931513-39-2 $12.95

ONE DEGREE OF SEPARATION by Karin Kallmaker. 232 pp. Sizzling small town romance between Marian, the town librarian, and the new girl from the big city. ISBN 1-931513-30-9 $12.95

CRY HAVOC A Detective Franco Mystery by Baxter Clare. 240 pp. A dead hustler with a headless rooster in his lap sends Lt. L.A. Franco headfirst against Mother Love.
ISBN 1-931513931-7 $12.95

DISTANT THUNDER by Peggy J. Herring. 294 pp. Bankrobbing drifter Cordy awakens strange new feelings in Leo in this romantic tale set in the Old West.
ISBN 1-931513-28-7 $12.95

COP OUT by Claire McNab. 216 pp. 4th Detective Inspector Carol Ashton Mystery.
ISBN 1-931513-29-5 $12.95

BLOOD LINK by Claire McNab. 159 pp. 15th Detective Inspector Carol Ashton Mystery. Is Carol unwittingly playing into a deadly plan?
ISBN 1-931513-27-9 $12.95

TALK OF THE TOWN by Saxon Bennett. 239 pp. With enough beer, barbecue and B.S., anything is possible!
ISBN 1-931513-18-X $12.95

MAYBE NEXT TIME by Karin Kallmaker. 256 pp. Sabrina has everything she ever wanted—except Jorie.
ISBN 1-931513-26-0 $12.95

WHEN GOOD GIRLS GO BAD: A Motor City Thriller by Therese Szymanski. 230 pp. Brett, Randi and Allie join forces to stop a serial killer.
ISBN 1-931513-11-2 $12.95

A DAY TOO LONG: A Helen Black Mystery by Pat Welch. 328 pp. This time Helen's fate is in her own hands.
ISBN 1-931513-22-8 $12.95

THE RED LINE OF YARMALD by Diana Rivers. 256 pp. The Hadra's only hope lies in a magical red line . . . climactic sequel to *Clouds of War*.
ISBN 1-931513-23-6 $12.95

OUTSIDE THE FLOCK by Jackie Calhoun. 224 pp. Jo embraces her new love and life.
ISBN 1-931513-13-9 $12.95

LEGACY OF LOVE by Marianne K. Martin. 224 pp. Read the whole Sage Bristo story.
ISBN 1-931513-15-5 $12.95

STREET RULES: A Detective Franco Mystery by Baxter Clare. 304 pp. Gritty, fast-paced mystery with compelling Detective L.A. Franco.
ISBN 1-931513-14-7 $12.95

RECOGNITION FACTOR: 4th Denise Cleever Thriller by Claire McNab. 176 pp. Denise Cleever tracks a notorious terrorist to America.
ISBN 1-931513-24-4 $12.95

NORA AND LIZ by Nancy Garden. 296 pp. Lesbian romance by the author of *Annie on My Mind*.
ISBN 1931513-20-1 $12.95

MIDAS TOUCH by Frankie J. Jones. 208 pp. Sandra had everything but love.
ISBN 1-931513-21-X $12.95

BEYOND ALL REASON by Peggy J. Herring. 240 pp. A romance hotter than Texas.
ISBN 1-9513-25-2 $12.95

ACCIDENTAL MURDER: 14th Detective Inspector Carol Ashton Mystery by Claire McNab. 208 pp. Carol Ashton tracks an elusive killer.
ISBN 1-931513-16-3 $12.95

SEEDS OF FIRE: Tunnel of Light Trilogy, Book 2 by Karin Kallmaker writing as Laura Adams. 274 pp. In Autumn's dreams no one is who they seem.
ISBN 1-931513-19-8 $12.95

DRIFTING AT THE BOTTOM OF THE WORLD by Auden Bailey. 288 pp. Beautifully written first novel set in Antarctica.
ISBN 1-931513-17-1 $12.95

CLOUDS OF WAR by Diana Rivers. 288 pp. Women unite to defend Zelindar!
ISBN 1-931513-12-0 $12.95